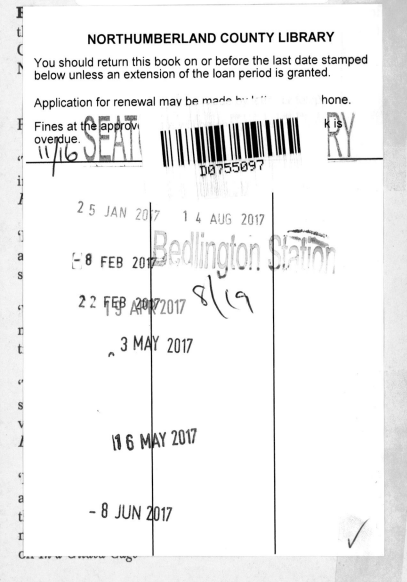

'Delightful . . . As ever, Bowen does a splendid job of capturing the flavor of early twentieth-century New York and bringing to life its warm and human inhabitants.' *Publishers Weekly* on *In a Gilded Cage*

'Winning . . . It's all in a day's work for this delightfully spunky heroine.' *Publishers Weekly* on *Tell Me Pretty Maiden*

'Sharp historical backgrounds and wacky adventures.' *Kirkus Reviews* on *Tell Me Pretty Maiden*

'With a riveting plot capped off by a dramatic conclusion, Bowen captures the passion and struggles of the Irish people at the turn of the twentieth century.' *Publishers Weekly* on *In Dublin's Fair City*

'Molly is an indomitable creature . . . The book bounces along in the hands of Ms Bowen and her Molly, and there is no doubt that she will be back causing trouble.' *The Washington Times* on *In Dublin's Fair City*

'The feisty Molly rarely disappoints in this rousing yarn seasoned with a dash of Irish history.' *Kirkus Reviews* (starred review) on *In Dublin's Fair City*

'A lot of fun and some terrific historical writing. Fans of the British cozy will love it, and so will readers of historical fiction.' Toronto *Globe and Mail* on *Oh Danny Boy*

Queen of Hearts
Malice at the Palace

The Family Way

Rhys Bowen

Constable • London

CONSTABLE

First published in the USA in 2013 by Minotaur Books,
an imprint of St Martin's Press, New York

This edition published in the UK in 2016 by Constable

1 3 5 7 9 10 8 6 4 2

A CIP catalogue record for this book
is available from the British Library.

ISBN 978-1-47211-850-9 (paperback)
ISBN: 978-1-47211-851-6 (ebook)

Typeset by TW Type, Cornwall
Printed and bound in Great Britain by CPI (UK) Ltd, Croydon CR0 4YY
Papers used by Constable are from well-managed forests and other responsible sources

MIX
Paper from
responsible sources
FSC® C104740

Constable
is an imprint of
Little, Brown Book Group
Carmelite House
50 Victoria Embankment
London EC4Y 0DZ

An Hachette UK Company
www.hachette.co.uk

www.littlebrown.co.uk

*Since this story is centered on family and religion,
I am proud to dedicate the book to my brother, Father Frank
Neville Lee, who after a high-powered career as a marketing
director has now been ordained an Anglican priest.
Our mother would have been so proud.*

Chapter 1

New York City, July 1904

Satan finds work for idle hands to do. That was one of my mother's favorite sayings if she ever caught me daydreaming or lying on my back on the turf, staring up at the white clouds that raced across the sky. I could almost hear her voice, with its strong Irish brogue, as I sat on the sofa and sipped a glass of lemonade on a hot July day.

Frankly, I rather wished that Satan would find me something to do with my idle hands because I was dying of boredom. All my life I'd been used to hard work, forced to care for my father and three young brothers after my mother went to her heavenly rest. (At least I presume that's where she went. She certainly thought she deserved it.) And now, for the first time in my life, I was a lady of leisure. Ever since I found out I was in the family way, back in February, Daniel had treated me as if I was made of fine porcelain. For the first few months I was glad of his solicitous behavior toward me as I was horribly sick. In fact I began to feel more sympathy for my mother, who had gone through this at least four times. But then, at the start of the fourth month, a miraculous change occurred. I awoke one morning to find that I felt well and hungry and full of energy. Daniel, however, still insisted that I did as little as possible, did not exert myself, took no risks, and generally behaved like one of those helpless females I so despised.

He wanted me to lie on the couch with my feet up and spend my days making little garments. I had tried to do this and the quality of my sewing and knitting had improved, but still left a lot to be desired. Besides, I knew that my mother-in-law was sewing away diligently and that my neighbors Sid and Gus would shower the child with expensive presents.

So this left long hours to be filled every day. Our little house on Patchin Place could be cleaned in a couple of hours. I did a little shopping, but Daniel's job as a police captain meant that he was seldom home for lunch and sometimes not even for dinner, so little cooking was required. I was glad of this when the weather turned hot at the end of June as my growing bulk meant that I felt the heat badly. Daniel suggested that he could fend for himself just fine and I should go up to his mother in Westchester County, where I'd be cooler and well looked after. I didn't say it out loud but I'd rather have endured a fiery furnace than a prolonged stay with Daniel's mother. Not that she was an ogre or anything, but her standards of perfection and her social interactions with members of high society left me feeling hopelessly inadequate. I knew that she was disappointed that Daniel had not made a better match than an Irish girl with no money and no family connections.

She never actually came out and said this, but she made it plain enough. 'I took tea with the Harpers yesterday,' she'd say. 'I remember that one of the Harper girls was rather sweet on you at one time, Daniel. She's gone on to make an excellent marriage with one of the Van Baarens. Her parents couldn't be happier.' And then she'd look at me.

So I was prepared to endure any amount of heat rather than Daniel's mother. I just wished these last months would hurry up and be over. I put down my lemonade glass and picked up the undershirt I had been attempting to sew. I could see sweaty fingerprints on the fine white cotton and several places where the stitches had been unpicked. I sighed. I just wasn't cut out to be a seamstress. As a detective I hadn't done at all badly, but that profession was now closed to me. Daniel had made me promise that I'd give up my agency when we married. I had hoped that Daniel would share his cases with me, that we'd sit at the kitchen table and he'd ask for my opinion. But he had claimed that his recent cases had been too commonplace to be worth discussing or else so confidential that he had to remain tight-lipped about them.

I looked up as the sun suddenly streamed in through the back parlor windows. A sunbeam lit the dust motes in the air and painted a stripe of brightness on the wallpaper. Now this room would soon be too hot for comfort and I'd be banished to the front parlor, dark and gloomy, until the sun set. I got up to draw the heavy velvet drapes across the window and noticed that the lace curtains looked rather dingy. That would never do. Having achieved lace curtains for the first time in my life, I should make sure that they remained a pristine white. I went into the kitchen and brought back a high-backed wooden chair. I proceeded to climb on this with some difficulty, then I reached up to unhook the first of the lace curtains.

I was at full stretch, standing on tiptoe, when a voice behind me boomed, 'Molly! What in God's name do you think you're doing?'

'Jesus, Mary, and Joseph,' I exclaimed. I teetered, and would have fallen if I hadn't grabbed at the velvet drape, which held fast. I looked around to see Daniel standing there with a face like thunder.

'The curtains needed washing.' I glared at him defiantly.

'You were risking the safety of our baby for the sake of clean curtains?' he demanded. He came over and helped me down from the chair. 'You nearly fell, and what might have happened then?'

'It was only a voice suddenly shouting right behind me that made me lose my balance,' I said. 'Until you showed up I was doing just fine.'

He looked at me more tenderly now. 'Molly, how many times have I told you to take it easy. You're in a delicate condition, my dear.'

'Nonsense. Women in Ireland have their babies one day and by the end of the week they're out helping their man in the fields again.'

'And how many of those babies die? Your mother didn't live long herself, did she?'

I chose not to acknowledge the truth in this. Instead I said breezily, 'Daniel, I feel fine and I'm bored to tears doing nothing.'

He took my arm and led me back to the sofa. 'Then invite some friends over to tea. I've introduced you to the wives of some of my colleagues, haven't I? It's about time you built up a circle of social acquaintances. And there are always your friends across the street,' he added grudgingly, not being as keen as I on my bohemian neighbors.

I sighed. 'They've gone to stay with Gus's relatives in Newport, Rhode Island, to escape the heat,' I said. 'You remember the mansion with the Roman pillars.'

'Very well.' We'd spent our honeymoon in Newport and it had hardly gone as planned. Daniel pulled up the kitchen chair and sat beside me. 'So why don't you go to my mother as I suggested? You know she'd love to make a fuss of you, and feed you well, and it's so much cooler out there.'

'Daniel, I'm your wife. My place is taking care of you,' I replied, not wanting to tell him the real reason. Isn't it amazing what marriage does to a woman? I was finally learning to be diplomatic. I was one step away from being simpering.

'I can fend for myself quite well. I've been doing it for years.'

'But you work long hours, Daniel. It's not right that you should come home to no supper and no clean clothes.'

He wagged a finger at me. 'What have I been telling you for months? Then this is the perfect time to get a servant.'

I sighed. 'Daniel, let's not go through that again. We really don't need a servant. This is a small house. I'm used to hard work. I'm happy to cook and clean for you, and for our baby too. If a few more children start to come along, then I may need some help, but for the present . . .'

'It's not just the amount of work, Molly. It's the principle of the thing. A man in my position should have a servant. When we start entertaining more, it wouldn't be right that you'd have to keep disappearing into the kitchen to see to the dinner. I want you to be the gracious hostess.'

'Oh, I see,' I said, my rising temper now winning out over my newfound meekness. 'It's not concern about me at all, is it? You're worried about how you appear in the eyes of society.'

He looked at my expression and took my hand. 'Molly, this is not for myself, it's for us. Everything I do from now on is for my family. I want the best for us and for our children. I want to rise in the world, it's true, and I'll be judged on the kind of home I keep and the people I associate with.' He paused. 'And I want the world to see that I married a beautiful woman.'

I had to smile at this. 'You may have been born in America, Daniel Sullivan,' I said, 'but you've certainly inherited your share of Irish blarney!'

He smiled too. 'I am thinking of you, Molly. If you're up all night with a crying baby, you'll appreciate a girl taking over from you so you can get your rest. You say you're bored and have nothing to do – well, what better time to train a servant so that she knows your wishes and how this household works by the time the baby arrives?'

I hesitated, then said, 'Well, I suppose I could start making inquiries.'

He jumped to his feet. 'I know,' he said. 'Why don't I write to my mother and ask for her help in this?'

Now my hackles truly were rising. 'Why does your mother have to come into every aspect of our lives?' I demanded. 'Do you not believe I'm capable of finding a servant for myself?'

'Of course you are. I'm simply trying to spare you extra toil and bother. I don't want you traipsing around the city at this time of year. They say there is typhoid in Brooklyn this summer and who knows when that will spread across the East River? We can't be too careful in your current condition.'

'Not all employment agencies are in bad neighborhoods,' I said. 'I went to a snooty one myself when I was newly arrived here and needed work.'

He frowned. 'I'm not sure we could pay the rates of a snooty agency. And I'm concerned that lesser agencies don't always vet their girls well enough. I don't like the idea of hiring a girl newly off the boat. How do we know she'll be trustworthy?' He put a hand on my shoulder. 'My mother knows the right sort of people, Molly. She'll be able to ask around and get recommendations. New York is a big place and full of crooks and swindlers, as I know only too well. We have to be extra cautious about who we allow into our house. One of the gangs would just love to place an informant in my home and have my comings and goings monitored.'

'But surely, if I go through a reputable agency . . .' I began, but he cut me off. 'Let's try my mother first and see who she can come up with, shall we? Then you can go out to her to interview likely girls and choose the one you like.'

I wasn't at all happy with this. If the gangs wanted to place a spy in our home to monitor Daniel's movements then it was just as likely that Daniel's mother would like to place her own spy to monitor mine. But I could hardly express that sentiment to Daniel. Men are funny about their mothers, seeing them as one step away from sainthood. So I told myself silently that I didn't have to choose any girl I didn't like and in the meantime I'd do my own asking around.

'I'll write the letter now,' Daniel said, 'if you'd be good enough to make me a quick bite to eat before I go back to work.'

With that he went through to his desk in the front parlor that had now become his study, and I went to my rightful place in the kitchen, trying to put aside thoughts that a woman's lot in life was not a fair one. I made him a cold beef sandwich and some pickled cabbage, and was pouring him a glass of lemonade when he returned with the letter.

'This can go out with the three o'clock mail if you'll take it to the post office for me.' He sat and worked his way quickly through the sandwich. 'I may not be home until late tonight,' he said.

I pulled up a chair and sat opposite him. 'Difficult case?' I asked, trying to sound casual.

'Several at once, that's the problem. I like to devote all my energy to one thing at a time, not to be running hither and yon. But the powers that be have saddled me with something I'd rather avoid.'

'Maybe I can help,' I suggested. 'If you'd care to discuss them with me.'

He shook his head. 'Nothing to discuss. No clever murderers to be outwitted. Just various types of petty crooks making life unpleasant for the populace.' He pushed his plate away. 'Very nice. Thank you, my dear. And you will make sure that letter gets to the post office, won't you?' He kissed my forehead and was gone.

I cleared away the remains of the meal and looked at that letter lying on the table. I didn't have to mail it, did I? But then I realized that I did. There has to be trust between husband and wife, however abhorrent it was to me that the task of finding my servant was being left to his mother. I glanced at the fruit bowl and saw that we were down to a single plum. Fruit was one of the things I'd been craving recently so I decided to treat myself to some peaches if I had to go out. I pinned my straw hat to my flyaway hair, put on my cotton gloves, and out I went.

The heat came up from the cobbles to hit me, almost as if someone had opened an oven door. I hugged the side of the alleyway that was in shade and made my way slowly to Sixth Avenue. I went into the post office and dropped the letter into the outgoing mail slot. I was about to leave when a large florid man leaned across the counter toward me.

'Excuse me, ma'am,' he said, 'but weren't you the young lady that used to collect the mail for P. Riley Associates?'

'That's right,' I said, P. Riley Associates being the name of the small detective agency I had inherited after the murder of Paddy Riley. 'But that agency is no more and the post office box has been closed.'

'I know that,' he said. 'It's just that a letter came in addressed to that establishment only a week or so ago, and I didn't quite know what to do with it, no forwarding address having been left with us. So it's still sitting there and I thought that maybe you'd know where to deliver it. Hold on a minute and I'll fetch it for you.'

He disappeared into a back room and then returned, panting and red-faced, but triumphantly waving an envelope. 'Here you are. So maybe you'll see that the right party gets his mail then.'

'I will,' I said. 'Thank you.'

With the letter in my gloved hand I went out into the heat of Sixth Avenue. I walked until I was standing in the shade of a sycamore tree before I stopped to examine it. Of course I knew that P. Riley Associates was no more, and that I had promised Daniel I would give up all such nonsense when I married him. That meant that I should throw the letter straight into the nearest rubbish bin. But then I told myself that it might be a belated payment for services rendered long ago and I couldn't risk throwing good money away. I looked at the envelope and saw the stamp with King Edward's head on it. From England then. I opened the envelope and found no money but a single sheet of cheap lined paper, such as one would find in an exercise book. I also saw from the address at the top that the letter came not from England but from Ireland, from County Cork.

Dear Sir or Madam: We are but simple folk and can't pay you much money, so if you're one of these big swank detectives then I'm thinking you'll not want to be bothered with the likes of us. But we're more than a little worried about our niece Maureen O'Byrne. She sailed for New York on the Majestic out of Queenstown just under a year ago, hoping to make a better life for herself in your country. Indeed things seemed to fall into place instantly for her. She hadn't been there more than a week or two when she wrote to us saying that she'd landed herself a good situation as under-parlor-maid with a Mrs Mainwaring and she hoped soon to be sending money home when she'd paid off her passage.

She had not given us an address to write to, so we could only wait for more news. Well, we waited and waited but heard nothing more. So now a year's coming up and we're concerned about her welfare. She was always a good girl and devoted to her uncle and me, as we were her closest relatives since her poor mother and father died. Something must have happened to her, or she would have written, I'm absolutely sure. Even if she couldn't send any money she would have at least written a note at Christmastime.

As I said, we are not wealthy folks and I have no idea what your usual fee might be, but we've a little set aside for our funerals and we're willing to do what's necessary to learn about our Maureen. Anything you can do to help will be appreciated. Please reply to the above address and God love you for your efforts.

Yours faithfully,

E. M. O'Byrne (Mrs)

P.S. *I have enclosed a picture of Maureen to help you with your inquiries. As you can see, she's a pretty girl, dainty, almost fairylike. We used to tease her that she was a change-ling as we're all heavyset and dark in the family except for her.*

Chapter 2

I stood staring down at the picture of Maureen. It had obviously been cut from a family group and showed her stiff, uneasy, and unsmiling; her hands folded in an unnatural position. Her hair was light, but it wasn't possible to tell the true color. I slipped the picture back into the envelope then reread the letter. By the time I had finished reading, my head had started buzzing with ideas. The missing girl had done something she was ashamed of and didn't want them to know. She'd run off with an unsuitable man, or she'd been sacked from her situation in Mrs Mainwaring's household and didn't want to write until she had found herself a new post. If I could locate this Mrs Mainwaring, no doubt this matter could be solved quickly. It shouldn't be too hard – Mrs Mainwaring must be a lady of some substance if she ran a household big enough to employ more than one parlormaid. And I knew people who moved in those circles. The first person to try should be my old friend Miss Van Woekem – she knew the Four Hundred personally. Or maybe some of my friend Emily's Vassar pals, or of course Gus came from a most distinguished Boston family who would have connections in New York. It wasn't definite that the lady lived in New York, but given that the girl landed here and found a situation immediately, one could surmise . . .

A horse and cart lumbered past, the poor horse with his head straining forward and breathing heavily as he attempted to drag a dray piled high with barrels. The clop of hooves and the rumble and rattle of the cart so close to me broke my train of thought and made me step back hastily from the curb. Then I realized that it was no use surmising. I would not be taking on this case. I had given up my detective business and promised Daniel that I would never again involve myself in stupidly dangerous situations. As hard as this was for me, I could see his point of view: I had narrowly escaped death on several occasions. I'd even suffered a miscarriage once that I had never found the courage to tell him about. He had been unjustly jailed at the time and in no position to marry me. As these thoughts passed through my mind I admitted that I had experienced some very dark hours. I had taken stupid risks. I was lucky to be alive and to be married to the man I loved with a bright future ahead of me.

I'd take the letter home, show it to Daniel, and ask if he knew of any reputable private detectives who might want to take on the job. I stopped at my favorite greengrocer on the corner of Ninth Street and bought a pound of peaches and some salad for Daniel's supper, since it would be too hot to think of cooking much. I looked longingly at those peaches in my basket, tempted to eat one on the spot, but reminded myself that the respectable wife of a well-known police captain does not behave like a street urchin. Instead I joined the throng attempting to stay in the shade under the elevated railway tracks, and was trying to avoid being bumped and jostled when I heard my name being called.

I stepped out into the sunlight, looked up, and saw a delicate vision in pale lilac waving at me. She seemed almost unreal, so out of place among the drab colors of the sturdy housewives and laborers that I had to look twice before I recognized her. It was Sarah Lindley, fellow suffragist friend of Sid and Gus. In spite of the fact that she came from an upper-class and wealthy family she was not only passionately involved in the suffrage movement but had been volunteering at a settlement house in the slums of the Lower East Side. She looked both ways and dodged between a hansom cab and a big black carriage to come to me.

'Molly, how lovely to see you,' she said, giving me a delicate kiss on the cheek. 'And how well you look. Positively blooming. How many months to go now?'

'Two and a half,' I said, 'and it can't go by quickly enough for me. I find this heat unbearable.'

'I know. Isn't it just awful.' She brushed an imaginary strand of stray hair back under her lilac straw hat.

'Surely you could escape from it,' I said. 'Don't your folks have a country estate? Or weren't you supposed to be making a European grand tour?'

'Already accomplished, my dear,' Sarah said, linking her arm through mine as we started to walk together. 'We went in May. France, Italy, Germany, you name it, we were there. Every art gallery and palace in creation. All very lovely, but not a single prince or count asked for my hand so Mama came home most disappointed.'

I glanced at her and we exchanged a grin. 'I don't

imagine you're in any hurry to marry after what you went through last year, are you?' I asked. Her last fiancé had turned out to be what we would have called a rotter who came to a bad end.

'Exactly,' she said. 'And I want to be like you. I want to marry for love. Mama is all for a good match, but I don't see why one should be unhappy for one's whole life just to have a title or a castle or something.'

'So what are you doing in this part of the city?' I asked.

'Coming to pay a call on your dear neighbors,' she said. 'I haven't seen them since I came back from Europe and I'm dying to regale them with all my stories. I know they'll love to hear about the fat German count who trapped me in the hotel elevator in Berlin and tried to kiss me.'

'How disgusting. What did you do? Scream for help?'

'Absolutely not, my sweet. I stuck the tip of my parasol into his foot. With considerable force. You should have heard him howl and hop around.'

I laughed. 'Sid and Gus would be proud,' I said, 'but I'm afraid you've come on a wasted journey. They are not home. They went to stay with Gus's cousin in Newport.'

'Oh, the dreaded Roman mansion.' She laughed. 'I wonder what made Gus endure that again? I thought she couldn't stand that particular cousin.'

'I gather they were prepared to suffer the cousin for the sake of sea air,' I said. 'It really is devilishly hot in the city. As I said, I'm surprised you haven't escaped.'

'Devotion to duty,' Sarah said. 'One of our volunteers at the settlement house is getting married so I promised to take over her shifts.'

'You're still working at the settlement house?'

'I am. It's hard work, but it brings me great satisfaction

to be able to make a difference in the lives of those people. We've expanded our educational programs and we're teaching so many poor mothers about hygiene and good nutrition. That's become my little pet project, actually. I love going out into the tenements and helping people. You'd be amazed how many mothers haven't the slightest idea about how to look after their babies – they let the little dears crawl around on absolutely filthy floors and put anything they find in their mouths and they even give them rags soaked in gin to keep them quiet.'

'You're doing a wonderful job,' I said.

She wrinkled her little button of a nose. 'Mama doesn't see it that way. I have to endure a constant barrage of comments about my chances of marriage slipping away and the bloom fading on the rose and the horrors of impending spinsterhood. But frankly, Molly, I'd be quite happy not marrying and doing this kind of work all my life. What's so wrong with it?'

'It isn't what your mother had planned for you, that's what,' I said. 'Every mother wants her daughter happily married and lots of grandchildren. You should see how excited Daniel's mother is about the arrival of the baby.'

'And your mother? I presume she's still at home in Ireland?'

I shook my head. 'My mother died when I was fourteen. My father's dead too. I have a brother who was part of the Republican Brotherhood, hiding out somewhere in France, and a younger brother still in Ireland, but that's all. No real family anymore.'

She touched my arm. 'Poor Molly. How sad for you.'

'I don't mind,' I said. 'I've got Daniel, and Sid and Gus have become like family to me. I'm so sorry they're not at home. I don't know when they plan to return. Would you care to come to my place for a cup of tea or a lemonade since you're in the neighborhood?'

'How kind of you. I'd love to.'

We turned, arm in arm, from Sixth to Greenwich Avenue and from there into Patchin Place, teetering on the cobbles in our dainty shoes. The house was now uncomfortably hot so I led Sarah through to our tiny square of back garden, where I had set a wrought-iron table and two chairs in the shade of a lilac tree, then brought out a jug of lemonade and a plate of biscuits I had made a few days previously. Sarah clapped her hands and laughed in delight.

'Molly, you have become so domesticated. Look at you, lady of the house and soon-to-be mother. Did you ever imagine when we met last year that your life could change so dramatically?'

'It certainly is changed,' I agreed as I poured the lemonade.

'How relieved you must be that you are no longer in danger and working in such uncomfortable circumstances,' she said.

I hesitated. 'Sometimes I feel that way, but I'm used to hard work, and I'm afraid I enjoyed the excitement of my job too. I find my present condition rather boring. I wasn't raised to leisure like you so I've no idea how to fill idle hours.'

She took a sip of lemonade. 'I was raised to leisure, as you say, but I have always rebelled against it. Croquet matches and coffee mornings seem such a waste of time to me. And all those discussions about new hats and dressmakers. I never could abide them. That's why I went to work at the settlement house and found like-minded people.' She looked up suddenly from her glass. 'You could always come and help me if you're bored,' she said. 'I'm sure you'd be splendid at educating families in the tenements on hygiene and I'd certainly relish a companion with me.'

'I would jump at a chance like that, but I'm afraid Daniel wouldn't agree. He's treating me as if I'm a dainty little flower at the moment and he's terrified I'll catch some awful disease if I venture into the slums.'

Her face grew somber. 'Well, he does have a point there. Remember that terrifying typhoid outbreak a couple of years ago? They are saying there is already typhoid in Brooklyn this summer and it can easily spread across the river. And there is always cholera in the hot weather. So maybe joining me wouldn't be such a good idea, Molly.'

'Don't you fear for your own health?'

She laughed. 'Me? I may look dainty, but I'm as strong as an ox. My brothers all came down with all the childhood diseases when we were young, but not I.'

'I was that way too when I was growing up, but I confess that I was horribly sick in the early months of my condition and for the first time in my life I did feel like a delicate china doll who needed looking after. Thankfully that has passed and I'm raring to go again. Daniel chided me earlier today because he found me standing on a chair, taking down the net curtains to launder them.'

'I think I might have chided you too,' she said.

'I need to keep busy, Sarah.'

She looked thoughtful. 'If you have time on your hands – you could always help our suffrage cause. I know you are a fellow supporter.'

'I am, most definitely, but I don't think I'm up to marching and carrying banners at the moment.'

'Of course not. But we always need help with flyers and brochures to be handed out. You could assist with things like that, couldn't you?'

'I could,' I said.

'We're having a meeting next week to plan strategy. Do you think you can join us?'

I started to say that I'd have to confer with Daniel first, but then the old Molly resurfaced. 'Yes, I'd like to,' I said. 'As long as it's not at a time when I should be cooking Daniel's dinner.' I saw her face and added swiftly, 'He works such long hours that I like to make sure he has a proper meal when he gets home.'

She nodded, accepting this, then put down her glass. 'I should be making my way to the settlement house,' she said. 'We have a couple of new volunteers and I'm afraid they both fit the expression, "The spirit is willing, but the flesh is weak." They love the idea of serving the poor, but they don't actually want to scrub floors and make beds.'

We both laughed as she got to her feet.

'I expect it's hard for people in your station to find themselves in such different circumstances for the first time,' I said. 'I don't suppose they've ever scrubbed a floor before.'

She nodded agreement. 'It is a shock when you first start and when you find your first bedsheet with fleas and lice all over it. But you soon get used to it. And it's so worth it when you see the change in the young women who come to us.'

'Where do they go when they leave you?' I asked.

'We try to find domestic situations for those who are suitable. Not all of them are, of course. Those who were ladies of the night or drug fiends don't take kindly to our ministrations on the whole.'

'And what happens to them?'

'I'm afraid they go back onto the streets, and probably will wind up floating in the East River someday.'

I stared at her, wondering how such a delicate creature could discuss such matters calmly. Most young women of her class would swoon at the words, 'drug fiends.' But as I watched her open the back door and step into the house an idea was forming in my mind. 'So some of these girls go into domestic service,' I said, following her down the narrow hallway. 'Do you place them yourselves?'

'We usually send them to an agency,' she said. 'We simply don't have the time to handle such matters.'

My eyes lit up. 'Then we may be able to help each other. Daniel has been adamant that we hire a servant – more for his status than for me, I suspect.' I smiled. 'He has just written to his mother to ask her for recommendations, but I'd rather choose my own girl if she's going to live in my house and work for me. Do you have anyone who might fit the bill at the moment?'

She paused, her hand on my front doorknob, thinking. 'Not really,' she said. 'But the agency that we use might be able to recommend a girl for you. They are most reliable and thorough. I'll take you and introduce you if you like.'

'That would be splendid,' I said. 'Where is this agency?'

'It's on Broome Street, not far from the Bowery. If you've nothing to do right now, I could introduce you on my way to work.'

Loathe as I was to step out into that heat again, I wasn't going to turn down this chance. 'Most kind of you,' I said. 'I'll fetch my hat and gloves.'

'What do you think?' I asked as we reached the entrance to Patchin Place. 'Should we chance the Sixth Avenue El and then walk along Broome or should we go across to Broadway and ride the trolley?'

'At this time of day they are both likely to be packed,' Sarah said. 'Not a good idea in your delicate condition. We'll take a cab.'

'A cab? But surely . . .' I began, but she was already stepping out into traffic, waving imperiously with her little gloved finger.

'There are some privileges of the rich that I still enjoy,' she said. 'And one of those is taking cabs whenever necessary. In fact Papa insists that I take cabs anytime I'm in undesirable parts of the city. He thinks I'm in constant danger of being captured and whisked off to white slavery.' And she gave a gay little laugh as the cab came to a halt beside us. I had to admit I was glad not to have to face a crowded rail car and the odor of sweaty bodies, my nose having become rather sensitive of late.

The cabby looked surprised when Sarah gave him the address. 'Are you sure that's where you want to go, miss?' he asked.

'Quite sure, thank you,' Sarah replied crisply.

We set off at a lively clip. I put my hand into my purse to find my handkerchief and my fingers closed around the letter. I pulled it out. 'Tell me,' I said. 'You don't happen to know a Mrs Mainwaring, do you?'

'Mainwaring? I don't think I do. Are they a New York family?'

'I couldn't tell you. I've just received this,' I said and handed her the letter. She read it. 'I thought you'd given up detecting work,' she said.

'I have, but I can't help being curious. If the Mainwarings had turned out to be a well-known New York family, I could have made inquiries and maybe been able to give these Irish folk an answer to their concerns.'

'The fact that I don't know them doesn't mean that they are not New Yorkers,' Sarah said. 'We are not among the Four Hundred, you know. Daddy started off in trade, which has limited our social rise, much to Mama's annoyance. And these Mainwarings could be fellow members of the middle class who have now made enough money for a big house and plenty of servants. Besides,' she handed me back the letter, 'you don't know that Mrs Mainwaring does live in the city, do you? She might live anywhere.'

'The fact that this Maureen found a situation so quickly after arriving in New York indicated to me that the family must be local. She'd either have seen an advertisement or visited a local agency like the one you are taking me to.'

Sarah nodded. 'Of course people from all over the country advertise in the New York newspapers. She might have seen an offer of employment in Pennsylvania or California for all you know.'

I shook my head. 'I can't see an Irish girl fresh off the boat being willing to set out for California, not knowing about the people she was going to.'

'It's a wild goose chase, Molly.'

'I know, and one I shouldn't be undertaking. But I just thought that if it might be easily solved, then I'd solve it and put the poor woman's mind at rest.'

'Your husband would not take kindly to your traipsing around New York, I fear.'

I chuckled. 'He certainly wouldn't. But if this agency finds me a good servant, then I'll have even more time on my hands, won't I?'

She returned my smile. 'Molly, you're incorrigible. No wonder Sid and Gus like you so much.'

The cab had slowed to a crawl as it entered the Bowery and had to follow a slow-moving procession of horse-drawn vehicles being forced into the curb to get around a stopped electric trolley. Sarah tapped imperiously with her parasol on the roof of our cab. 'It's all right, driver. You can let us disembark here. It's quicker to walk the rest of the way.'

The driver jumped down to help us from the cab. 'You're sure you'll be all right, miss?' he said again. 'Watch out for pickpockets around here, and less savory folk too.'

'Don't worry, I come to this part of the city every day,' she said. 'I work in the settlement house on Elizabeth Street.'

'Well, blow me down,' he said, mopping his brow with a big red handkerchief. 'Good luck to you then, miss.' He looked at the coin she had given him then tipped his cap. 'And God bless you too.'

Sarah slipped her arm through mine and steered me through the traffic. We had to break into a sprint as a trolley car came toward us at full speed, its bell clanging madly. One always forgets how fast mechanized vehicles can go. Once on the other sidewalk we were in the shadow of the El and had to force our way among the housewives shopping for tonight's meal, children getting out of school, and factory workers coming off the early shift. When we turned into Broome the scene was even more chaotic with pushcarts lining both sides of the street and the air resounding with the cacophony of hawkers calling their wares, children shrieking at play, and the ever-present Italian organ grinder on the corner, cranking out a lively tarantella. Sarah seemed impervious to it all as she proceeded briskly, pushing aside ragged children and shopping baskets. She was moving at such a great pace that I found it hard to keep up with her and almost collided with a nun, bearing down from the opposite direction. She was wearing a black habit with a cape over it and carried a shopping basket over her arm. The habit was topped off with a peaked bonnet that jutted out, hiding her face in shadow, apart from a long nose that protruded, giving the impression of a black crow.

'Sorry, Sister,' I muttered, remembering the trouble I had gotten into at school when I'd run around a corner during a game and knocked one of the nuns flying.

'No harm done. God bless you, my dear,' she said softly, then crossed the street, nodding to two other nuns in severe black habits topped with white coifs who were chatting with a priest and couple of round, elderly women.

'I'm glad I'm not a nun,' Sarah said, echoing my thoughts. 'To be wearing all those garments in this weather must be unbearable.'

'They're probably so holy they don't notice,' I replied with a grin.

A bell started tolling, a block or so away. The little group broke apart and looked up. The two women crossed themselves. The priest nodded to them and then started walking briskly toward that tolling bell. The crowd on the sidewalk parted magically to let him through. It was clear that the Catholics held sway in this part of the city.

Sarah pulled me out of the stream of the crowd. 'Ah, here we are,' she said, stopping at a dark entryway. 'It's on the second floor. Are you able to make it up the stairs, Molly?'

'Yes, of course.' I peered up a long, narrow flight of stairs, then added, 'I'm not quite an invalid, you know.'

Up we went. I found it more of an effort than I had

expected and that long dark stair seemed to go on forever, but I tried not to let Sarah see that I was out of breath and perspiring by the time she tapped on a dark wood door and then ushered me inside.

I had been to employment agencies myself when I was first looking for work in the city. They all seemed to have been staffed by haughty dragons of women, but the white-haired, soft-faced lady behind the desk could not have been nicer. She listened to my request then nodded. 'You'll be wanting someone who has experience with babies then. Most of the girls we see don't have much of a clue. Oh, to be sure they've helped look after siblings, but their ideas on safety and cleanliness leave much to be desired. So let me give the matter some thought. How soon would you want the girl?'

'There's no hurry,' I said. 'I want someone who'll be just right. I'd rather wait.'

'Of course you would.'

'So did you already place Hettie Black, Mrs Hartmann?' Sarah asked.

'Oh, yes. Snapped up instantly. She would have been good,' Mrs Hartmann said. She had me write down my name and address. 'I'll have a note sent to you the moment I find a suitable girl,' she said.

We were about to leave when it occurred to me that Mrs Hartmann was the perfect person to ask about Maureen O'Byrne.

'You keep a list of past clients, presumably?' I started to say when there came a scream from the street below.

'My baby! Someone has taken my baby!'

Chapter 3

We rushed over to the window. Below us we could see a young woman, fair-haired and attired in the usual white shirtwaist and cotton skirt of the Lower East Side, looking around desperately, her light eyes wide with terror.

'My baby!' She screamed again. 'She was here. In her carriage. I left her for a second while I went into the butcher's and now she's gone.'

Instantly there was chaos as the crowd closed in around her. We didn't wait a second longer but went down the stairs as fast as we could, then were caught up in the crowd and swept across the street to the young woman. She was gesturing to a battered baby carriage that was now empty, apart from a crudely made cloth rabbit and one knitted bootie.

Older women had already come to her side to calm her screams. One of the nuns we had seen was first to reach her, patting her shoulder with a comforting meaty hand. 'Don't fret, my dear,' she said in a strong Irish accent. 'Perhaps someone from your family picked the baby up. Perhaps she was crying and one of your other children is carrying her around.'

'I don't have other children. She's my only child.' Her eyes continued to dart up and down the street. 'Who can have done this? Where have they taken her? My baby. Somebody find my baby for me.'

I felt a wave of terror, of almost physical sickness, come over me, and as if in response my own baby gave an almighty kick. I clutched at a lamppost to steady myself. Sarah had gone ahead of me, pushing through to the center of the little group. 'Somebody go and find the constable,' she said. 'And you children – spread out. Go and look to see if you spot anybody running away with a baby. They can't have gone too far with her.'

'Does anyone have smelling salts?' the nun demanded. 'This poor woman is about to pass out.'

Sarah rummaged in her delicate little purse and produced hers. The nun proceeded to wave them under the woman's nose. For once I could almost have used them myself. But I got a grip on myself and stepped forward. 'Did anybody see a person near the baby carriage? Did anyone see someone carrying a baby away?'

Heads were shaken.

'You see people carrying babies all the time,' a small girl answered. She spoke with a trace of Italian accent and had the black hair and big dark eyes that betrayed her ancestry and the fact that this quarter was known as Little Italy. She looked no older than seven or eight but she herself had a squirming toddler on her hip. 'We have to take the babies out and look after them so mother can clean up the apartment. Stop it, Guido,' she added as the toddler wriggled even harder. 'You're not getting down.'

The woman was no longer screaming but sobbing, her thin body shaking with great gulps.

'It's another of those kidnappings they're talking about,' a woman next to me muttered.

I turned to ask her what she meant when the crowd parted and two constables pushed their way toward the distraught woman.

'Stand aside please!' one of them bellowed. 'Move back now. Go on, about your business, all of you.' The crowd backed up a little as his bully club was brought out. He reached the woman. 'Now, what's happened here?'

Fifty people tried to talk at once, shouting in various accents with much hand waving. If the circumstances hadn't been so terrible, it would have been a comical scene. The constable held up his hands. 'Ladies. Quiet. One at a time.'

I glanced at Sarah, then decided it was about time I helped. I stepped forward. 'This woman's baby has been stolen from the baby carriage,' I said.

He looked at me, determining immediately from the way I was dressed that I was not a resident here. 'Did you witness it, ma'am?' he asked.

'No. We heard her screams when we were in that building across the street and came straight down. We have asked, but it seems that nobody actually witnessed it.'

He nodded. 'It's easy enough to lift a baby from a buggy around here without anyone seeing,' he said. He looked across at his fellow constable. 'You'd better let them know at HQ. We might be looking at another one.'

The younger policeman nodded, fought his way back through the crowd then disappeared down the street at a great rate. The constable turned back to the young woman, who was visibly shaking, hugging her arms to herself as if she was cold. 'Now then, what's your name, my dear?'

'It's Martha, sir. Martha Wagner.'

'So tell me exactly what happened, Mrs Wagner,' he said.

The young woman fought to control her sobs. 'I was shopping for my man's dinner, the way I always do. I went into the butcher's for sausages and I left the baby outside because there's no room for a buggy in the shop. I was only in there a moment. Not more than a minute or two, and when I came out . . .' she paused and gulped. 'She was gone!' Her voice rose in a hysterical scream again.

'You were alone? No other kids to guard the buggy?'

'She's my first. We've only been married a year,' the woman said. 'We just moved here from Pennsylvania. My man has just found a job on a river steamer.'

The nun was patting her arm again. 'We'll pray for you, my dear, and for your little child that the good Lord watch over her and deliver her safely back to you.'

The young woman shook her head furiously. 'I want her back now,' she said.

'We'll do what we can,' the constable said, 'and these things usually turn out well. So give us a description of the child.'

'They say she takes after me,' she said. 'She's three months old, real dainty like a little china doll with big blue eyes. Just a tiny amount of light hair like mine. Everyone says she's like a little angel. Her name is Florrie. Florence after my mother who passed away last year.'

The constable duly wrote this down. He shifted uncomfortably as if unsure what to do next.

'I heard that there have been other kidnappings,' I said. 'Does this fit the pattern?'

He looked at me as if I was speaking a strange tongue.

'That's not my job, ma'am,' he said. 'I couldn't say.'

'But surely the police must have some ideas? Haven't you been asked to be extra vigilant?'

Sarah tugged at my sleeve. 'Molly, we shouldn't get involved in this. I need the help of these men. I don't want to antagonize them. I'm sure they're doing all they can.'

'They don't seem to be,' I said angrily. 'He doesn't seem overly concerned. If it were my baby . . .' I stopped short as that awful vision flashed through my mind. My baby. If somebody stole my baby.

'The good sisters here will keep an eye open for your child,' the constable said, nodding to the nuns.

'We will indeed. And we can alert the sisters at the Foundling Hospital to be on the lookout as well.' She looked at her fellow nun for confirmation.

'But who can have taken her? Why would anyone do this?' The words came out as gulping sobs.

'I'm sure the baby will turn up again safe and sound,' the constable said. 'Now why don't you give us your address and . . .'

'Here we are, sir.' The young constable had reappeared, red-faced from running. 'Another kidnapping, so they are saying.' He forced his way through the crowd. 'Stand aside, ladies, and let the captain through.'

And to my horror Daniel materialized between the heads of the crowd. He strode impatiently to the center of the group with that confidence that bordered on arrogance.

'What's going on, McHale?' he demanded.

'This woman's baby's been snatched from the buggy,' the constable said. 'Just like the last one on Hester.'

'Are we sure it's a kidnapping this time?' Daniel

demanded. 'Remember the last time they dragged me out only to find that the child's grandmother had picked it up and gone into another store with it.'

'This lady doesn't seem to have any relatives around here,' McHale said. 'Newcomer to the city.'

Daniel glanced briefly at the woman who was now silent, but who clung to the sleeve of the nun's habit. He turned back to the constable. 'Any witnesses? The whole damned street was crowded with people. Someone must have seen something.'

His eyes searched the crowd. I had been standing holding my breath, not daring to move. His gaze reached me, went to pass on, then he started in surprise.

'Molly, what the devil are you doing here?' he demanded.

'I came with Sarah,' I said. 'You remember Sarah Lindley? She introduced me to an employment agency for domestics. We heard the screaming and . . .'

'An employment agency?' he snapped, glaring at me. 'I thought we'd agreed to put this matter into the hands of my mother. I asked you to mail the letter.'

'Which I did,' I said, 'but I met Sarah and it seemed like a good opportunity to check out some girls for myself.'

'But I thought I said clearly that—' He broke off abruptly. 'We've no time to go into this now.' He turned to the younger constable. 'Please escort Mrs Sullivan away from here and find a cab to take her home.'

Chapter 4

The young constable came over and offered me his arm. Every fiber of my being was itching to resist, to shake him off, to tell Daniel that I was not going to be ordered around by him and would make my own decisions. But I also realized that I was his wife and I couldn't question his authority in front of these people without jeopardizing his standing among them. Besides, the law gave husbands complete authority over their wives. This was really the first time I had had a true taste of Daniel exercising that authority, and I didn't like it.

'Go home with the constable now, please, Molly,' Daniel said, 'and we will discuss this later.'

I saw some of the women tittering behind their hands and others looking at me with sympathy. Sarah looked white-faced and shocked.

'I'm sorry,' I said. 'I'd better go. I don't want to complicate matters.'

She nodded. 'I understand. We'll be in touch.'

I let the constable lead me away. We had to walk all the way to the Bowery before he found a hansom cab for me.

Anger and humiliation thundered through my head all the way home. I was not going to accept this treatment from Daniel. I was not going to allow him to order me around like some servant. I was his wife, his partner, his equal. I would make that perfectly clear when he came home. When I reached Patchin Place I looked longingly at Sid and Gus's red-painted front door. If only they were home they'd take me in, allow me to let off steam, offer sympathy and advice, ply me with wine and whatever exotic delicacy they were cooking up at the moment. And at some stage we'd probably laugh over the stupidity of men and I'd come away feeling so much better. But they weren't home. They were miles away, enjoying the brisk sea air in Rhode Island. I heaved a sigh and put the key in my front door.

When I took off my hat and gloves I found the letter from Ireland stuffed into my handbag. In all the excitement I had completely put it from my mind. I took it out and reread it, looking with sympathy at the unschooled hand that wrote it and sensing her fear. I certainly wasn't just going to discard it or send it back to Ireland, that was for sure. Presumably I'd have to hand it over to Daniel and ask him to find another investigator to look into the disappearance of Maureen O'Byrne. Then my feisty nature resurfaced. The way Daniel had treated me, it would serve him right if I went behind his back and did the investigating myself.

A glance at the kitchen clock on the wall told me that I should think about preparing my husband's evening meal.

'He can go to hell first,' I said out loud. I'd not prepare anything for him tonight. He could come home to a bare table and fare for himself. That might remind him what life without a wife was like and how lucky he was to have me. Then those words 'go to hell' echoed around my head. *Be careful of what you wish for.* One of my mother's other favorite sayings. Daniel lived close to hell every day. I never knew when he might be dealing with a ruthless gang or a violent criminal, or when I'd open the door to find a policeman standing on my doorstep with bad news. I felt tears stinging in my eyes. I should not have said such a terrible thing, even if I didn't really mean it. After all, he was just behaving like any other man, wasn't he? Most women in the world were treated by their spouse like helpless, simple creatures who needed guiding and protecting – and chastising when they did something wrong. It was rather like being a pet dog.

Grudgingly I washed lettuce and radishes and put out a pork chop ready to fry. The sun sank lower through my kitchen window until it disappeared behind the silhouettes of tall buildings to the west. I ate my own light supper. Night fell and still he didn't come. I tried to read by the gaslight. Finally when the clock struck ten I went up and prepared for bed. But I couldn't begin to sleep. My mind was racing with terrible thoughts. I had made him angry and because of this he wasn't as vigilant as usual. I got up again and started to pace, going to the front window to peer down at Patchin Place, my ears straining for the sound of feet on the cobbles.

When I saw a constable coming, my heart nearly leaped from my throat, but it was only our usual constable on his nightly rounds and I heard his heavy boots die away into the rumble and roar of the distant city.

I sat in bed hugging my knees. 'Don't let him die,' I prayed. Images of myself trying to raise a fatherless child hovered in my brain. I heard a distant clock striking midnight and the city sounds fell silent one by one until all I could hear through the open window was a baby crying and a pair of tomcats yowling at each other on a distant rooftop.

Then suddenly I heard the sound of an automobile. A door slammed. Imperious feet came closer and the front door opened. I was out of bed in a shot.

'There you are at last,' I said as I appeared at the top of the stairs.

He looked up at me. 'What are you doing awake? You didn't wait up for me, I hope?'

'I was worried sick.'

'But you never know what time I'm coming in,' he said. 'As it happened I finished working late and went for a bite with a friend.'

The worry and anger exploded together. 'A bite with a friend?' I stomped down the rest of the stairs until I was facing him. 'While your wife worries about you and pictures you lying dead in a gutter? It's quite clear that you don't care about my feelings at all.'

He stepped back, clearly not expecting this onslaught. 'Steady on, Molly. You know I don't keep regular hours. I didn't leave my office until after ten and I didn't think you'd be up that late to cook for me.'

'I had your meal all ready and waiting,' I said, but even as I said it I decided that I sounded rather pitiful. 'And you're lucky I went to the trouble,' I said, 'after the humiliating way you treated me this afternoon. I was absolutely furious, Daniel.'

'I wasn't too pleased myself,' he said. 'I thought I made it quite clear to you that I didn't want you in the Lower East Side with all that dirt and disease. I can't believe that you deliberately went against my wishes.'

My hackles were truly rising now. That Irish fighting spirit was coursing through my veins. 'For one thing I was on Broome Street, which isn't the Lower East Side, it's Little Italy,' I said.

'You know what I meant,' he snapped back. 'I meant any of those areas of pushcarts and crowded tenements.'

'Greenwich Village isn't exactly a rural haven, is it? I'm risking dirt and disease just as much when I go to the grocery on Charles Street to buy your food.'

'I agree. That's precisely why I wanted you to go to my mother for the hottest months,' Daniel yelled back.

'If I'd known you'd rather eat out in a restaurant than come home for dinner, then I'd have gone long ago. I only stayed out of loyalty and devotion to you, but the way you order me around, you don't deserve either.'

'For your own good, Molly. I do it for your own good. You've become too accustomed to taking risks. You're no longer making decisions just for yourself, as I am no longer making decisions just for myself. We're a family, Molly. We have to pull together.'

I had been raring for a fight, but his rational approach and the tender way he was looking at me took the wind out of my sails. In my heart I knew he was making sense. It did seem as if I were deliberately undermining him. I took a deep breath. 'Daniel, you have to understand that I've been responsible for my own life and my own decisions for a long time now. If you take my own choices away from me and put them in the hands of your mother, it makes me feel that I'm worthless and useless and have no control over anything. I feel like a damned spaniel.'

I knew I was swearing and did it deliberately to show

that women were allowed to use as many bad words as men. He didn't even react to it.

'But it makes sense to use the experience of others. My mother moves in circles where people are used to hiring servants. Surely it is better for us to find a girl who comes with personal recommendations, rather than letting a complete stranger into our house, isn't it?'

I hated it when he was right. 'I suppose so,' I admitted grudgingly.

He put his hands on my shoulders, drew me toward him, and kissed me. 'Now up to bed with you. You need your sleep.' Then his arms wrapped around me, pulling me closer to him. 'And you don't look a bit like a spaniel,' he said. 'Your ears are much nicer.' And he nuzzled at one of them.

'Wait,' I said. 'I'm dying to know about the kidnapping I witnessed today. What did you find out? Did the lady get her baby back?'

'Molly, it's past midnight. You need your sleep and so do I. And you know I shouldn't discuss police matters with you.'

'But I witnessed it. I've a right to know.'

'Curiosity killed the cat,' he said, touching a finger to my lips. 'We'll talk about it in the morning. Off to bed with you.'

He slipped an arm around my waist and was about to escort me up the stairs when I said, in my most casual voice. 'By the way, a letter came for my old detective agency today.'

'I hope you returned it to the sender,' he said.

'Hold your horses,' I said. 'I was going to hand it to you to see if you knew of another private investigator who could look into the case. But the Irish woman who wrote it clearly has no money. She won't be able to pay normal rates and you probably wouldn't find any professional detective willing to take on her case. And this poor woman is worried sick about their niece who came to America and now has stopped writing to them. So I thought that since I had time on my hands . . .'

'Oh, no . . .' he began. 'Molly, what were we just talking about?'

'Just a minute!' I snapped. 'Would you stop behaving like the lord and master and listen to what I have to say. You know that raises my fighting spirit.'

'But, Molly – you are expecting a child. We have agreed that you should be taking it easy and not running any kind of risk, have we not?'

'I don't intend to run any kind of risk. The person who wrote to me has the name of the household in which this young woman was employed. I thought I might ask some of our friends if they have heard of this family. You know, people like Miss Van Woekem who move in society. It's a fairly uncommon name so what could be the harm in asking if anyone has heard of this family? And it would give me something to occupy myself with.'

He shrugged. 'I have no objection to your visiting our friends, as you know very well. But . . .'

'I understand. If no one we know has heard of the family in question, I have to turn the case over to another investigator or write to the Irish people telling them I can't help them.'

'Finally you're showing some sense,' he said. 'Now we've talked quite long enough. If you don't need your sleep, I certainly do.'

He put his arm around me and led me firmly up the stairs.

Chapter 5

I must have been really tired because I awoke with the sun streaming down on me and Daniel no longer in the bed. I arose hastily, pulled on my robe, and went downstairs. Daniel was sitting at the kitchen table, dressed and ready for work, with a mug of coffee in front of him.

'I'm sorry,' I said. 'You should have woken me.'

He looked at me with concern. 'You looked so peaceful lying there that I didn't have the heart. And you had a bad night, didn't you? Moaning and crying out in your sleep.'

'Did I?' I tried to remember. Something disturbing was lurking at the edge of my consciousness. 'I must have had a bad dream. But I can't for the life of me remember—' I broke off suddenly as a flash of memory came back. 'Oh, I do remember now. The stolen baby. I dreamed that someone had stolen my baby and I was desperately searching for it. That poor woman, Daniel. She was distraught. Did you manage to help her?'

He shook his head. 'I'm afraid it's just going to be a matter of waiting. That baby will materialize again when the parents pay the ransom.'

'But how can they afford to pay a ransom? They were obviously dirt poor.'

'It's been no more than a hundred dollars so far,' he said. 'And people can usually scrape together that much from relatives and friendly societies and unions.'

'So it's true what one woman said. It really was one in a string of kidnappings?'

He nodded. 'It seems to be. Five of them now that we know about in the last couple of weeks, all over the Lower East Side. Of course there could be more cases that we don't hear about. Parents might have been scared that something would happen to their child if they went to the police so they kept quiet, paid the ransom, and the child was returned.'

'And it was the same method of operation in each case?' I asked.

'As far as we can tell. Child snatched from its baby carriage, ransom note delivered to the parents, ransom money paid, and child returned safely.'

'That's awful. And you have no idea who is behind it?'

'Not yet. I suspect it's the work of a gang of some sort. Not one of the big gangs because they assure me they are not involved.'

'You take their word?'

'In this case yes. We have a sort of gentlemen's agreement that they provide cooperation if I overlook certain things.'

'What sort of things?'

He chuckled. 'I certainly couldn't share this information with you. It's entirely confidential. But I do trust Monk Eastman enough that when he tells me it's not his men, I have to believe him. No, I believe we're looking at a gang of petty thieves who maybe tried this once and realized they were onto a good thing. It's easy money with little risk. Who's going to notice if someone takes a baby in those crowded streets?'

'So how will you ever catch them?'

'We'll catch them in the end because like most criminals they'll become more greedy and more daring. The first three babies were left to the care of their older sisters and they were all Jewish families who could find a local synagogue or benevolent society to come up with the money. So now they've branched out further afield – an Italian baby and now this one – an American-born couple from Pennsylvania, and they've started taking babies from under the noses of their mothers. Soon they'll start demanding more than a hundred dollars, or start moving uptown to better neighborhoods, and then we'll nab them.'

'Could you gain no clue from the ransom notes? What kind of hand wrote them?'

'No kind of hand. They were made up of words cut from a newspaper or magazine.'

'So the kidnappers are literate, then.'

'They can read, if that's what you mean. Or at least one of them can read English, which might rule out a foreign gang, like those new Italian fellows. And frankly I don't think they'd stoop to baby snatching. The one thing they value is the family.'

'What about fingerprints on the ransom notes?' I asked suddenly as the idea occurred to me.

Daniel laughed. 'You're too sharp for your own good. We haven't been able to take any prints that we recognize yet. The trouble is that we need to build up a bigger repository of fingerprints. Most police departments don't bother with them since they've never been admissible in a court of law. Myself I think they are the way of the future, but it's hard to make people change their thinking.'

I poured myself a cup of coffee and sat down across the table from him. 'You'd think that some nosy old lady would have seen something from an upstairs window, wouldn't you? Or a woman hanging out laundry.'

'If some man had sneaked up and furtively grabbed a baby and run with it, then yes. But if the kidnapper was smart he'd have leaned over the buggy and acted as if the child was his. Then who would have noticed?'

'You speak as if it was a man,' I said. 'What if a woman is doing the actual kidnapping – a gangster's moll?'

'Quite possibly,' he said.

'That would make more sense, wouldn't it? The woman comes along, wheeling a baby carriage of her own, whisks the sleeping baby into her carriage, and pushes it away.'

'I'm glad you're married to a policeman or you might have ended up as a devious crook,' he said, smiling at me as he got to his feet. 'I've already shared more than I meant to, and I have to go.'

'Have you had breakfast? Let me at least cook you an egg.'

'I'll survive,' he said. 'I've a meeting at eight-thirty. We have something a little more worrisome on our plate at the moment. We've been tipped off about a new anarchist group who have apparently set up shop in the city. I'd like to hand these kidnappings over to a junior officer, but we're shorthanded at the moment, and since I'm the only one who is on good terms with Monk Eastman, I had to take this on myself or risk losing the goodwill I'd worked hard to establish.'

He took his hat from the peg on the wall and bent to kiss me.

'I could help,' I said, making him stop in his tracks.

'Help doing what?'

'With these kidnappings. I am an experienced detective, after all. I could help patrol the streets, keeping my eye open for kidnappers.'

'Molly.' He smiled, shaking his head at the same time. 'Even if I didn't mind you wandering through disease-ridden streets there's nothing you could do. They won't strike again until these people have paid the ransom and then there is no guarantee where they'll show up next. We'll probably have to wait until they slip up – which most crooks do in the end, I'm glad to say.' He started for the front door. 'Oh, and, Molly, I'd like you to get in touch with that employment agency and let them know that you'll not be requiring their services.'

The front door slammed behind him. I got up and started to clear away the coffee cups. I turned the water on in the scullery sink so violently that it splashed up all over me. I was brimming over with frustration and futility. That woman's face hovered in front of me, her panicked eyes darting from side to side. Surely I'd have been able to help. I was a woman, after all. I wouldn't stand out, like a constable in uniform. I was so tempted to go against Daniel's wishes, but a small voice in my head whispered warnings. What if I did catch some terrible disease and I lost the baby or died myself? Besides, I ran the risk of being seen by one of Daniel's men or even Daniel himself and then I'd never hear the last of it.

I went upstairs to wash and dress. A cool breeze was stirring the net curtains at the window. I took off my robe and sat on the bed, enjoying the feel of the breeze through the thin cotton of my nightgown. Surely there was something I could do to help. After all, I'd come out onto that street at the very moment that the woman screamed. Hadn't I seen anything? I closed my eyes and tried to re-create that street in my mind. But all I could see was the woman, standing there screaming, people running toward her, not running away.

My hand stroked across the silky fabric of the comforter and I turned my thoughts to last night's dream. It was strange that I hadn't remembered it when I awoke. Sometimes I had the most vivid dreams, but all I could recall of this one was the feeling of panic and dread as I stared into an empty baby carriage.

Nothing. There was nothing I could do, except leave it to the police, as Daniel had told me so many times before. But there were times when I had ignored him and I had succeeded when the police had not. I had been a good detective, I reminded myself. The thought of doing nothing was more than I could bear, and yet this was how it was going to be for the rest of my life.

Then I remembered the letter. Now here was something I could do. Daniel had told me he wanted me to contact the employment agency to tell them I'd no longer be requiring their services. He didn't say how I should contact them, so I'd pay a visit in person this morning and this time be able to find out if they'd ever had a Maureen O'Byrne on their books or had heard of a Mrs Mainwaring. If they hadn't then they could give me the addresses of other employment agencies that Irish girls fresh off the boat might have used.

Having a plan of action before me, I now dressed in a

hurry, cleaned up the house, and then set off. The weather was changing. Clouds were scudding across the sky from the west, bringing with them a strong breeze that stirred up the dust as I crossed Washington Square. The square was populated with people enjoying the fresh air before it became too hot. Mothers sat on benches fanning themselves in the shade, while children ran around with hoops and jump ropes, doing what children do.

I looked at the baby buggies stationed beside the seated women. Two women were deep in conversation, their arms waving expressively as they talked, and I realized how easy it would be to walk past, reach down, sweep up a baby, and go on walking. Had the kidnappers a particular target in mind before they took a child, or were the kidnappings random? Somehow they had to find out the name and address of the victim to be able to deliver the ransom note, but that wouldn't be hard. I remembered that the woman yesterday had been asked for her address by the police while I was there, and presumably had given it within the hearing of those around her. An accomplice of the kidnapper could have been among the crowd, ready to overhear and take down the particulars.

I left the square behind me, walked to Broadway, and took the trolley to Broome. Then I faced the long climb up the stairs to the agency. How did women manage at home in Ireland when they walked several miles into town with one baby on their hip, another in their belly, and a basket full of shopping on their arm? Obviously I was not as strong as I thought.

Mrs Hartmann nodded in sympathy when I explained my predicament. 'I didn't realize he'd already asked his mother,' I said, not wanting to admit that I'd gone against my husband's wishes.

'I quite understand,' she said, her gaze indicating that husbands were infernally annoying creatures, 'but I'll still keep my eyes open for you, Mrs Sullivan. Your husband's mother may not be able to find a suitable girl in a hurry and I think it's very important that your servant learns your ways and the running of your household well before the baby arrives.'

'Thank you,' I said. 'You have my address. If the perfect girl shows up, I'd certainly like to meet her.' I stood up to go, then lingered. 'There's one more thing,' I said. 'I was going to ask you yesterday before we were interrupted. Is it possible that a girl called Maureen O'Byrne came to your agency about a year ago?'

She frowned. 'The name doesn't ring a bell, but we deal with so many girls. A year ago, you say?' She called into the outer office, 'Jessie, would you check the books and see if we ever had a Maureen O'Byrne as a client, about a year ago?' She turned back to me, 'Was this a girl you possibly wanted to hire?'

'Possibly,' I said. 'Actually I'm trying to find where she is employed now for her relatives at home in Ireland. She hasn't written for a while and they're worried. I just thought that Maureen might well have been to an agency such as your own.'

Jessie poked her head around the door. 'Nobody by that name that I can see, Mrs Hartmann.'

'Thank you, Jessie,' she said. 'I'm sorry, Mrs Sullivan. We can't help you.'

'What about a Mrs Mainwaring?' I asked. 'Have you ever supplied her with servants?'

'Does she live in New York? We don't really handle clients outside of Manhattan.'

'I don't know. That's the problem,' I said. 'Maureen wrote to her relatives that she'd found a good position with a Mrs Mainwaring. And that was the last they heard from her.'

'I've never dealt with a woman of that name,' she said. 'But there must be twenty or more agencies like ours in this part of the city, not to mention the more exclusive ones further uptown.'

'Would you be kind enough to give me the names of some of those agencies?' I asked.

'I can have Jessie write out a list of those we know,' she said. 'Was this Miss O'Byrne a relative of yours? You're going to a lot of trouble for her.'

'I like to help when I can,' I said. 'I'm sorry to have taken up so much of your time.'

'Not at all. Always glad to help a potential future client.'

I came down the stairs again with a list of similar agencies in my purse. Unfortunately they seemed to be in areas that Daniel wouldn't want me to go. I suppose that made sense if they wanted to attract girls straight from the boats – but they were off limits to me. I fought back annoyance again until I told myself I was, as usual, being too impatient. I could easily write to the addresses I had been given. It would only be a question of waiting a few days, and her family had already waited months. A week or so longer wouldn't make much difference.

Thus appeased for now, I came out to the street and stood staring across at the shop window where the kidnapping had taken place. Other women pushed baby carriages past the shop, some pausing to chat as they met a neighbor. The scene was peaceful and ordinary as if no tragedy had happened there. I wondered if the couple at the center of yesterday's drama had received their ransom note yet and how they would possibly come up with the money. I wondered what would happen if they couldn't come up with the money. Would the baby then wind up floating in the East River with a note tied to it to warn future victims to pay up? It made me feel sick to think about it.

I was about to make my way home when I froze. Someone I recognized was hurrying straight toward me. He was absolutely the last person that I ever expected to see again – my brother Liam.

Chapter 6

It couldn't be true. For a second I wondered if my eyes were playing tricks on me, but the sunlight was falling directly onto that flame-red hair, making it glow brighter even than my own, and the way he swung his arms in that rolling, jaunty way when he walked was so familiar to me. The last time I had seen him was two years ago, when we'd had to flee together from Ireland after a failed prison break that had killed my other brother Joseph. I'd left Liam hiding out in France, wanted by the English. So what on earth was he doing walking down a busy street in New York in broad daylight?

'Liam!' I exclaimed in delight and moved forward to throw my arms around him.

Instead he took a backward step. He looked startled, afraid, and for a moment I thought he was going to bolt on me. But his eyes lit up and he managed the ghost of a smile. 'Molly. It's good to see you. How are you?'

'Well, thank you.'

His eyes traveled over my person and reacted when he noticed my belly. 'It's a little one you're carrying, is it?

Does that mean that–' He broke off, trying to phrase the question correctly. I could see he was trying to catch a glimpse of my left hand.

I read his meaning and laughed. 'Yes, in case you're wondering, Liam, I'm rightly and properly married. To a captain in the police force no less. I'm Mrs Daniel Sullivan.'

I saw his glance become wary. 'A captain of police. Well, well.'

'I would have written to tell you the news, but I had no way to contact you.'

He nodded. 'It's better that way.'

He looked thinner than when I'd last seen him and he never had had more than an ounce of meat on those bones. And older too. A grown man and not a boy. A man who had seen too much suffering for his years.

'Holy Mother of God, Liam,' I said. 'It's grand to see you. How long have you been in the city?'

'A week or so.'

'Why didn't you let me know?'

He shifted uneasily from one foot to the other. 'It's a big city, Molly. How would I have found you?'

'I left my address with you, didn't I?' I felt frustration rising inside me. This was my brother, whom I hadn't seen for years, and he was treating me like a causal acquaintance, almost like a stranger.

'You might have done so. But I destroyed all the papers I had; everything, just in case we got caught. No sense in involving other people in our struggles. That's why I didn't try to seek you out, Molly. It's better if no one knows I'm here.'

'What are you doing here, for God's sake?' I demanded.

He looked around warily, although nobody on the street seemed to be paying either of us any attention. 'I can't tell you that, Molly.'

'Look, why don't you come back to my place for a meal?' I said. 'Then we can have a grand old chat.'

Again that guarded look. 'I'd rather not, if you don't mind. Better for both of us that way.'

I touched his arm lightly. 'Liam, are you in trouble?'

At this he laughed. 'Trouble? Me? Oh, no, only a price on my head from the English and me in this country with false papers. Otherwise everything's just grand.' He shifted uneasily again. 'I shouldn't be standing out here, for anyone to see.'

'Then come and have a cup of tea. There are plenty of little cafés on the Bowery.'

He shook his head again. 'I'd rather not, if you don't mind.' He must have seen my face fall. 'Look, I don't want to involve you in anything, Molly. Far better if you've not seen me and don't know that I'm here.'

'But I'd like to help if I can,' I said. 'Is it on Brotherhood business that you're here?'

'Of course, but I can't tell you about it so don't ask me.' He glanced past me up the street. 'I should be going. It was lovely to see you. I just wish I could stay and have a "grand old chat." '

'Liam, don't go yet.' I grabbed his sleeve this time. 'You're the only family I've got, apart from young Malachy, and I don't even know where he is anymore.'

'He's doing just fine from what I hear,' Liam said. 'He's still being looked after by Mr O'Brien of the Irish League up in the north. I get reports on him from time to time. He's a big strapping lad now, they say, as tall as me. Maybe

I'll see him again if he decides to come and fight for the cause.'

'But surely you can never go back to Ireland, can you?' I asked. 'You said yourself there was a price on your head.'

'There's a price on the heads of all those who fight for our freedom, Molly. But we're not just going to sit by and do nothing. We've a right to govern ourselves and we have to do what it takes to claim back what's rightfully ours.'

My mind went back to the events in Dublin, the bomb and the chaos and the dead bodies at that jail and our other brother Joseph sprawled dead in the street. It all seemed as remote as something I'd read about in a book. And yet Liam was still living it, clearly still planning to go on fighting.

'God be with you then, Liam,' I said. 'I'm at ten Patchin Place if you need me. Can you remember that? It's in Greenwich Village, just north of Washington Square.'

He looked at me, long and hard, as if trying to memorize my face. 'I'll not be involving you in this, Molly. Better if you forget you've ever seen me, all right?' He patted my shoulder and attempted a jaunty smile. 'Good luck to you, and to your captain and the little one. You can always name him Liam after me. Someone needs to carry on the name.'

Then he pushed past me and crossed the street to the other side. I stood and watched him go until he turned the corner into Elizabeth Street.

After he'd gone all I wanted was to retreat to the safety and security of my own little home. I hurried to the Broadway trolley and back to Patchin Place. The wind had really picked up now, buffeting me full in the face as I crossed the north side of Washington Square and sending scraps of paper twirling. And those white fluffy clouds were now heavier. It would rain before the day was out.

As I entered my house I saw the curtains in the kitchen billowing out and realized that I'd left the windows open to cool down the place. I closed the windows then sat at the kitchen table, trying to catch my breath. I had walked far too fast for my current condition and I could feel my heart hammering in my chest. As if in response, the child wriggled and squirmed. I put my hand on my belly to quiet it and felt the strong little kick against my fingers. He or she would be born in a few weeks and would probably never meet his Uncle Liam. I felt tears pricking at my eyes.

My brothers and I had never been that close. I was the big sister, the one who cooked for them and mended their torn clothing and broke up their fights. Joseph had only been two years younger than I – a co-conspirator in my adventures – but Liam was five years younger – the little one who tagged along and who ratted on us to our mother if we did something wrong. I'd never really known him. For a few brief moments we had been together in Dublin, but only as fellow soldiers in a failed uprising. And yet he and Malachy were all the family I had in the world and he was clearly risking his life by being here. I wanted to help but he wouldn't let me.

'Oh, Liam,' I said out loud, overwhelmed with futility and grief. I sank my head into my arms on the table and stayed there, feeling the cool of the scrubbed wood against my cheek. I suppose my disturbed night's sleep must have had something to do with what happened next, because I awoke to find someone shaking my shoulder.

I sat up, heart thumping and with no idea where I was. Daniel's concerned face came into focus above me.

'Good God, Molly. What's wrong?' he asked. 'You look terrible.'

I could feel my cheek smarting as it came back to life. 'Nothing's wrong. I must have nodded off, that's all.'

'Doing too much again, I'll wager,' he said. 'And too late to bed last night. I don't know how many times I've told you that you have to take it easy. Go and wash your face, there's a good girl, and spruce yourself up. I've brought a guest home for lunch.'

I was instantly galvanized into action. 'A guest? Why didn't you warn me? I could have made something special.'

'It was rather spur of the moment. We had a meeting together and then he asked after my wife and said how much he'd like to meet you again. Since it was around lunchtime I suggested we come back here.'

'Who is it?' I asked.

'You'll see. I've put him in the front parlor and I'll bring him a glass of whiskey to keep him happy until you have lunch ready.'

I crept upstairs and started in horror when I saw my face in the bathroom mirror. Lying against the wood of the table had flattened one side of my cheek, giving it a strange, villainous expression. I splashed cold water and massaged my cheek to bring it back to life, then brushed my disheveled hair, all the while trying to think what on earth I could serve to Daniel and a nameless male visitor. Really men were hopeless, weren't they – expecting their wives to produce a meal out of thin air, like a conjurer drawing a rabbit from a hat.

By the time I had made myself look respectable I had decided that I had enough eggs in the larder to make an omelet with cheese and parsley. I had some salad greens from the day before that shouldn't have wilted too much and I had those lovely peaches to serve for dessert. I could hear the sound of deep male voices in the front parlor as I came down the stairs, followed by hearty male laughter. Of course my curiosity got the better of me. I had to know for whom I'd be cooking lunch.

They both looked up and got to their feet as I appeared in the doorway.

'Ah, Molly, there you are,' Daniel said. 'You remember Mr Wilkie, don't you?'

Chapter 7

Mr John Wilkie, head of the newly formed Secret Service, came toward me, his hand extended. 'My dear, Mrs Sullivan, how good to see you again. And looking so radiant too. Your husband informs me that congratulations are in order.'

His hand gripped mine in a powerful grasp.

'How good to see you again, Mr Wilkie,' I said. 'Although if Daniel had informed me in advance that he was bringing a guest to eat with us, I'd have been able to make you a better meal.'

'I'm sure whatever you prepare will be just fine,' Mr Wilkie said. 'And I assure you that my desire in coming here was to see you again, not to sample your cooking skills.'

'I hope an omelet will do,' I said.

'It will fit the bill perfectly.' He gave me a beaming smile. From his jocular manner it was hard to believe that this was a man who was responsible for the security of the nation and who dealt with spies and anarchists.

As I excused myself to go through to the kitchen I heard

him say to Daniel, 'It's too bad you've chained her down with a family, Sullivan. I could have used her to work for me. She's one gutsy little woman. And sharp too.'

'Too sharp for her own good, sometimes,' Daniel retorted. 'I'm glad she'll soon have a baby to occupy her and keep her out of mischief.'

I set to work beating the eggs, wondering all the while why Mr Wilkie had insisted on coming to meet me again. Perhaps he wanted me to do something for him. He had hinted at my wedding that he'd like to use me again some-time. Of course Daniel would flat out refuse. Once more it passed through my mind that Daniel didn't have to know. If I worked for Wilkie I'd be some kind of spy, wouldn't I, and spies weren't supposed to confide in their spouses.

Then I laughed out loud at the ridiculousness of this thought. A fine spy I'd make with my bulging belly and then with a baby on my hip, demanding loudly to be fed while I tried to tail dangerous, international criminals. I managed a presentable omelet and salad, then peaches and cheese for dessert. The conversation was limited to harmless and general subjects – the recent hot weather, the political situation in Washington, possible names we might choose for our child. I remained the gracious host-ess until I couldn't stand it a moment longer.

'Mr Wilkie, you clearly didn't come to New York to discuss the weather with the Sullivans,' I said. 'Are you needing Daniel's help with a new case?'

'Molly!' Daniel gave me a warning glare.

John Wilkie laughed. 'I told you your wife was sharp as a tack, didn't I, Sullivan. Of course I didn't come to New York in midsummer for the sake of my health. And your husband's knowledge of the city should prove invaluable. Actually we're keeping tabs on a new group of anarchists.'

'Is Emma Goldman still at their center?' I asked.

He laughed again. 'Now, how did you know about Emma Goldman?'

'I was involved in the assassination of President McKinley,' I said, then corrected myself. 'What I meant to say was that I was investigating a murder that brought me into contact with Mrs Goldman, so I know a lot about her.'

'My, but you would be useful to me,' Wilkie said.

'The answer is no, Wilkie,' Daniel said. 'Rope me in to help with your cases as much as you like, but my wife is no longer available for your little schemes.'

Wilkie was still smiling. 'In answer to your previous question, Mrs Sullivan, from what we can gather this is a new and completely separate group of anarchists with no ties to previous cells. They seem to be popping up like mushrooms all over the globe at the moment, I'm afraid, and with very different goals. Some of them idealistic about creating a new order in countries like Russia, some of them seeking only destruction and collapse of regimes. And all of them quite ruthless, which is why we have to nip in the bud any threat against our government.' He pushed his plate away from him. 'Fine lunch, Mrs Sullivan, but we should be getting back to work. So good to see you again.'

He held out his hand to me and shook mine warmly. I followed them out of the dining room.

'I may be late again tonight, my dear,' Daniel said.

'So now you're working with Mr Wilkie, does that mean that you're no longer supervising the kidnapping case?'

'Kidnapping – what's this?' Mr Wilkie asked and I saw Daniel give me an annoyed look. 'I've heard nothing about it. Don't kidnappings fall under my jurisdiction?'

'Not these particular incidents,' Daniel said. 'They all involve poor families in the Lower East Side, with ransoms of less than a hundred dollars. We suspect the work of a small gang, who have stumbled upon an easy way to make money.'

'Have the children been returned safely?'

'So far,' Daniel said. 'At least in the cases we know about. I presume some parents never go to the police out of fear.'

Wilkie nodded. 'If it's a small gang, then you shouldn't have too much trouble. They'll become too bold. That sort always do.'

'You're right, sir,' Daniel said. 'We should be on our way, then. Good-bye, Molly.' He gave me a peck on the cheek. 'And no more roaming around, remember. Take a rest this afternoon.'

'Yes, Daniel,' I replied, giving my best imitation of a good wife, making both of the men smile.

After they had gone I cleared away the remains of the meal, then wandered around the house, wondering what to do next. My nap at the kitchen table had taken away my need for an afternoon siesta, but the weather now looked as if it might rain any moment. I considered going uptown to Gramercy Park and visiting old Miss Van Woekem, who knew everybody worth knowing in New York, but I had no desire to get soaked to the skin. Besides, when it rained the trolley cars and Els became packed with people.

So I set to work on my other task – writing to the

employment agencies inquiring about Maureen O'Byrne and Mrs Mainwaring. On the sofa I noticed my latest piece of sewing, lying rumpled and unattractive, waiting to be finished. If I managed to locate Maureen, I'd accept a modest fee that would enable me to buy all the under-garments a baby needed. I was on my fourth letter when I heard a tap at the front door. I went to open it and found Mr Wilkie standing there.

'Mr Wilkie,' I exclaimed.

'Mrs Sullivan, I'm sorry to disturb you, but I believe I may have put down my gloves in your parlor,' he said.

'I don't think so,' I began, 'but please do come and take a look.'

He strode ahead of me into the parlor, looked around briefly, and then said, 'No, you're right, they're not here. Then I must have left them in the police department auto-mobile. No doubt your husband will find them.'

He hesitated, as if reluctant to leave, and it suddenly came to me that the gloves had been an excuse to return here. He wanted to find me alone. He was going to ask me to work for him, in spite of Daniel's protests. I felt a thrill of excitement rush through me. I would have to turn him down, of course. But nevertheless it was flattering to be asked.

'Was there something else, Mr Wilkie?' I asked. 'I sensed when you came for lunch that important men like you don't take time out of a busy schedule to pay social calls on the wives of colleagues for no reason at all.'

Wilkie chuckled. 'What did I say? Sharp, Mrs Sullivan. Sharp as a tack. There was something, that I didn't want to bring up in front of your husband, but I never found the opportunity for a second alone with you during luncheon.

May I sit down?' He chose Daniel's leather club chair and sat, motioning me to take a seat on the sofa. I tried not to look too keen or interested as I assumed a modest pose with hands folded in my lap.

'Mrs Sullivan this is a rather delicate matter,' he said. 'One I don't wish to share with your husband for obvious reasons.'

For one absurd second it crossed my mind that it was my body he was interested in, and not my sharp brain. Then I reminded myself that no man would choose as a mistress someone in my present condition. He cleared his throat as if trying to find the right words. I was really intrigued now.

'You have a brother, I believe,' he said at last.

'I have two brothers still living,' I said.

'Would it surprise you to know that one of them, Liam Murphy, is in New York at this very moment?'

I checked myself before I answered, 'Liam?' I feigned surprise. 'In New York? That can't be true.'

'So he has not contacted you then?'

'He'd have no way of contacting me. He doesn't know my address or anything about me. We were never close and I haven't heard from him in years. Are you sure it's my brother? There are plenty of young Irishmen called Liam Murphy, and plenty more with red hair.'

'It's him right enough,' Mr Wilkie said. 'My counterparts in Britain have been keeping tabs on him and his Republican Brotherhood and they notified me that he'd sailed from Le Havre in France, heading for the United States.' When I said nothing he looked up, his gaze holding mine. 'You did know that your brother is part of the Republican Brotherhood, I take it?'

I realized then that nobody had connected me to that failed prison break in Dublin. One of them had given his life to spirit me away. 'I suspected as much,' I said. 'Liam always did have a strong sense of justice, and what red-blooded Irishman would not want to fight to gain independence for his own country? We've been an occupied country for three hundred years, you know. And America did exactly the same thing in 1776 to free themselves from the British yoke.'

Mr Wilkie had to smile at this. 'It's not my place to judge the righteousness of his cause,' he said, 'but I am bound to cooperate with my counterparts in Britain and your brother is wanted on a capital charge over there.'

'Do you know what made him come to America?' I demanded and I could hear the belligerent tone in my voice now. 'Is it possible he's seen the hopelessness of the Republican cause and has decided to try for a better life for himself in America, the same as all those other immigrants?'

'If that were true, I'd say good luck to him,' Mr Wilkie said. 'But I'm afraid that we have credible intelligence that he's here on Republican Brotherhood business.'

'Raising money, you mean?'

'Possibly. The Irish in America are known to be more than generous when it comes to the Home Rule cause. And not just with money. Weapons too. It could be that he's here to acquire weapons.' He paused. I remembered being involved in smuggling a trunk full of rifles to Ireland, but tried to keep my face composed. 'It's possible, I suppose,' I said.

'But we are concerned it may be more than that,' Wilkie continued. 'I mentioned a newly formed anarchist group to you. We have gotten wind that they are planning some kind of coup, and the Irish Republican Brotherhood may be involved.'

'Why are you telling me all this?' I asked.

'Because your brother may well try to contact you, to ask for assistance,' Mr Wilkie said.

'And if he does?'

'Then I'd like you to let me know.'

'You want me to betray my own brother?' I rose to my feet.

'It's a question of whether family loyalty should come before the greater good. If this group is planning something that involves the killing of innocent people, for example – where would your loyalties lie then? And how would it look if the wife of a distinguished police captain might be implicated as an accessory if you did not turn in your brother?'

'Would you turn your own brother in to the authorities, knowing that he'd be hanged when all he tried to do was rescue our other brother from jail?' I stood there, hands on hips and really angry now.

'Maybe we can come to some sort of arrangement,' Mr Wilkie said softly. 'I may be able to find a way for him to stay here in America, with a new identity – a chance for a new life, if he agrees to give up his connections to the Brotherhood. What do you say – wouldn't you rather your brother was here safely, able to make a good life for himself?'

'Of course I'd want that,' I said, 'but I'm not my brother. That decision would have to come from him. But this is all a moot point, Mr Wilkie. Liam has not tried to contact me and I think it's unlikely that he will for the very reason you suggested. He would not want to implicate me in any of his schemes.'

Mr Wilkie had also risen to his feet. 'I've taken enough of your time, Mrs Sullivan, and I'm truly sorry to have caused you any distress. All I can say is that I will do what is within my power to help your brother if he puts himself in my hands. You'll tell him that at least, won't you, if he shows up on your doorstep one night?'

'I'll tell him that,' I agreed. 'If he shows up on my doorstep.'

Mr Wilkie picked up his hat and placed it on his head. 'Then I take my leave of you. Oh, and I see no reason to mention this conversation to your husband. He doesn't know anything yet about your brother's possible involvement in this matter. Good day to you, Mrs Sullivan.'

'And to you too, Mr Wilkie,' I said.

'I can let myself out,' he said and went.

Chapter 8

I slumped back onto the sofa, the wind knocked from my sails. Actually I felt quite sick. He wanted me to work for him as a spy all right, but only to ensnare my own brother. I had sensed that Liam was in danger, but I hadn't realized how serious his situation was. And now I realized that I could never attempt to seek him out to warn him. It was all too possible that John Wilkie would have someone tailing me wherever I went and I wasn't going to risk leading his men straight to Liam.

No wonder Liam had looked so anxious when I stopped him in the street. I tried to think how I could get word to him that the authorities were looking for him. If I couldn't go into the Lower East Side myself I'd have to send someone else. The person who came immediately to mind was Sarah. Her settlement house was only a block away from where I had encountered Liam. If he was staying nearby there was a good chance she'd see him. I must somehow get a letter to her, that she could hand to Liam, warning him. But that posed another problem. I couldn't risk going to that settlement house in case I bumped into Liam again. If only Sid and Gus were here.

I jumped as there was a knock at the front door again. Who could that be now? Maybe Mr Wilkie regretted what he had just asked me to do and was returning to apologize. And to think that two days ago I had complained about being bored. I smoothed down my skirt and opened the front door.

Standing before me was the most welcome sight in ages.

'Molly, we're back!' said my dear friend Augusta Walcott, usually known as Gus, as she wrapped me in a hug.

'I'm so delighted to see both of you,' I said, turning to hug my other friend, Elena Goldfarb, nicknamed Sid, in turn. 'Come on in. I've lemonade or iced tea.'

'Just what we hoped,' Sid said. 'We're parched after that long uncomfortable train journey. We had to wait for the connection in Providence for over an hour. Some sort of trouble on the line.'

They followed me through to the kitchen and sat at my kitchen table.

'So how was Newport?' I asked as I put a kettle on the stove. 'I kept thinking of you enjoying that ocean breeze.'

'The breeze was fine,' Gus said. 'And the sea bathing was delightfully cool, and we went for a sail or two. Those were the good parts.'

'And the not so good?' I asked.

Sid grinned. 'Nonstop social functions – croquet and tennis parties and luncheons, dinners, formal balls. Also Gus's cousin was determined to set her up with a young man.'

'A ghastly young man,' Gus added. 'He talked with a

lisp and sprayed when he said his esses. And he talked about himself all the time and how wonderful he was and how brilliantly he played tennis.'

'Sounds delightful,' I said dryly.

'Oh, and he came from the best of families, as Gus's cousin kept reminding us,' Sid said. 'And when Gus told her cousin that she was quite happy in her current situation and saw no reason to change, the cousin was frightfully huffy.'

'She said that friendships such as ours were quite acceptable among young girls, before they knew the way of the world and were ready for a husband, but quite unacceptable thereafter,' Gus added with a grin at Sid.

'So we packed up and escaped,' Gus said, giving Sid a conspiratorial glance. 'I don't really know what made us accept the invitation in the first place. We knew how unbearably snobbish and conniving my cousin would be and how she'd keep trying to make a suitable match for me.'

'Hurray for your cousin. I can't tell you how glad I am that you're home again,' I said.

'You've been dying of boredom, I knew it,' Sid said. 'What did I tell you, Gus. I said we should have spirited Molly with us to Newport.'

I put a plate of cookies on the table and took down the best china from the cupboard. 'Until two days ago that was true,' I said. 'But things have been happening thick and fast.' And all details of the letter and Sarah and the kidnapped baby came spilling out and I finished by telling them about bumping into Liam and Mr Wilkie's visit. I should probably have kept quiet about the latter, but I had come to rely on my friends and their good sense, and

I needed to tell someone. Also I've never been good at holding my tongue.

'Goodness me,' Gus said. 'You've been having far too much excitement without us.'

'I feel rather shaken up by all of it, if you want to know,' I said. 'Seeing that poor woman so distraught when her child was kidnapped really upset me.'

'Well it would, given your current condition,' Gus said.

'And then running into my brother like that, only to find that the Secret Service is on the lookout for him. I really want to warn him, but I don't see how I can risk going anywhere near him without putting him in even greater danger.' I got up as the kettle began to sing on the stove.

'Molly,' Gus said carefully, 'you say your brother is in great danger and you want to warn him, but if he's really part of some kind of anarchist plot, should you really stand in the way of the authorities and tip off these people that the Secret Service is onto them? I mean, what if they plan to assassinate the king of England or our president? I know blood is thicker than water, but . . .'

'I don't want you to think that I condone anything like that. If I try and warn Liam it will be to go back to France and have nothing to do with this plot. I can't believe he'd want to be part of something that involved innocent lives.'

I saw my friends exchange a hurried glance.

'I thought maybe I could write him a letter, telling him that he should leave the country right away. Maybe Sarah could keep an eye out for him to deliver the letter for me. I saw him on the corner of Elizabeth Street, not too far from her settlement house. But Daniel doesn't want me going to that area. Do you think you'd be able to deliver the letter to her?'

'Of course,' Gus said.

'Better than that,' Sid said. 'You can enlist us, Molly. We can scour the Lower East Side looking for your brother, can't we, Gus.'

'I can't ask you to do that for me,' I said quickly.

'Nonsense, we'd love to do it. You know we always jump at the chance to help you with your sleuthing.'

'Yes, I know,' I said with slight hesitation. Sid and Gus had always been keen volunteers, but the trouble was that to them life was a great and glorious game.

'Oh, come on, Molly, do say yes,' Gus said. 'We're itching to do something useful after all those days of mindless chatter and tea parties.'

'I don't think you understand how serious this is,' I said. 'The police are looking for him. If you approach him and say anything that anyone could overhear, you're sealing his death warrant.'

Sid looked rather haughty as she said, 'Molly, I think we can be trusted to show a little common sense. We are women of the world, after all. And our work with the suffrage movement has required guts and diplomacy.'

I realized this was true. They took terrible risks for the cause and had been to jail on at least one occasion. 'Of course. Forgive me,' I said. 'I'd be most grateful if you undertook this task for me. I'll write the letter today.'

'What does your brother look like – do you have a photograph?'

'No, but he looks like me,' I said. 'His hair is even brighter red and he's thinner and rather gaunt-looking now, but the resemblance is very strong. You'd recognize him if you saw him.'

'Well then, that's settled,' Sid said. 'You write the letter. We'll get unpacked and sorted out and then we'll be at your disposal.'

'You're the tops,' I said. 'I'll never be able to repay all the kind things you've done for me.'

'Nonsense,' Gus said. 'Our life would be awfully boring if you didn't live across the street. We love a little spice and danger from time to time, don't we, Sid?'

'Just a little,' Sid said.

I poured each of them a glass of iced tea and put the sugar bowl in front of them.

'Then can I also ask you to keep your eyes open for more potential kidnappings when you're going through the Lower East Side?'

'More kidnappings? Are you expecting more?' Gus sounded shocked.

'I'm afraid so. The one I witnessed, or almost witnessed, was the fifth recently that the police know about. Daniel thinks that a gang has found taking babies an easy way of making money.'

'That's despicable,' Sid said. 'We shall certainly keep our eyes open and if we do witness one, then heaven help the kidnapper.'

'Oh, do be careful,' I said hurriedly. 'These gangs are quite ruthless.'

Gus put her hand over mine. 'Don't worry. I'll make sure she doesn't do anything too daring or stupid. But I have to confess I'm a teeny bit excited about apprehending a possible kidnapper myself. Do you have any description?'

'None at all. The police have nothing to go on. I'm afraid snatching a baby is all too easy in those crowded streets.'

'We'll just do our best then,' Gus said. 'You can rely on us, Molly.'

And she saluted. I laughed. 'Now I can concentrate on the other matter,' I said. 'That letter about the missing Irish girl.'

'I thought you promised Daniel no more detective work.' Sid wagged a finger at me. 'What does he think about this?'

'She hasn't told him, naturally,' Gus said with a smirk at me.

'Actually I have his blessing,' I said. 'At least I have his blessing to ask our friends if they have come across a family called Mainwaring, which was the name of the family where the girl from Ireland found employment.' I took a sip of my own tea, then looked up at them. 'You don't happen to have come across anyone called Mainwaring in your travels, I suppose?'

'The name doesn't ring a bell.' Sid looked at Gus for confirmation.

Gus shook her head. 'I don't think I know anyone called Mainwaring. Did you say she lives in New York?'

'I don't know where she lives,' I said. 'I made that assumption because the girl found a job so quickly after landing here. I'm writing to employment agencies to see if any of them remembers placing the girl.'

'Why don't you just put an advertisement in the *Times*?' Sid said. 'Wishing to contact a Mrs Mainwaring who recently employed Maureen O'Byrne as a domestic.'

'I could do that,' I said doubtfully. 'Would it be very expensive?'

'I shouldn't think so,' Sid shrugged, money to her being no object.

Money was an object to me, but I didn't want to admit this. 'I thought of going to see Miss Van Woekem,' I said. 'She knows everybody who matters.'

'It depends if this Mrs Mainwaring matters or not then,' Gus said. 'Most people can afford a maid or two.'

'So what would you do if you wanted to locate somebody?'

'Go to City Hall and take a look at the electoral roll. That is if there is a Mr Mainwaring; women, of course, not being on anyone's electoral roll.'

'Yet,' Gus finished for her.

'That's a good idea,' I said, cheering up immensely. 'I can do that.'

'Providing the Mainwarings are citizens and can vote in elections,' Sid pointed out.

'Sid, you're making difficulties,' Gus said. 'If they are not on the electoral roll, they'll be on some other kind of list. If they own a house, they'll pay property tax. City Hall will have them listed somewhere.'

'And then there are the electoral rolls in the other boroughs too,' Sid added. 'People with money are moving out of the city these days to the new suburbs.'

'Other boroughs,' I said. 'I don't think Daniel would want me to go charging off to the Bronx.'

'Molly, you're beginning to sound like the dutiful little wife,' Sid said. 'Where is that spunky girl we used to know? Surely Daniel doesn't monitor your every movement.'

'No, but . . .' I began.

'She did agree not to take on any more cases, Sid,' Gus added for me. 'And she shouldn't get too tired, rushing all over the place.'

I shot her a grateful smile.

'Maybe we can take on that for you too,' she added.

'I really can't expect you to run all over the place for me,' I said. 'I'll go to City Hall and if the Mainwarings don't show up there, I'll hand over the case.'

'We've made the offer, Molly. We're at your disposal, but I really don't think you should take on too much to worry you at the moment. I read something recently in a journal of medicine, written by a professor of psychology who claimed unborn children can pick up all kinds of stimuli in the womb that may affect their later life. They recommend mothers think kind and beautiful thoughts all the time.'

I laughed. 'Oh, dear. I don't think I'm the sort of person who only thinks beautiful thoughts. But you're probably right about taking on too much. I'm certainly feeling the heat this summer.'

'Why don't you go out to your mother-in-law?' Gus said. 'It's lovely and leafy out in Westchester.'

'For the same reason that you returned from those cool ocean breezes in Newport,' I said. 'A day or so of my mother-in-law and I'd rather endure the heat. Besides, it's cooler today. I think it's going to rain.'

'Then we should get going, Gus,' Sid rose to her feet. 'We have to buy food or we'll starve tonight.'

'I'd invite you to dine here,' I said, 'but I've only two pork chops and I don't think they'll stretch to four.'

'We need to stock up the pantry anyway,' Sid said. 'The larder is bare and the poor dog will have nothing if we don't get going. Come over for a glass of wine later. Thank God we still have a well-stocked cellar awaiting us.'

I escorted them to the front door and watched them cross the alleyway to their own house. Then I went to the desk in the front parlor and thought carefully before I composed a note to Liam. Sid was right. It had to contain nothing that might implicate me, but he had to know that it came from me. Something from our childhood . . . Then I remembered that my brother Joseph always teased him by calling him Freckle Face. Liam hated it. Our mother told him to stop and threatened the strap if he used the words again, so he resorted to calling Liam FF.

Dear FF, I wrote.
They know you're here. They are looking for you. Leave the city immediately. God be with you.

There. Nothing that could tie it to me, but would make it quite clear to him. I put the letter into an envelope and carried it across the alley to Sid and Gus who promised to set out on their quest the next morning. I felt as if a great load had been lifted from my shoulders. My friends were home and everything was going to be all right from now on.

Chapter 9

The rain started that evening and when Daniel came home he was drenched to the skin. Then in the middle of the night there was a thunderstorm with lightning flashing and rain drumming hard on the roof. I lay awake, waiting for the next flash and crash while my mind raced with so many worrying thoughts. Would Liam be caught before Sid and Gus could find him and deliver my warning? What if they called his name out loud and thus gave him away? And what if that woman couldn't come up with the money to ransom her kidnapped baby? Would the kidnappers kill it? In the end I went downstairs and made myself some warm milk, and drank it sitting in the cold empty kitchen while the thunder raged outside and Daniel slept on peacefully.

In the morning it was still raining and I decided to wait to pay my visit to City Hall. No sense in getting crushed in a crowded El train. By afternoon the sun was out again and when I set off the sidewalks were steaming. Little boys took great delight at stomping in puddles and when a carriage went past me at a great clip it sent up a spray of muddy water, spattering my skirt. I made it down to City Hall on the trolley and then was made to wait while clerks decided if I was important enough to be helped, before one of them disappeared into the cavernous filing rooms, only to return empty-handed. It became clear that there were no Mainwarings of note living in the borough of Manhattan – at least not able to vote or be affluent enough to own their own homes.

Reluctantly I turned my steps for Patchin Place. I had done everything I could at the moment and would have to rely on Sid and Gus to contact Liam. I'd have to check my housekeeping account to see if it would stretch to an advertisement in the *Times* as Sid had suggested. Then I decided that I had to learn to let go of my former life. I was no longer private detective Molly Murphy. I was Mrs Molly Sullivan, soon to be a mother. There was no turning back now. A nagging thought whispered that if I didn't take on the case, who would? I hated the thought of those people in Ireland sitting there worrying and waiting while nobody worked on their behalf.

I didn't get a chance to mention it to Daniel that evening as he didn't come home until I was asleep and was gone again at crack of dawn. I heard nothing from Sid and Gus all day and made constant trips to the front window in vain to see if they had returned. When they did, they had no news.

'No sign of your brother or of any kidnappers,' Sid said. 'We walked our feet off to no avail. Really that part of the city is too tiresome for words. Too many people and one has to look so carefully where one puts one's feet. And my dear, the smells! I don't think anyone we saw ever washes.'

'Don't feel you have to go back,' I said. 'Please leave the

letter with Sarah on the off chance that she spots him and that's all we can do.'

'Never let it be said that a Walcott deserted her post,' Gus said. 'We'll keep going until we succeed, Molly.'

I felt awful that I had asked them to do such a loathsome task while I sat at home, trying not to worry. The problem with not having enough to do is that one has too much time for worrying thoughts.

The afternoon post brought a letter from Daniel's mother. I opened it with trepidation and was relieved to read that she would keep her eyes open for a suitable girl but that we'd probably have more luck with finding a servant through one of the employment agencies in the city. At least that brought a smile to my lips. The next day was Sunday and Sid and Gus informed me regretfully that they had a luncheon to attend out on Long Island. I asked them to inquire after any Mainwarings who might live on Long Island, since it was an area of impressive mansions.

'Put the advertisement in the *Times*, Molly. So much simpler,' Sid said.

Daniel had left early on Sunday morning, having to work again. He apologized when he kissed me good-bye, as I still lay in bed.

'I know it's hard on you,' he said, 'but this is a policeman's life.'

He looked so weary. I longed to take him into my arms. 'I don't suppose it's much fun for you either,' I said, stroking his cheek. 'Are you still working on those kidnappings?'

'They are the least of my worries,' he said.

'Did that poor woman get her baby back yet?'

'Not that I heard. I don't even know if they managed to come up with the ransom money.'

'Are your men not watching her house to catch the kidnappers red-handed?' I asked indignantly.

'We have to be very careful, Molly,' he said. 'We can't jeopardize the safety of the child. We have a constable keeping an eye on the place, but it won't do any good. The ransom note came through the mail and the woman didn't want to show it to me, because it said clearly, "Do not show this to the police, or else." '

'How terrible,' I said.

He nodded. 'So we're no nearer to catching them. I have put my feelers out with all the known gangs, and so far nothing.'

'Will the baby be returned to the parents' address? Maybe you can nab them then.'

He started for the stairs. 'The last child was dumped in a basket outside the Foundling Hospital,' he said. 'Others have been left in churches. I have to go.' And he blew me a kiss.

The frustration had returned. I could really be helpful if only he'd let me. I'd stand watch outside the woman's house. I could follow her when she went out and nobody would be any the wiser. Why did Daniel have to be so protective and so insistent that I not get involved with his work? I knew he was acting this way to keep me safe, but it still irked.

Two more frustrating days dragged on with no sightings of Liam and no sign of kidnappers, and no Daniel around from dawn until late at night. When I asked him questions he answered with a snapped monosyllable, clearly exhausted and frustrated himself. I had an advertisement written and ready to put in the *Times*, but I couldn't bring myself to do it. Then on the Wednesday I was just returning from shopping for Daniel's evening meal when I heard my name being called and saw Sid and Gus hurrying toward me, waving excitedly.

'Molly, listen to this. Great drama.' Gus called.

'You've found him?' I asked.

'No, sorry. I'm afraid we haven't. Still no sign of him. But big excitement with the kidnapping you told us about.'

'Was the baby returned safe and sound?' I asked, filled with hope. 'Were the kidnappers caught?'

'More dramatic than that,' Sid said. 'We just happened to be in the right place at the right time. It was on Broome Street, wasn't it, Gus?'

Gus nodded. 'We were just feeling rather hot and tired and had decided to make our way home when we saw a police wagon pull up and a policeman got out, carrying a basket, covered with a cloth, looking for all the world like a picnic basket. Well, naturally we were intrigued so we hung around to watch. While he was asking for confirmation of an address a young woman came running down from a tenement above – pretty little thing, very fair and German-looking. And she screamed out, "You've found my baby?"'

'And the policeman said, "Safe and sound, ma'am. Left right outside police headquarters on Mulberry."

'He pulled back the white cloth that was over the basket. She rushed forward and then she stopped dead and said, "That's not my baby." '

'Then she got quite hysterical,' Sid continued. 'The police were trying to calm her and telling her that she'd forgotten what her own child looked like and all babies look alike, but she was quite insistent.'

Gus leaned closer. 'She said, "My baby is beautiful.

Everyone says so. This baby is ugly. Take it away. I don't want to see it again." '

'And she was right, wasn't she, Gus?' Sid said with the hint of a smile. 'The baby was a homely little creature, all red and wrinkled the way some babies are, like little old men.'

'How strange,' I said. 'What can have happened? Do you think they kidnapped more than one baby at once and mixed them up?'

'I'm sure I don't know,' Gus said. 'The woman and the policeman got into the wagon and went off with the baby, so we can't report what happened next.'

I went on home, and started to prepare Daniel's supper. But I found it hard to do the task at hand as I felt quite sick with worry about what Sid and Gus had told me. I knew it didn't concern me and was none of my business, but I couldn't get the woman's face out of my mind. Surely any woman knows what her own child looks like. What would happen now? And, more to the point, where was her baby?

I held off from cooking dinner until about eight and was rewarded at eight-thirty with the sound of the front door opening.

'You're home. What perfect timing,' I said, going to greet Daniel. 'I'm so glad. I've made you liver and bacon because I think you need building up and . . .' I broke off. 'What's the matter?' He looked as if he might explode with anger any second.

I went up to him, touching his lapel gently, 'Daniel, what on earth is it?'

'I have been betrayed by my own wife, that's all,' he said in a clipped voice he was fighting to control. 'Exposed, made to look a fool. Betrayed.'

'What are you talking about?' I demanded. 'I have never done anything to betray you.'

'Come into my study. We need to talk.' He was glaring at me in a way that made me feel almost sick. He took my arm and manhandled me into the front parlor.

'Let go, you're hurting me,' I shouted angrily. 'I don't know what this is about, but you are behaving like a boor.'

'Sit.' He pushed me down to the sofa. I was actually rather frightened. I'd never seen him like this, but I certainly wasn't going to let him see it.

'All right,' I said. 'In what way am I supposed to have betrayed you?'

'Because you failed to mention to me that you knew your brother Liam was in town and failed to mention that you had been meeting secretly with him, when half the police force in New York has been looking for him.'

'Just a moment,' I said, now as angry as he was. 'Who exactly told you I had had secret meetings with my brother?'

'You were seen with him, Molly.' His voice was rising now, loud and frightening. 'Talking together on the corner of Broome and Elizabeth. While I've been trying to catch him, you've been undermining my efforts and warning him off, haven't you?'

'I have absolutely not been undermining your efforts.' I was shouting too now. 'If you'll listen for a minute, I'll tell you exactly what happened.'

'Go on.' He sat opposite me, arms folded and still glaring. I took a deep breath, fighting to remain calm and reasonable. 'Remember you told me you wanted me to cancel my request for a maid with the employment agency? I went back there to tell them I didn't need their services after all, came out into the street, and the first person I bumped into was my brother. I was stunned, as you can imagine. I tried to greet him the way you'd greet a long-lost family member, but he made it quite clear that I was the last person in the world he wanted to see and my meeting him was putting him in danger. I told him he was stupid to be here and to go straight back where he came from. We parted. I haven't seen or contacted him since. End of story.'

'You could have mentioned it to me,' he said, more quietly now.

'I could have. I chose not to for Liam's sake. He is my brother, after all.'

'Did he tell you what he was doing here?'

'He told me nothing. As I just said, he wanted nothing to do with me and told me to forget I'd ever seen him. I tried to give him my address, but he wouldn't take it. I guessed he was probably over here to raise funds for the Republican cause.'

There was a long silence then he said at last, 'I'm sorry. I should not have behaved in that way.'

'No you should not,' I said.

Another long pause before he said, 'I was caught wrong-footed at a meeting with John Wilkie and several Secret Service men. They asked how I was getting on with trying to locate the anarchist group and then one of them told me, with great satisfaction, that my wife had been meeting secretly with her brother – one of the men we were trying to find. Imagine what a fool I felt.'

I continued to give him a frosty stare. 'I would have thought that any loyal and devoted husband would have said that he couldn't comment on the statement until he had asked his wife in person.'

'You're probably right.' He sighed.

'I know I'm right. You're always going on about husband and wife having to trust each other and now it's quite clear that you don't trust me.'

'I wouldn't have gotten so upset but it's such a crucial matter, Molly.'

'Do you know that Liam is involved in some kind of anarchist plot or are you just putting two and two together because he's here at the same time as a new anarchist group has sprung up?'

'I'm afraid we have good information that this plot is somehow linked with the Irish Republican Brotherhood. And your brother's name is on John Wilkie's wanted list.'

'John Wilkie asked me to report to him if my brother tried to make contact,' I said.

Daniel looked up, suspicious. 'He did? When?'

'He came back to the house after that luncheon. He asked me to report straight to him.'

'The devil he did.' Daniel's face flushed with anger again. 'Going behind my back with my own wife. I see it now. They want my cooperation and the use of my men, but it's still their case and they want all the glory when it's busted open. Typical.'

'Then leave them to it. Withdraw your men.'

'I'd love to, but the directive comes from President Roosevelt himself. I can hardly go against him on a matter of national security.'

'Do they think the anarchists might be plotting to strike here in America?'

'We just don't know. They are working in utmost secrecy and we haven't managed to get anywhere near them yet. We only have hints of names but not where they might be meeting or what they might be planning. I'm just praying we don't have to wait until a bomb explodes on the president before we find out.' He looked up at me. 'So did you report your encounter with your brother to Wilkie?'

'I had already met Liam when I spoke to Mr Wilkie and I saw no reason to mention my encounter to him, since Liam had given me no information of any kind.'

He was still staring at me, 'And would you have gone to Wilkie if your brother had chosen to contact you again?'

'I suppose it depends what Liam had wanted of me. If he had contacted me again I would have warned him that the police were after him and he should get out of the country immediately.' Another point occurred to me. 'And if you had asked me to let you know if I made contact with my brother, I might have done so. But you choose not to share any information with me and keep me completely in the dark on your cases.'

'I have to, Molly. You know that.'

I stood up. 'Your dinner is in the oven. You'd better eat it before it's dried out.'

He got up too. 'Molly.' He put a tentative hand on my shoulder. 'I'm sorry I yelled at you. We have to think what would be the best thing to do next. Your brother gave you no idea where he was staying, I take it?'

'I told you once, Daniel. He wanted to get away from me as quickly as possible.'

'I don't want you going back to that part of the city in the hope of bumping into him again.'

'I'm not stupid, Daniel. I'm not going to be used as bait to catch my brother.'

He sucked in air through his teeth. 'This is a tricky situation. I don't want John Wilkie putting pressure on you either. I think the best thing would be to get you away from the city altogether. I keep suggesting that you go to my mother during this hot weather, and that would seem like an admirable solution to remove you out of harm's way.'

I was about to stand up for myself and say I refused to be shipped off like a piece of baggage, when it struck me that this time it was an admirable solution. If I was not in the city I had absolutely no chance of running into Liam again. Sid and Gus could continue to be my spies while I was safely far away in the country.

I nodded demurely. 'Very well, Daniel. If that's what you want.'

He looked at me suspiciously for a moment, trying to gauge if there was any underhand reason for my sudden meekness. Finding none, he came over to me, put his hands on my shoulders, and kissed me. 'That's my girl,' he said. 'I'll send a wire to my mother in the morning to say that you are coming.'

For the only time in my life I did not protest.

Chapter 10

The rail journey north to Westchester County proved to be quite delightful after we crossed the Harlem River and city streets gave way to woodland and meadows. I tried to enjoy the vistas, but I was filled with the usual apprehension I felt at the thought of facing Daniel's mother, coupled with concern over those I had left behind. I had told Sid and Gus that both the Secret Service and the New York police were actively looking for my brother, and I recounted what Daniel had told me. They promised to be extra careful, but seemed excited at the challenge. Daniel had assured me that he had been perfectly all right on his own for thirty-two years and would not starve to death in my absence. I didn't tell him it wasn't starvation I feared. Anarchists were known to be ruthless. They wouldn't hesitate to kill if anyone got in the way of their plans. I knew that policemen like Daniel faced death every day, but I hadn't been married long enough to become used to it yet.

As I stared out the window I wondered whether Liam really was working with anarchists and what would happen to him if he was caught. Surely the death penalty. I shuddered and remembered the fatalistic way he had said, 'Someone has to carry on my name.' He was practically the only family I had. A woman across the compartment was bouncing a healthy toddler on her lap and I pictured myself doing the same thing this time next year. It was hard to believe that I'd soon have a little one of my own. Then another face came into my head – that poor woman on Broome Street, so sure that the baby returned to her was not the right one. How could that have happened? What would she do now? Try to love a child that wasn't her own? I felt almost sick at the thought.

I was met at White Plains Station by Mrs Sullivan's man, Jonah, with the pony and trap, and we set off through leafy lanes for the hamlet of Elmsford, some two miles away. I felt the cares and worries slipping away with the gentle swaying of the trap and the sweet smell of honeysuckle and green meadows. I should learn to stop worrying about things I couldn't change and enjoy the life I had. I was going to be spoiled by Mrs Sullivan, and . . . I remembered the best part . . . I was going to see little Bridie again. Bridie was the child I had brought across from Ireland who had become dear to me. In fact I would have liked to have her live with us when her father and brother went off to Panama to build the canal, but Daniel had objected. She was ten years old now and Daniel's mother had volunteered to train her for domestic service, but had taken to her so well that I didn't think service was in her future.

I found I was smiling when, at long last, we turned off the lane into Mrs Sullivan's driveway. The house was one of those simple older homes built of local bluestone in the days when the Hudson Valley was a sleepy backwater of small farms. That had all changed when the railroad granted speedy access to the city and the barons of industry built their own extravagant mansions along the river's banks. Mrs Sullivan's house was not in any way extravagant but was of pleasant appearance with a climbing rose spilling over the porch and French windows opening onto a lawn bordered by a spreading elm and oak tree.

Bridie came rushing out to meet me at the sound of the horse's hooves, her face alight with excitement. As I was assisted down from the trap she flung her arms around me. She had grown since I saw her last and was looking healthy and well cared for, her hair neatly braided and her pinafore edged with lace. Mrs Sullivan followed her out onto the porch and gave me a surprisingly warm welcome.

'Well, there you are,' she said. 'Isn't this nice.' And she let me kiss her on the cheek. Bridie took my hand and tried to drag me up the stairs. 'Come and see your room, Molly. I picked fresh flowers for you and the pillow on your bed has lace around the edge that I sewed myself,' she said.

'Heavens, child, give Molly a chance to catch her breath first,' Mrs Sullivan scolded, but with a smile. She turned to me. 'She was up with the sun this morning, so excited about your arrival.' She led me through to the spacious front parlor. 'Sit down and we'll have Bridie bring us some iced tea before you do anything else.' She examined me critically. 'You're looking tired, my dear. It's not good for you to exert yourself too much. I'm sure the city heat was overwhelming in your condition. I kept telling Daniel he should send you out here for the whole summer.'

'He wanted me to come out to you, but I didn't want to leave him alone when he has to work so hard.'

She nodded. 'I was exactly the same when my man was with the police. I expect you've gathered by now that it's no fun being a policeman's wife. If his father had had his way, Daniel would have gone into the law and then into politics instead of following his footsteps into the police force. Of course there is still time to pursue a political career.'

'Daniel loves his job,' I said. 'I think he even enjoys the danger and the long hours.'

'Maybe he'll change his mind when he has a family and wants to spend more time with them,' she said. 'Ah, that's right, Bridie. Put the tray down on that table and see if you can pour very carefully without spilling. Good girl.' She turned to me. 'She's turning into a grand little helper. She'll make some man a fine wife someday.'

Bridie came to perch on the arm of my chair, waiting impatiently to show me the room she had prepared for me. At last she was allowed to lead me upstairs. The windows were open and the sweet scent of roses and newly mown grass wafted in. Doves were cooing on the rooftop. There were flowers on my bedside table and clean white linens on the bed. It all looked very inviting and I reminded myself that I could have been enjoying it all summer, but for my own stubbornness.

Mrs Sullivan refused to let me do a thing. She set up a wicker chaise for me under the oak tree and instructed me to put my feet up. 'You can't be too careful at this stage,' she said. 'I've some fine white knitting yarn if you've a mind to start on a little jacket.'

I lounged in the shade, sipping iced tea and nibbling on plums from a tree in the orchard. *This is the life of Riley*, I thought. The contentment lasted all of an hour before my thoughts turned to Liam and Daniel and what was happening in the city. I fetched my note paper and wrote to Sid and Gus, asking them to let me know the moment they had any news, then to Daniel, emphasizing the warm welcome his mother had given me. Then I made a valiant attempt at starting the little jacket before, I'm ashamed to say, I nodded off to sleep in the shade.

I was glad I had that afternoon nap as my sleep was disturbed that night. My windows were open and I was jarred awake by unfamiliar nightly noises – the hoot of an owl, the bark of a fox. When I did fall asleep it was to troubled dreams and someone holding up a hideous and malformed infant to me. 'That's not my baby!' I screamed and awoke sweating. Maybe it was a good thing that I had removed myself from the tensions of the city. Soon I'd learn to slow myself to the calm rhythm of the country-side . . . at least I hoped I would.

When I awoke the next morning I was full of energy and wanting to be doing something. I went for an early morning walk, read the paper, tried to help clear away breakfast but was told to go and sit down.

'I'm not used to being idle,' I said.

'You have to learn to do what's best for the baby,' Mrs Sullivan said. 'When it arrives you'll think back wistfully to the time when you had a minute to rest. Make the most of it.'

She did allow me to deadhead the geraniums, but refused any more strenuous gardening. 'If you feel up to it,' she said, 'we've been invited to tea with my neighbors, the Blackstones. Letitia Blackstone was a famous society beauty in her youth.'

I was all set to say I was too tired. I tended to agree with

Sid and Gus that society gossip was very tiresome, especially when one didn't know any of the people who were being talked about and when one's mother-in-law was likely to drop hints about the sort of girls Daniel might have married.

'We needn't stay long and they are anxious to meet you,' she added. 'You'll probably find that some of the ladies attending came to your wedding.'

After that I had to agree. I could see she really wanted to go. She looked pleased. 'They are very well connected and could be useful to Daniel someday.'

We were driven in the pony and trap by Jonah. The Blackstones' house was much grander than Mrs Sullivan's – a proper mansion with a portico, terraced gardens, and a small ornamental lake. My mother-in-law mentioned at least a dozen times what a good match Letitia had made and how happy her parents had been for her.

Tea had been set up in the shade of trees beside this lake and there were several other ladies present, mostly of Mrs Sullivan's generation. I was made a great fuss over when I arrived.

'To think that Daniel is going to be a father at last,' Mrs Blackstone said as she escorted me to my chair. 'And you despaired that he'd never marry, Mary.'

'What ever happened to that other girl – the Nortons' daughter, wasn't it?' an older woman asked from her deckchair.

There was an uncomfortable silence. Arabella Norton had been Daniel's intended when I first met him.

'I gather she's married – into a Philadelphia Mainline family, so in fact a better match than . . .' the speaker broke off and cleared her throat in embarrassment.

'And is your family from this area, my dear?' another of the women asked me, rapidly changing the subject.

'Molly is from Ireland,' Mrs Sullivan said for me, before I could disclose that I'd come from a peasant's cottage.

That pretty much put an end to the topic of conversation, since we knew no people in common, and the talk reverted to local matters. I sat and listened as they discussed people and events that meant nothing to me, eating my slice of cake and sipping at my tea. My attention wandered to a pair of mallards on the lake, to a flock of chickadees in the tree above us while unfamiliar names washed over me.

'Don't tell me they mean to divorce? I know he behaved badly, but how shocking that she really plans to divorce him. Rather short-sighted of her, when you consider the fortune he will inherit one day. How tragic for Marjorie. And they are related to the Wetherbys, aren't they?'

'The Wetherbys? That big brick house on the road to White Plains?'

'You know, Estelle Wetherby. You met her at a dinner party at the Van Horns.'

'Was she the one whose daughter married that Mainwaring fellow?'

I was instantly alert and sat up in my seat.

'Leonard Mainwaring? That's right. She did. Estelle thought it was a good match at the time, but I'm not so sure personally. Of course he has plenty of money and comes from an important English family but . . .' The women leaned closer into a tight little group from which I was excluded. Their voices were lowered.

'But he was a bit of a rake, wasn't he? Got into trouble with gambling debts?'

'And an eye for the ladies, so I heard. Perhaps he's settled down now he's married. They often do, don't they?'

'Do they live nearby?'

'Closer to the river, don't they? Estelle told me once. Irvington, I think.'

'Big fancy house, so I hear. At least Estelle's daughter has got something out of it.'

The talk moved on to other people I didn't know, but my brain was buzzing. Mrs Mainwaring, of the right social class and with a big enough house to be able to afford more than one parlormaid! I couldn't believe my luck. Now I had to work out how I could manage to pay a call and find out if they had employed Maureen O'Byrne.

I gave myself a stern talking to when we returned home. I was not supposed to be pursuing any kind of work. I should have handed over this case to another detective by now. But it was no good. I was experiencing that familiar feeling, like the hound that picks up the scent of the fox, that we were finally on the trail of the quarry. I was convinced that I'd found the answer and would soon locate Maureen O'Byrne for her relatives. I waited until we were sitting at the supper table before I asked casually, 'How far away is Irvington?'

'Irvington? About three miles. Charming little town on the Hudson. Do you know it?'

'I've never been there,' I said, 'but I've been told that it's very pretty and the river should be delightfully cool in this weather. Is there any kind of transportation that I could take to go there one day?'

'Transportation? You're not in New York, my dear. We've the pony and cart if Jonah is free to drive.'

This was looking promising. I pressed on. 'I heard your friends mention a family called Mainwaring. A friend of mine in New York knows some Mainwarings in Westchester County. In fact she's been to stay with them. I wonder if it's the same family.'

'It's an unusual name,' Mrs Sullivan said. 'It probably would be. I'm not personally acquainted with them but I have met Mrs Mainwaring's mother, Estelle Wetherby, so it would be acceptable to pay a call upon them if we happen to be taking a trip in that direction.'

Oh, Lord. I hadn't counted on my mother-in-law wanting to come with me. That would make things rather difficult. But I could hardly ask to borrow her pony trap and go without her.

She seemed quite taken with the idea. 'We could take a picnic one day. That sounds like a good idea, doesn't it, Bridie my dear?'

'To the river? Can I come?' Bridie wriggled excitedly.

'Of course. I'll arrange it with Jonah.'

'Can Jonah show me how to catch fish? He promised.'

'We'll see,' Mrs Sullivan said.

So things were finally moving along. All I had to do was to come up with a person in New York who might possibly be a friend of Mrs Wainwaring. Not Sid or Gus. They were frowned upon by polite society and tried to steer clear of it. I thought of other young women of good family I might know. I had become acquainted with several of Sid and Gus's Vassar classmates and I remembered Fanny Poindexter, who had died so tragically a year ago. Dead women tell no tales, I thought. She'd be perfect. Now all I had to do was to wait patiently.

The next day brought no letter from Sid and Gus,

which meant that they still hadn't found Liam. Also no letter from Daniel, but he was not good about writing. Men aren't. They only resort to letters if there is something important to say that can't wait. But at least I took it to imply that he hadn't caught Liam either. Mrs Sullivan showed no intention of making the trip to Irvington and I began to wonder if she had forgotten. I couldn't think of a way to remind her about it without seeming over-eager and rude. So I had to lounge around the house and garden, trying to fill the hours with my sad attempts at knitting, or with writing letters while Mrs Sullivan busied herself with household matters, pausing to give me the occasional lecture on the correct cleaning of silver or the right way to mend a scorch mark on a tablecloth. To my annoyance she decided that the plums were ready for bottling and took Bridie and me with her to the shed while she hunted for suitable jars. I had a horrid feeling that this might be a process taking several days and wondered if she'd possibly let me go to Irvington alone.

Indeed the next morning we were rounded up after breakfast to pick plums. By afternoon she had great pots of plums bubbling on the stove and by nightfall there were jars sitting on the kitchen window ledge to cool.

'I hope you made a note of everything I did, Molly,' she said. 'I know you live in the city now, but there will come a time when you'll have to preserve your own fruit.'

As we sat down to a late cold supper she looked at us in satisfaction. 'A job well done,' she said. 'I think we deserve a day off, don't you? Why don't we take that trip to the river tomorrow. Are you feeling up to it, Molly?'

I managed to suppress any emotion when I replied, 'What a good idea. Yes, I think I might be up to it.'

Chapter 11

We set off for Irvington after breakfast, the picnic basket at our feet and Bridie sitting up beside the driver. It was pleasantly cool as we passed along leafy lanes, with no sound except the gentle *clip-clop* of the pony's hooves and the cooing of pigeons in the trees above. After an area of thick woods we came to a point where the road started to descend to the river below us, sparkling in the morning sunlight. A paddle steamer was making its way upstream and the sound of music floated across the water from its deck. Bridie gave a squeal of delight.

'Sit still, or you'll fall off,' Mrs Sullivan warned, yanking on the back of her pinafore. The pony descended the hill slowly until we were riding down the main street with its clapboard stores and old brick taverns. It had as old a feel to it as any town at home in Ireland, like stepping back in time.

'Should I inquire where the Mainwarings live?' I asked, trying not to sound too eager.

'We'll leave that for later,' Mrs Sullivan said. 'One does not pay a social call before noon.'

I glanced across at her and thought how interesting it was that she started life as the child of Irish immigrants who fled from the potato famine, yet now behaved as if she'd been born with that proverbial silver spoon in her mouth. Perhaps that was why she wasn't too keen on me – I reminded her of her own past, which she had chosen to forget. Jonah assisted us down from the cart, my back now stiff from sitting on the hard bench, and we went for a walk along the waterfront, with Bridie commenting excitedly about the river traffic that passed us. 'Do you think the ship my father and brother went on was bigger than this one?' she asked as a cargo steamship came down carrying bricks and stone.

'Much bigger,' I said. Her father and brother had gone off to Panama to help build the new canal and she hadn't heard from them for months. I knew Seamus was not much of a writer, being barely schooled, but I wondered if they were all right. A few stories about the conditions at the canal had trickled through to New York and they didn't sound good. Strangely enough, her father's decision to go to Panama had been Bridie's good fortune. Instead of living precariously in slums wherever Seamus could pick up laboring work, Bridie was now on her way to becoming a young lady and would no doubt end up as snobbish as Mrs Sullivan if my mother-in-law had anything to do with it.

When the sun became too hot we retreated to a riverside park and spread out our picnic cloth in the shade of a big elm tree. Then followed my absolutely favorite kind of meal: ham sandwiches, cold meat pie and pickles, tomatoes and radishes fresh from the garden, peaches and plums and currant bread, washed down with homemade ginger beer. We lay replete in the shade watching the boats on the river glide past us.

'I don't think we'll bother about calling on those people today,' Mrs Sullivan said, as we reluctantly packed up the remains of the meal. 'Far too hot for social calls. We shall look as if we've been perspiring, and that would never do.'

'Oh, but I'd really like to,' I said, more vehemently than I'd expected.

She looked at me strangely. 'But you don't even know them.'

'But my friend in New York would never forgive me if I was in the vicinity of her dear friends and didn't call upon them,' I said.

She frowned. 'Surely, you don't have to mention it to your friends.'

I wasn't sure how to proceed from here. 'I only need to go through the motions and leave my card. It wouldn't take long. How would it be if you and Bridie stay by the water where it's cooler and I'll see if their house is within walking distance?'

'My, but you are determined in this matter,' Mrs Sullivan said, dabbing her face gently with a cologne-soaked handkerchief. 'We don't even know if this is the same family.'

'Is it likely there are two lots of Mainwarings in Westchester County? It's not a usual name, is it?'

'Well, no,' she admitted. 'I can't say I've come across anyone else with that name and I know a good many people in the county. Very well, if it means so much to you. Take the trap while Bridie and I will go to see if there is a soda fountain nearby. She has been such a big help to me recently that I think she deserves a soda or an ice cream.'

'Ice cream?' Bridie's face lit up. 'Can it be strawberry flavor?'

'Bridie, remember I've told you it's not ladylike to ask for things. Help me up, child, and then help Molly.' Bridie did so. Mrs Sullivan dusted herself off.

'It will probably be more fitting to have you call on the Mainwarings alone, rather than three strangers descending on them at once,' she added.

I let out a sigh of relief. We walked back into town and asked for directions to their house. It seemed they were well known in the vicinity, but not, one got the feeling, well liked.

'Oh, yeah, the Mainwarings,' the greengrocer didn't elaborate and went back to piling peaches onto his display. 'Big house. Up the hill. You can't miss it.'

So Jonah and I set off, back up the hill. When the pony and trap reached the top, there facing us was a gateway worthy of a palace, its brick columns topped with seated lions and the gates themselves of fancy ironwork.

'In here, Jonah,' I said.

Mrs Wetherby was probably right in thinking that her daughter had made a good match. Jonah got down to open the gate and through we went, up a driveway lined with flowering shrubs. There were fountains playing in the forecourt, and the portico, with its marble columns, was as grand as described. I was beginning to have second thoughts about this whole mission. If Mrs Mainwaring was part of Westchester society, then word would undoubtedly get around that I had been looking for her housemaid, and that word would finally reach Mrs Sullivan. She would then know that I'd made up a story and conned her into going to Irvington in the first place.

She'd probably even tell Daniel, which would not be a good idea.

I was almost ready to have Jonah turn the trap around and retreat when the front door opened and a nursemaid in crisply starched uniform came out pushing an impressive perambulator. She looked at me with interest, nodded, then went on walking. A gardener appeared from the side of the house. 'You'll want some water for the pony, no doubt,' he said to Jonah. 'Hot day like this. Bring the trap around this way.'

So I had to dismount whether I liked it or not and walked with trepidation up the marble steps to the front door. I handed my card to the maid who opened it and I asked if Mrs Mainwaring was at home. I was ushered into a cool marble foyer with a sweeping staircase on one side.

'She's resting, ma'am,' she said. 'May I tell her what this is about?'

'I'm inquiring about a maid who might have been employed here,' I said. 'Her family in Ireland is anxious to track her down.'

'What was the maid's name, may I ask?'

'Maureen O'Byrne,' I said.

I saw her expression falter, just a little. 'Maureen,' she said. 'Oh, yes. She was here.'

'But not any longer?'

'Not any longer,' the girl said.

'How long ago did she leave?'

'About six months ago, ma'am.' She was looking around as if she was trying to find a reason to conclude this conversation and leave me.

'Do you know why she left?'

'Harriet, with whom are you gossiping?' came an

imperious voice from the top of the staircase. The mistress of the house stood there, tall, slim, and haughty-looking, dressed in a gray, silk tea dress.

'This lady wants to know about Maureen O'Byrne, ma'am,' the girl said, her voice sounding taut and nervous now.

'Who is she?' The words were snapped out.

'Mrs Daniel Sullivan from New York, Mrs Mainwaring,' I called up the stairs. 'I received an urgent letter from a family in Ireland, who are trying to trace their niece. In her last letter home she wrote that she had found employment in your household.'

Mrs Mainwaring came slowly down the stairs, taking in the cut of my clothing and the quality of my hat, I've no doubt. She was working out whether I was somebody of sufficient importance to talk to. In the brighter light of the foyer I could see that she was not as young as I had expected and her face was rather gaunt. Not a great beauty and with a hard look to her eyes.

'Maureen left our employ several months ago,' she said.

'Could you possibly tell me where she went?'

'I have no idea.'

I decided I had better stretch the truth a little if I wanted to learn anything more. 'I should have mentioned that I am currently visiting my mother-in-law – Mrs Sullivan of Elmsford – who is a friend of your mother's.'

'Oh, I see.' The gaunt look softened a little. 'And what connection does Maureen have to you?' Again her eyes traveled over my outfit. Not the best quality, she was thinking, but not entirely shabby either. 'Is your mother-in-law with you?'

'She found the heat too oppressive to undertake the

trip,' I said, not mentioning that she was currently eating ice cream at the bottom of the hill.

'Well, you'd better come in and sit down, I suppose,' she said. She turned to the girl who was hovering in the background. 'Bring some iced tea through to the Blue Room, Harriet.'

'You're most kind,' I said and followed her through to a small sitting room at the back of the house. It had a fine view of the river and was decorated with blue Chinese plates. The sofa was upholstered in blue silk and the walls painted white with blue panels inset. A pretty room, one of good taste. She indicated I should sit and I did.

'I'm sorry, you asked what connection I had to the girl,' I went on, thinking that for once the truth might be the best plan of action. 'At one time I used to own a small detective agency in New York City. Naturally I gave it up when I married. However, this letter arrived out of the blue a week ago. I intended to pass it on, but when I was at a gathering of one of my mother-in-law's friends – Letitia Blackstone? You probably know her–'

She nodded. 'Yes, I've met Mrs Blackstone.'

'–and your name was mentioned, it seemed too fortuitous to ignore. I'd like to be able to put these peoples' minds at rest. I do hope you'll forgive the intrusion.'

'Of course,' she said, none too graciously. 'And I wish I could help you more. Maureen was indeed in our employ. She was a pleasant enough girl, good-looking, nice personality, hard worker, but with too much of an eye for the young men, I'm afraid. She got herself . . .' She paused and coughed as if the words offended her sensibilities too much to utter. '. . . in the family way.' And she blushed bright red, picking up the fan that hung at her belt and

fanning herself. Harriet reappeared carrying a crystal jug
and glasses on a tray. She put it on a Chinese lacquered
side table. We watched in silence as she poured and
handed each of us a glass.

'So you dismissed her,' I said as Harriet departed.

'I am not a monster, Mrs Sullivan,' she said. 'We sent
her to the nuns. There is a convent not far away who make
it their mission to take in fallen girls, such as Maureen.
They allow them to stay until they have had their babies
and then try to find good homes for the children. They
do wonderful work and have saved many a poor girl from
complete ruin.'

'What is the name of this convent?'

'The convent of the Holy Innocents, very appropriately,'
she said. 'I believe the sisters are of a French order. They
came down from Quebec originally. I'm not Catholic
myself so these things are somewhat of a mystery to me.'

'And that was the last you saw of her, when you sent her
off to the nuns?'

'It was,' she said. 'And I'm surprised. She was a good
worker and we offered to take her back when she had
fully recovered. But she never came.'

'She might have felt too ashamed,' I suggested.

Mrs Mainwaring shook her head, 'I very much doubt
it. I got the impression the young woman thought a lot of
herself. Ideas above her station, you know.'

'Then she might have gone off in search of a better
position.'

She gave me what can only be described as a wither-
ing stare. 'What better position would be open to a girl
from the bogs of Ireland with no education, background,
or family? Girls like that wind up with the only job open

to them – and we all know what that is.' She paused to let this sink in.

'Is it not possible that she has married the young man who is the father and kept her child?'

'Oh, I don't think so.' She shook her head. 'She would not name the father, but I got the distinct impression that he was not in a position to marry her.'

'It wasn't one of your staff then?'

'No,' she said curtly. 'It was definitely not one of my staff. I would have found out and forced him to marry her.'

I had been sipping the iced tea, which was deliciously refreshing.

'I'm sorry I can be of no further help to you, Mrs Sullivan,' she said, putting down her own glass and making it perfectly clear that this interview was at an end. 'The girl could be anywhere by now.'

I got to my feet. 'Thank you for your time, Mrs Mainwaring. You have my card. If she does contact you again, would you please let me know?'

'She would not be getting a reference from me, Mrs Sullivan. I made a more than generous offer and it was rejected. My generosity cannot be relied upon twice.'

As we came out into the foyer a butler was passing. 'Soames, is Mr Mainwaring back yet?' she asked.

'I believe not, madam,' he said.

'If he does show up in the next hour or so, please remind him that we are expected for dinner with the Rothenburgers,' she said. 'And that he promised to say goodnight to his son.'

'Certainly, madam. I will tell him–' a significant pause '–if he comes home in the next hour or so.'

This was clearly a household of tension, I thought, and I wondered if all the tension was caused by the brittle Mrs Mainwaring. Perhaps Maureen had good reason not to wish to return here after her confinement and had managed to find something better.

'You have a little boy then,' I said because I felt uncomfortable standing in the foyer. 'My congratulations.'

She smiled then. 'My husband comes from an old and distinguished family. An heir is important to him.' Her eyes went to my own shape. 'I'm sorry I could not be of assistance to you.'

I stepped out into the heat of the afternoon and had just been assisted back into the pony trap when I heard the scrunch of wheels on the driveway and an automobile came toward us, driving fast. It screeched to a halt only a few yards from us. The pony danced and snorted nervously and a young man jumped out, vaulting neatly over the closed door. He was handsome in a way that would go down well on the Broadway stage – hair parted in the middle, jaunty little mustache, wearing a striped blazer and white flannels. He came up to me.

'Sorry about that. Didn't see you until the last second. Hope I didn't scare the little mare too much.'

'She seems to have calmed down, thank you,' I said.

'Been visiting my wife have you? That's splendid. She needs more visitors. Needs to get out more.' He gave me a once over with his eyes then added, with a rakish smile, 'And I wouldn't object to seeing a pretty face around here once in a while. Do you live in the neighborhood?'

I adopted a polite tone, not wanting to be accused by Mrs Mainwaring of encouraging her flirtatious husband. 'No, I'm staying with my mother-in-law in Elmsford and

I just paid your wife a courtesy call, because the family is acquainted with your mother-in-law.' I saw no reason to tell him the truth. He was the sort of man who'd have no interest in the hiring and firing of servants.

'Well, do call around again. Bring your husband with you,' he said.

'My husband is unfortunately hard at work in the city.'

'Nose to the grindstone type, is he?'

'A police captain,' I said.

Did I detect a flicker of alarm in his eyes?

'Well, bless my soul. It takes all types, I suppose. I'd better let you go on your way then.'

And he ran up the steps into the house.

Chapter 12

Bridie sat beside the driver, sticky but content as the pony walked slowly home. Mrs Sullivan fanned herself. 'So what was she like, this Mrs Mainwaring?' she asked as we left Irvington behind us and plunged once again into the shade of the trees. 'Are you glad you made all that effort to visit?'

'Not really,' I said. 'She didn't exactly welcome me with open arms. I rather got the feeling that I was a little beneath her and thus not worth the effort.'

'I told you it wasn't a good idea to make social calls unexpectedly in this heat,' Mrs Sullivan gave me a triumphant look. 'People are not at their best when they are perspiring and she was probably in no mood to be sociable.'

'Well, I've done my duty to my friends and don't need to go back,' I said. 'But I'm glad we came to Irvington. It was delightful by the river, wasn't it?'

'The ice cream was certainly delightful,' Bridie said, echoing the words in such a grown-up way that it made us smile.

We lapsed into silence. I was wondering how I could

come up with a way to visit the convent that had taken in Maureen. It had been hard enough to convince Mrs Sullivan to visit the Mainwarings. I couldn't at the moment think of a good excuse to visit a convent. I wasn't known for my religious fervor, in fact I'd only agreed to being married in the Catholic Church for Daniel's sake. I certainly didn't think my mother-in-law would believe I had another friend whose sister was a nun and would want me to call upon her.

I sighed. It was hopeless. A wicked little idea crept into my mind that I could pretend to have received an urgent summons to go home, then go instead to a local inn and investigate at my leisure, but deceiving my mother-in-law left a bad taste in my mouth and it was bound to lead to complications with Daniel when his mother wrote to ask him why I was needed at home so urgently and I hadn't turned up. I sighed. Why couldn't I give up my former life gracefully and accept this new stage of my life? I knew the answer. Because I was so close. The convent was nearby. A few questions and I'd find out the truth. I'd most likely be able to write to the folks in Ireland with news of Maureen. All I needed was one day to myself. This required some serious thought.

As we approached the lane leading to our house I said casually, 'Mrs Mainwaring suggested that I go to look at some of the fine mansions nearby.'

'There certainly are some fine homes closer to the river,' Mrs Sullivan agreed. 'Mr Washington Irving's Sunnyside, and the Octagon House. But I expect she means that monstrosity that Vanderbilt has constructed at Hyde Park. Some people would be impressed by all those pillars and whatnot.'

'She also said there was a convent nearby that was worth a look?' I suggested, wondering if I was stabbing in the right direction. 'Interesting old buildings with some history?'

She frowned. 'A convent? I don't know what she was referring to. There's only one convent that could be described as nearby and that's the one in North Tarrytown. I wouldn't say the buildings have any architectural merit. It used to be the old fever hospital before the nuns took it over in the last century. Depressing-looking place if you ask me, up on a hill and exposed to the gales. All Gothic arches from what you can see of it. And of course you can't go inside. They are an enclosed order.'

'Oh, then it can't be the same one,' I said. 'This one takes in mothers and babies. Mrs Mainwaring said they did wonderful work.'

Mrs Sullivan was eyeing me curiously now. 'They take in fallen young women. Not the sort of place for respectable people like you or me. And I wonder why this Mrs Mainwaring is so keen on it? Is she a Catholic? I've not seen her at any Catholic charitable functions in the county.'

'I've no idea,' I said, with a shrug of the shoulders. 'Not everyone's idea of interesting architecture is the same. Perhaps she likes places of Gothic horror.' I smiled, to show that this was of no importance.

'Mrs Mainwaring sounds most disagreeable. I'm glad I didn't accompany you and that you have no reason to visit her again.' She dabbed at her forehead. 'I think we have had enough excursions for the time being. It's not good for you to go running around the countryside in your delicate state. I noticed when you climbed into the trap that your ankles are starting to swell up.'

When we reached Mrs Sullivan's house and went inside I found a letter from Sid and Gus waiting for me on the hall table. 'Oh, what a pleasant surprise,' I said. 'My friends have written to me. Would you excuse me, please?' And I took it up to my room to read.

I think we have combed every inch of the Lower East Side, Gus wrote in her neat sloping hand, *and haven't seen anyone resembling your brother. If he is still here, he is not venturing forth, at least during daylight hours. Sid has decided enough is enough and has other fish to fry – she's been asked to write an article on the state of the suffrage movement in America for a British journal. And I must admit I yearn to get back to my painting. We really did our best, Molly. We have left your note with Sarah, just in case she spots your brother.*

Of your dear husband we have not seen hide nor hair. He must be going to work at an ungodly hour before we're awake and returning after dark. Really you should per-suade him to take up a more sensible profession, Molly. The man will wear himself out before he's forty.

Oh, and remember the incident of the wrong baby we reported to you? It made all the newspapers and now there is a general public outcry to catch the kidnappers. Could it be that this is what is keeping Daniel busy to all hours? Frankly the publicity will not help, I'm afraid. The kidnap-pers will surely lie low until the fuss has died down.

I trust you are enjoying the tranquility of the countryside with no such drama. It is still frightfully hot in the city and Sid talks of renting a cottage out in the Hamptons.

Your devoted friend,
Gus

I folded the letter and put it onto my bedside table. Again I experienced that simmering frustration. Surely I could have found my brother by now? Surely I'd have been able to come up with the answer to the wrong baby – at least I could have given it a darned good try. I liked a case I could sink my teeth into. And now here I was, cut off and powerless in Westchester County while the rest of the world had come to a standstill. It seemed that nobody was making any progress in any direction, almost as if we were all suspended in a giant limbo of summer heat. And now it looked as if Sid and Gus would be heading out to the tip of Long Island – too far away for me to contact them if I needed them.

I gazed out of the window. Jonah was raking the grass. 'I wonder,' I said. I picked up my writing set and wrote back, telling them of the trip to Irvington, the beauty and tranquility of the river.

There are some charming little inns along the Hudson and the breeze is delightfully refreshing. There are also some very fine residences – no doubt Gus will know their owners and could even secure herself an invitation to one of them. If you've a mind to escape from the city, you could do worse than come up this way and thus do a good deed by saving your poor friend from dying from boredom and from lectures on being a good homemaker. Is it really essential that I know how to preserve plums?

After I had given the letter to Jonah to take to the mail, I felt a trifle guilty at making such a preposterous suggestion. I was always prevailing upon their good nature, wasn't I? They could exist quite happily without me but I really needed them. I had grown up with no close female friends, the local girls thinking that I was strange because I wanted to read and educate myself, and dreamed of a better life. It had been such a treat to discover women with whom I could share opinions, hopes, and fears. But would they not grow tired of such an annoying neighbor eventually? It was too late now. The letter was already winging its way to New York.

It did cross my mind that if Sid and Gus came to the Hudson, I'd have a perfect excuse to escape occasionally and wondered if I might push my luck by asking to learn how to drive the pony trap. Obviously not at the moment as Mrs Sullivan was still recovering from today's outing. She was sitting on the sofa and fanning herself with the magazine she had been reading as I came into the room. 'I don't know if it was quite wise of us to go on an excursion in weather like this,' she said. 'I feel like a limp rag and it must be even worse for you. You must put your feet up immediately and have Bridie bring you an ice bag for your ankles.'

'I'm really just fine,' I said.

'Nonsense, you're looking quite drawn and tired around the eyes,' she said. 'I should never have let you go on that wild goose chase to visit Mrs Mainwaring. You should take it easy for a while, at least until the weather changes.'

I chose the wicker armchair by the French window.

'You had a letter from your friends then,' she said. 'Good news from the city?'

'No news of any consequence,' she said. 'They have seen nothing of Daniel which means he is still working incredibly hard.'

'That poor boy will work himself into the grave. We

must do something about it, Molly.' She leaned over to me. 'His father had connections with all kinds of political figures and I know they'd be only too happy to introduce Daniel to the world of politics. He only has to say the word.'

'I don't think he wants to go into politics, Mother Sullivan,' I said.

'He'll change his mind once he has a family,' she said, and went back to her magazine.

I decided to take the risk. 'My friends say they are finding the city unbearably hot,' I said. 'I told them how lovely it was by the river today and suggested that they come and stay at an inn out here.'

'I suppose they could always stay here,' she said.

'Very kind of you, but I think they'd prefer the breezes on the river. And they do like their privacy. But of course they'd love to pay a visit to you – maybe to luncheon or tea.'

'Of course,' she said, looking relieved.

Conversation turned to other matters but the seeds were sown. Now all I had to be was patient. I spent two days as a model prisoner, lying with my feet up, even finishing the back of the tiny jacket with not too many dropped stitches. I made an attempt at a watercolor painting of the roses. I read a book. I helped pick raspberries for jam. And all the time a thought was nagging at my brain. *When can I go to the convent and find out what happened to Maureen?*

Then on the afternoon of the third day I received a letter from Gus.

Molly, as usual you make the most brilliant suggestions. As Sid said, we have already enjoyed the ocean this summer.

It should surely now be the turn of the river, and the way you describe it, it does sound inviting. Added to which we can visit you and take a trip upstream to relive our happy time at Vassar. I seem to recall we spent the night once at a delightful little village called Tarrytown. It had a magnificent view across the river where it widens into the Tappan Zee. I presume the inn is still there – can't remember its name, but it was something charmingly romantic and rural like Green Gables or Sleepy Hollow – didn't Washington Irving live nearby? Either way, I'm sure we'll be able to locate it, or one like it. So expect to hear from us in a few days. I can't remember how close you are to Tarrytown. Would you be able to take a look for us and see if our inn is still there?

By the way, we finally saw your industrious husband and told him that we were thinking of staying on the Hudson ourselves. He said it was a capital idea but we were to make sure you did nothing too strenuous. So you see, Molly, we have been charged with watching over you.

I heaved a sigh of content. Now that my friends were expected in a few days, I permitted myself one small stretching of the truth.

I came out to the porch where Mrs Sullivan was resting on the swing after another session of jam making. I sat beside her. 'You remember my friends – the two women who were my bridesmaids? Misses Elena Goldfarb and Augusta Walcott?' I mentioned the names to remind her that Gus came with family connections and my strategy obviously worked as she nodded and said, 'Of the Boston Walcotts, wasn't it? Such a charming young woman. Such good manners.'

'Well,' I continued. 'I believe I mentioned to you that they were thinking of coming to stay on the river nearby. I've received another letter from them. They wondered if I could check on a little inn they remember in Tarrytown. Unfortunately they can't recall its name but have described it to me. Tarrytown is not too far from here, is it?'

Mrs Sullivan's lips pursed in a gesture I had seen all too often. 'Do your friends know of your condition?'

'Of course.'

The pursed lips remained in place. 'I don't call it very considerate of your friends to want you to go running all over the place for them in this heat.'

'Oh, I'm sure they wouldn't want me to exert myself,' I said hastily. 'It's not as far as Irvington, is it? Only a mile or so? So if you could spare Jonah one morning, maybe I could do marketing for you at the same time and thus save you a trip into town.'

She was still frowning, but at last she spoke. 'Well, we are running low on sugar. And there is a butcher in Tarrytown who provides excellent chickens. I thought we might treat ourselves to a roast chicken after our industrious jam making.'

'I'd be happy to run those errands for you,' I said. 'Would you like me to go in the morning?'

'I think that would be all right,' she said. 'You could take Bridie with you. You know how she loves the river and she has been such a willing little helper with the fruit picking.'

I could find no good reason not to take Bridie, but I didn't want her reporting back to Mrs Sullivan that I'd been to a convent. Maybe I could send Jonah off with her to get an ice cream while I snooped around. But at least I'd succeeded in the first part of my plan. By this time tomorrow I'd know the truth about where Maureen O'Byrne had gone.

Chapter 13

I chose to set off early so that we would be back before the heat of the day. It was another pleasant ride, shaded by trees the whole way. Bridie chattered excitedly about what we were going to see and whether one could swim or catch fish in the river.

'We don't have no fishing poles with us,' Jonah said, 'but I'll ask the mistress if I can take you fishing someday, if you've a mind to learn.' Clearly Bridie had become the favorite of the household.

Tarrytown was another of those charming riverside towns with clapboard and brick houses lining narrow streets that descended to the river, which had here begun to widen into something closer to a lake. Jonah said it was called the Tappan Zee, presumably by the early Dutch settlers in this region, and today it sparkled in sunshine, with the hills on the distant Jersey shore adding to the pleasing appearance. On the shoreline was a ferry dock and beside it a low white lighthouse, presumably to remind mariners heading downstream that the lake diminished into a river again just beyond. I soon found not one but two charming inns with views of the river, checked out the bedrooms and inquired about availability. I bought sugar at the grocers and paid for a chicken at the butchers, to be collected on our way home. Then I suggested that Jonah take Bridie down to the riverfront and let her look at the fishermen and at the ferry crossing to New Jersey while I ran some personal errands. I also slipped him some money and suggested an ice cream.

Now for the real business of the day. I inquired about the convent in the dry goods store, where Mrs Sullivan had asked me to buy white baby ribbon, and was given directions – up on the hill in North Tarrytown.

'Is it within walking distance from here?' I asked.

The woman behind the counter looked at my figure, then shook her head. 'It's a mile or more, I'd say.' She turned to the man serving at the other counter. 'Wouldn't you agree, Seth?'

Seth nodded. 'More than a mile,' he said, gloomily, 'and uphill too. A good way out of town.'

The shopkeeper was looking at me with interest and I sensed that she was trying to decide whether I was one of those fallen women, in need of the nuns, or not. I was about to say that I was looking for a young relative who had gone there when I hit upon an absolutely marvelous idea.

'I'm thinking of offering one of those young women employment as a maid,' I said.

She nodded with enthusiasm. 'I've heard of folk around taking the girls into service afterward,' she said. 'That's a good Christian act, for you.' She glanced across at Seth again, whom I presumed was her husband. 'You were going to make that delivery of the canvas in North

Tarrytown, weren't you? You could run this lady up to the convent.'

'I was going to wait until later,' he mumbled, but the woman said firmly. 'It has to be done sometime and it might as well be now.'

He sighed, took off his apron, and started for the back door, glancing back at me. 'Come on, then,' he said. 'Can't wait around all day.'

So I rode beside the uncommunicative Seth through the town and up the hill until the houses gave way to meadows and small farms. Then we left the road for a narrow rutted track, bordered by tall somber evergreens, until we turned a corner and there before us was a grim building of rough-hewn gray stone. It was only about two stories high at this point, but it had square towers at both corners facing the river and I glimpsed a higher sloping roof of what was probably the chapel on the far side, adorned with a simple cross. No windows looked out toward us, but in the middle of the wall was a big wooden door. It was about the most uninviting building I had ever seen and reminded me of the medieval strongholds of my childhood in Ireland.

'This'll be it then,' Seth said. 'How long do you reckon you'll be?'

'Not more than fifteen minutes or so,' I said, eyeing that foreboding door. 'Will that suit you?'

'I suppose so,' he said grudgingly. He didn't offer to help me down, so I clambered down from the seat none too elegantly, I suspect.

'If I come out and you're not here, I'll walk up the track to meet you,' I said.

'No point. I have to come this far to turn the cart,' he

said. 'You'd best wait in the cool until I get you. And don't let those nuns lock you in there.' He gave a dry chuckle. 'There are some as say that girls go in there and aren't seen again.'

I could tell that this was his attempt at humor, but all the same I felt a chill run down my spine as I walked toward that massive door with as much bravado as I could muster. I rapped firmly on the knocker and waited. I heard Seth turning the cart around and then the horse clopping away before suddenly a panel right in front of my face slid back and a voice from the other side said, 'Can I help you?'

I handed my card through the dark slot to an invisible female person. 'Mrs Molly Sullivan of New York,' I said. At the last moment I decided to keep to the story I had invented. 'I wonder if I might have a word with the mother superior. I'm in need of a servant and I understand that there might be a young woman staying here who would fit my needs.'

'I'll see if Mother is available,' the voice said. 'Please come in.'

The enormous door creaked open and I stepped into cold darkness. After the bright sunshine I could hardly make out where I was, but gradually the figure before me came into focus. She was a young girl, wearing a light-colored pinafore that failed to mask the large round belly beneath it. She looked absurdly young to be having a child, no more than a child herself, and she smiled at me shyly.

'I'll take you into the parlor,' she said. 'This way please.'

'What's your name?' I asked.

'It's Katy, ma'am. Katy Watson.'

She held open a door for me and I stepped through

into a dismal, spartan room. It had a vaulted ceiling and a stone floor like a dungeon, and the dungeon effect was completed with a small barred window, overlooking a courtyard with a kitchen garden and beyond that a high brick wall. The furniture in the parlor consisted of a table with a Bible on it and a couple of shabby upholstered chairs, both the worse for wear. Katy indicated that I should sit on one of them.

'I'll go and tell Mother that you're here,' she said.

It smelled old and damp and musty. No sunlight came into the room and I shivered as I sat there. I hoped the quarters for those poor girls were a little more cheerful than this – or perhaps the object was to make sure they knew they were being punished for their sins. At least they were only here for a short while, whereas the nuns–

'*Dominus vobiscum,*' said a voice right behind me, making me jump. I hadn't heard the door open and looked around to see I was still alone in the room. 'Don't be alarmed, my child,' the voice said again and I saw that a shadowy figure, draped head to toe in black, had appeared behind a carved wood grille built into the wall.

'I'm sorry, Mother.' I laughed nervously. 'I hadn't expected the wall to be talking to me, like a confessional.'

'I'm not the mother superior,' she said. 'She's at her prayers and we didn't want to disturb her. I'm Sister Perpetua, her second-in-command. And surely you knew that we are an enclosed order.' The voice was soft, gentle, ageless with an Irish lilt to it. 'We keep the grille between ourselves and the outside world.' Even though she spoke in little more than a whisper, her voice echoed around that dismal room.

'What about the girls who come here?' I asked before

I could stop myself. 'Do you keep yourselves shut away from them?' I spoke louder without meaning to and my voice howled back at me.

'As much as possible. There is strict division between our convent life and the life of our charges. The young women essentially take care of themselves and sleep and eat apart from us. It would not be wise for our sisters to see the babies. It would remind the younger ones too much of what they have chosen to give up to enter here. Now how can I help you?'

'I have two reasons for coming here,' I said. 'I understand that when the girls leave here they are sometimes placed in domestic service.'

'That is correct. Are you looking for a servant at this time?'

'I am.'

'Any particular type of servant?'

I was tempted to say 'under-parlormaid,' but I replied, 'Just a maid of all work to help me in a small New York household. The work would not be overly taxing but I would want a reliable, cheerful girl.'

'Of course you would,' she said. 'I'd have to confer with Sister Jerome, who is in charge of these young women and their babies, but I don't think a suitable candidate springs to mind at the moment. We've a couple of lovely young women who recently delivered, but they have both expressed a desire to enter the convent.'

'Does that happen often?'

'Oh, yes,' she said. 'Quite regularly. You see these girls have experienced the unfairness and cruelty of the outside world and they compare it to the tranquility of our lives. It's an easy choice.'

I decided to take the plunge. 'You had a girl here called Maureen O'Byrne,' I said. 'Is she no longer with you?'

'Maureen? Why, no, my dear. She left us more than two months ago. Was it Maureen you particularly wanted to hire?'

'Not particularly, but I'm acquainted with her family back in Ireland and they wrote to me expressing concern about her. So I hope to be able to give them news of her. Do you happen to know where she went?'

'I understood she was going back to her former place of employment.'

'I've been to visit Mrs Mainwaring, her former employer, but Maureen did not return there.'

'Oh, how strange. Of course I have no direct contact with the young women, but we sisters are certainly privy to what is happening on the other side of the grille. I could swear that she left to go back to her former employers because we sisters were cheered by this woman's generosity and Christian charity.'

'I see,' I said. 'Is there perhaps one of Maureen's particular friends still here in whom she could have confided a secret plan she didn't share with the sisters?'

'I'm not sure if any of them are still here. They are usually required to go back into the world as soon as they are fit and strong, so that we have room for another girl to take their place. Unfortunately there is always more need than we can fill in our small way. It's a wicked world out there, as I'm sure you know.'

'Do they ever take their babies with them?' I asked.

'We discourage that strongly. There is no future for an unmarried woman with a child and Sister Jerome works wonders in finding adoptive families for the babies. Almost every one of them goes to a good home.'

'And those that don't?'

'I'm afraid it's the Foundling Hospital for them. But we try our very best, and there are always childless couples who long for a little one of their own, aren't there? Luckily we've developed quite a reputation and so they come to us from far and wide.'

'That's good news,' I said. 'So would there be nobody here who can tell me anything more about what happened to Maureen?'

'No doubt Sister Jerome would know. She's now in charge of the maternity cases. It used to be our dear Sister Francine but she died recently. Sister Jerome is the order's bursar and thus responsible for the placement of the girls and their babies. She's most efficient. She would have signed the order to release the girl.'

'Could I possibly speak to her?'

There was a distinct pause before she said, 'I'm not sure if she's occupied at this moment, or maybe still at her prayers. If you'll open that door behind you and call for Katy for me, she can go and search for her. But I can't guarantee that she'll come.'

My feet echoed from the stone floor to the vaulted ceiling as I crossed the room. And even though I spoke in a low voice, it echoed into unseen darkness as I called for Katy. She appeared right away, brushing down her apron.

'Are you leaving, ma'am?' she asked.

'No, Sister Perpetua wants you to run an errand for me.'

Katy stepped into the parlor. 'Yes, Sister,' she asked reverently. 'What do you need?'

'This lady would like to talk to Sister Jerome,' the voice

said. I still had no idea what she looked liked, whether she was large, small, old, or young. She was just a black shape with a lighter oval of featureless face that spoke. 'Could you go and find her and see if she has time to come to the parlor grille?'

'Very good, Sister,' she said and I heard her neat little feet tapping away down a hall.

'That one's a good child,' Sister Perpetua said. 'They all are, at heart. Just foolish, most of them. Not evil. She'd make you a good servant in a month or so, if you're prepared to wait.'

'Thank you,' I said. 'I think that might work splendidly.' I had already taken to her.

We waited in silence. Actually I wasn't even sure that she was still behind the grille. There was no question of small talk. At last a sharper, deeper, more powerful voice said, 'Sister Perpetua tells me you want to see me.'

I stared at the grille and could make out a taller, thinner shape – so tall and thin that any hint of a face was cut off from my view above the grille.

'This lady is looking to hire a servant, Sister,' Sister Perpetua said. 'And she's inquiring after Maureen O'Byrne.'

'Maureen?' the sharp voice said. 'She left us a while ago.'

'Do you know where she went, Sister?'

'We do. She was going back to the family she worked for previously. They were generous enough to forgive her sin.'

'I've been to visit them,' I said, 'and she never came back.'

'She didn't? Silly girl. I'm afraid she had ideas about

bettering herself. I just hope she hasn't run off to the city. No good will come of that.'

'Didn't she just up and go without saying good-bye?' Sister Perpetua asked.

'She did, ungrateful child,' Sister Jerome answered. 'Slipped out while the sisters were in chapel at matins one morning and her fellows were asleep. It wasn't until breakfast that we realized nobody had seen her. A stupid thing to do really. She was due to be released anyway within a couple of days.'

'Is it possible she ran off with a young man?' I asked. 'The baby's father?'

Sister Jerome sucked through her teeth. 'I suppose that is possible, although I got the impression that the baby's father wasn't in a position to marry her. A married man, I'd always thought.'

'I just wondered,' I said cautiously, 'whether she might have confided in another girl here of a secret plan she didn't share with you. Whether she had a special friend here.'

'Sister Francine was still in charge when Maureen was here. I had little contact with her,' Sister Jerome said. 'But from what I understand she was a religious girl. Her religion meant a lot to her and I suspect she felt her shame strongly, which would have kept her from making friends here.' Before I could speak again, she added, 'Besides, I suspect all those who were here with her have departed by now.'

I wasn't sure if she was being deliberately obstructive or just matter of fact. I took a deep breath. 'Would you be kind enough to tell me where I could find any of those girls now? Are any still living in the area?'

'May one ask why this interest in the girl? If you're wanting to hire her, I think you'd be out of luck. If the Mainwarings weren't good enough for her, then I suspect you'd have to be a Rockefeller.' And she gave a dry little half laugh, half cough.

'No, I wasn't wanting to hire her,' I said. 'I received a letter from her family in Ireland, concerned because they hadn't heard from her in a long while and wanting news of her.'

'She wouldn't have written home, would she?' the sharp voice said. 'In fact she told me herself that she could never go home again and face them, after what she'd done. She said they'd die of shame and grief.'

'I think she'd be surprised. They are very fond of her. Very worried about her.'

'Are you a relative?' she asked.

I wondered if I'd be given more information if I said I was. 'No. I'm not a relative, just someone whom the family knew how to contact in New York. They wrote me such a sad letter, I wanted to help if I could. I know what it's like to be worrying about somebody and imagining the worst.'

'I wish we could help you put their minds at rest, my dear,' Sister Perpetua said in her soft voice. 'But if Sister here knows nothing about where she's gone, then I'm afraid we have lost her. All we can do is offer to pray.'

'We will certainly pray for Maureen,' Sister Jerome said. 'And hope that she sees the error of her ways and returns to the family who were kind to her.'

'I'm staying nearby in Elmsford,' I said. 'If you hear any news of her, would you please let me know? I'll write the address on the back of my card and give it to Katy.'

'You may certainly do that,' Sister Jerome said. 'But I

doubt we will hear anything. We keep ourselves purposely shut away and hear little news from the wicked world outside. I bid you good day. *Pax vobiscum*. Katy, would you show this lady out?'

I heard the swish of black robes behind the grille.

Chapter 14

The sunlight was overwhelmingly bright as Katy opened the big front door for me. I stood there blinking, feeling the heat radiating from that stone wall and the high demented screech of cicadas in the trees. 'Thank you, Katy,' I said. 'You've been most kind. When is your own baby due?'

'In about two weeks, they say,' she said, looking down at the ground and not meeting my eyes.

'I'm sure you'll be glad to get it over with,' I said.

She nodded, her eyes still averted from me. 'I'm not looking forward to the birth, though. I've heard the other girls. It sounds awful. They scream and curse and call for their mothers – and some of them die.'

'You're a good strong girl. I'm sure you'll come through it just fine,' I said. 'I have to confess I'm just a tad apprehensive about it myself, but we women all have to go through it, don't we?'

'It seems so unfair,' she said, looking up at me now. 'I mean he was the one who forced me to do it with him and his life hasn't changed at all. If I went home again, I'd be soiled goods. No respectable man will want to marry me.'

'It's very unfair, I agree,' I said. 'Look, Katy, after you've had the baby, I'd like to offer you a job working for me in New York City. I've only a small house and the work wouldn't be hard and you'd be experiencing life in the big city – maybe you'd be able to make something of yourself there. You'd certainly have a chance to meet some nice boys who don't know about your past.'

Her whole face lit up with unconcealed joy. 'You'd do that for me? Oh, ma'am. I promise you I'd be the best servant ever. I come from country stock so I'm not afraid of hard work. I was dreading having to go back to Red Hook.'

'Then we'll call it settled, shall we? My name's Mrs Sullivan. I'll call back after the baby is born and see how you are doing.'

She nodded.

'I'd better be off then,' I said. 'I'm getting a lift back into town.' I thought I could see a cart approaching between the trees.

'There is one thing, ma'am,' she said in a low voice as I went to move away. 'You were asking about Maureen.'

'Yes,' I said. 'Did you know her?'

'A little. I arrived just before she was due to leave so I never got to know her well, but I got the impression that she was going back to the family she'd come from. At least I heard her say, "What choice do I have? Who else would take me in?" '

'But Sister says she just escaped early one morning?'

'She did. When we filed in to take our places at breakfast she wasn't there and nobody had seen her. Sister Jerome was annoyed because nobody was allowed to sleep in late. Then when we searched and found she'd gone, Sister was really furious. She kept saying what an ungrateful girl Maureen was and how the rest of us better appreciate what was being done for us.'

'You say you didn't know her well. Can you think of any girls who might have known her better – a girl she might have confided in what she planned to do?'

Katy chewed on her lip, making her look like a five year old. Again I was struck with how absurdly young she was. 'There was Emily Robbins. Those two were thick together. I don't know why Sister didn't mention her.'

'And do you know where Emily was going when she left here?'

'I believe she was going home,' Katy said. 'She came from a respectable family. They have a farm not too far from here. Near Cortland, I think she said. So she was planning to go home and they were giving out that she'd been on a trip abroad with a family friend.'

'Thank you,' I said. 'I'll try to pay her a visit. People usually confide in someone if they are planning something, don't they?'

The lip was still being chewed. 'That was what was so hard when I found out about the baby. There was nobody to tell. I kept it to myself until it started to show, not knowing what to do. And then my mother noticed and she told my dad and he threw me out of the house and said never to come back.' There was a long pause. 'And my mom didn't say a word. Not even good-bye.'

'Katy, I'm so sorry.' I touched her shoulder gently. 'I'll make sure you have a good home with me, all right? And you'll have a baby to look after too.'

She managed a smile. Seth and the cart appeared between the last of the fir trees. 'I have to go,' I said.

She moved closer to me. 'There was one other thing

that was strange,' she said. 'Like Sister said, Maureen was religious. She had this little statue of Our Lady. A lovely little thing, beautifully carved, it was. She said her grand-dad made it for her first communion. She kept it on the table beside her bed. Well, after she'd gone, I was told to strip her bed and clean out her cubby and I found she'd left things behind.'

'What kind of things?'

'Her hairbrush, for one. It was a lovely hairbrush with a tortoiseshell back and Sister said I could keep it if I liked so I still have it. But I mean – I can understand that she left in a hurry, but who doesn't take their hairbrush with them?'

'And the little statue of Our Lady?'

She leaned very close to me and said in a whisper, 'I found it in a wastebasket. So I'm puzzled. She'd never have left that behind unless . . .'

'Unless what?'

'Unless she had to leave in a real hurry.'

'Katy?' a voice boomed from the darkness inside.

Katy shot a fearful look around. 'I have to go. I'm not supposed to be out here, talking.'

'I'll see you soon, Katy. I'll be back,' I called as she ran inside. The big wooden door closed with a resounding boom. I went to meet Seth and hauled myself up onto the cart.

'I see they didn't lock you in one of their cells then,' he said as he flicked a whip at the horse.

'I didn't get a chance to see any cells. I was only allowed in the parlor.'

'I don't understand it myself,' he said as the horse picked up speed. 'Shutting themselves away from the world like that. It ain't natural. No wonder they go funny.'

We came back into the center of Tarrytown and I met Jonah and Bridie at the appointed place.

'You're back too soon,' Bridie complained. 'We didn't even have a chance to buy an ice cream yet.'

I glanced up at the clock on the train station and saw that I'd been away for less than an hour. It felt more like a lifetime.

After Bridie and I had shared a sundae in the soda fountain, we got into the trap, picked up the chicken from the butcher, and headed back to Elmsford. Bridie chatted excitedly about everything she'd seen – a man catching a big fish and a sudden breeze that had blown another man's hat into the river and a fisherman who had managed to hook the hat and fish it out. And a girl had waved to her from the top deck of a paddle steamer. Her only regret was that she had not been allowed to swim like the little boys who jumped off the jetty.

I tried to be receptive and encouraging as she talked to me, as she had been a shy, reticent child until recently, but words were screaming in the recesses of my brain. Not Bridie's words but Katy's. *Unless she had to leave in a real hurry.* What would have made Maureen leave in such a hurry that she left her prized statue behind? Had someone turned up outside the front door? The young man she was hoping for, perhaps, saying, 'Come with me now. I've a trap waiting and we can be far away before they find us?'

When I saw Katy again I must ask which of her things Maureen had actually taken with her. The hairbrush she could have overlooked in her haste. I'd left things behind before when I'd had to pack in a hurry. But the little statue – she'd have made sure she took that.

'Sorry, dear, what did you say?' I asked as Bridie's words cut into my consciousness.

'You weren't paying attention, Molly,' she said, giving me her best frown. 'I was telling you that Jonah is going to teach me fishing and then I'll catch fish for dinner. Right, Jonah?'

'That will be just grand,' I said. 'Your daddy and brother would be proud of you.'

'They think I'm just a little kid and no use for anything,' she said.

'Then you'll surprise them when they come home.'

There was a pause before she said quietly, 'Do you think they'll be home soon?'

'I really couldn't say, sweetheart.' I stroked her hair. 'I think it takes a long time to dig a canal across a continent.'

I heard the visible sigh of relief. 'Because I want to stay with Mrs Sullivan and you for a long, long time,' she said. 'I want to go to a proper school and learn how to be a lady.'

'Of course you do, and you will.'

'I hope so,' she said and snuggled against me. I put an arm around her, and she fell asleep against me. I began to feel drowsy too until I was jolted awake by a most disturbing thought. Maybe Seth's jokes had not been just idle chit-chat but had some substance to them after all. What if the nuns had tried to force Maureen to take the veil and had locked her in a cell, from which she managed to escape and flee at the only time she could, while they were in chapel? That would explain why she had to leave behind her most precious possessions.

And I knew I could not let the matter lie. I had to find out what had happened to her some way or another.

Chapter 15

When we got home I presented Mrs Sullivan with the ribbon, the sugar, and the chicken. She nodded with satisfaction over the quality of the latter. 'We'll have that on Sunday then, shall we? Is there any chance Daniel might be able to come and join us?'

'I'll write and ask him, if you like, but I doubt he'll take time off when he has so much to do. From what I understand he's trying to juggle several cases at once.'

She shook her head, making a *tut-tutting* noise. 'If we're not careful, he'll be facing an early grave like my husband.'

'I think Daniel thrives on hard work,' I said. 'I'll write to him.'

'After you've had your lunch,' she said firmly. 'It's all laid out and ready in the dining room.'

The lunch was ham and salad, with newly baked rolls, followed by a plum tart and cream. I ate ravenously. I hadn't realized how hungry my escapades had made me. Mrs Sullivan looked on with approval. 'That's right. You're eating for two now.'

Then she forced me upstairs to lie down. As soon as

she had closed the door behind her I tiptoed to my writing case and took out paper and envelopes. Then I wrote my letters while lying on the bed. First I wrote a short note to Daniel saying that I'd had a pleasant excursion to the river, all was well and his mother hoped he could join us for lunch on Sunday. I added a postscript that I missed him. Then I wrote to Sid and Gus, describing the two inns (not the Green Gables or Sleepy Hollow, but The Lighthouse Inn and The Hideaway). I recommended The Lighthouse Inn as the upstairs rooms had a spectacular view across the Tappan Zee and it was not likely to be as noisy as the other, which was near the train station. In addition, the innkeeper seemed to be a pleasant woman, not too nosy and round enough to indicate that she was a good cook.

I smiled to myself. Soon I'd have my friends nearby and all would be right with the world. I suppose I should have been more excited at the prospect of my husband coming to Sunday luncheon and of course I wanted to see him, but he was not good company when he was overworked like this and would undoubtedly begrudge the time away from work. If he came at all, that was.

I sealed the envelopes, put on stamps, then crept downstairs to find Jonah. I found him easily enough, hard at work mending the outdoor pump, muttering to himself and using words a lady should never overhear. I backed away carefully and decided I could walk the letters to the nearest mailbox myself. It was a decision I regretted as soon as I reached the end of the lane leading into Elmsford. I hadn't realized quite how hot the afternoon had become and every step became an effort. I had thought that the nearest mailbox was only a short walk away but the road seemed to stretch on forever. I wasn't going to give up, having come this far, but the sweat was running into my eyes by the time I pushed the letters through the slot and turned for home.

I hadn't gone far when I was overcome by an attack of dizziness and had to sit on a tree stump in the shade. This was something I hadn't experienced since the early days of my pregnancy and it alarmed me. I wasn't the sort of woman who succumbed to an attack of the vapors! Grudgingly I had to admit that maybe my husband and mother-in-law were right and I should not be doing anything too strenuous. I had been rushing around all morning and should have taken a proper rest. Maybe this quest to find Maureen O'Byrne was too much for me.

I looked up as I heard the sound of a horse's hooves coming from Elmsford at a brisk trot. A small black closed carriage approached. As I watched it I caught a glimpse of the person inside. It was a tall, gaunt, hooded figure in black and it resembled Sister Jerome, the harsh nun I had met earlier today. I watched the carriage pass with interest. Curious. If those nuns were an enclosed order, then didn't that mean that they never left the convent? So what was one of them doing alone in a carriage, and a rather fine-looking carriage at that? And weren't nuns always supposed to travel in pairs?

I got up and headed back to the house. There was something strange about that convent and the way that Sister Jerome had deliberately tried to put me off from looking for Maureen. Another thought crossed my mind – what if she hadn't run away at all, but was still locked up, a prisoner of the nuns? And I knew I couldn't let the matter rest. My curiosity and concern wouldn't let me. I also realized that I had a perfect opportunity to do some snooping. Sid and Gus could invite me to stay on the river with them for a few days. And from there I could take the train up to Cortland to call upon Emily Robbins who, according to Katy, had been thick with Maureen. I could even go back to the convent on the pretext of interviewing Katy for future employment in my household.

I found a new spring in my step. I had the bit between my teeth now and nothing was going to stop me.

Two days later I received two letters. The first was from Sid and Gus, thanking me for my research and telling me that they had sent a wire to The Lighthouse Inn, booking themselves in from Friday onward, and couldn't wait to see me. The other letter was from Daniel. His mother was right. He had been working too hard for too long. He had decided to come up for Sunday lunch and maybe even to stay on for a couple of days.

'Oh, what wonderful news,' Mrs Sullivan said as I read the letter out loud to her. 'He obviously misses you terribly, my dear.'

I nodded. I knew I should be ecstatic that my husband missed me so much that he was coming all the way to Elmsford to see me, but the first thought I'd had was that I'd now have to wait until he left before I'd have a chance to visit Sid and Gus at The Lighthouse Inn. And who knows, they might have found life in Tarrytown too boring by then and flitted to pastures new. They rarely stayed in one spot for long and if they went I'd have no opportunity to carry on with my quest to find Maureen.

On Sunday morning the house was in a flurry of activity. First we all had to go to church at eight. I went along too, not because I wanted to, but because I knew that my lack of religion would distress my mother-in-law, who expected everyone to go to church. Then we had a hurried breakfast before Daniel's mother had my things moved to her own bedroom so that he and I could have the big four-poster bed.

'We can't turn you out of your room,' I protested.

'It's only right that a married couple should have the one good bed in the house,' she insisted, and there was no budging her.

Daniel arrived about eleven. He came up the path slowly, as if every step was an effort, but his face lit up when he saw me.

'Well, look at you,' he said, bounding up the last two steps to me. 'Positively blooming. The fresh air obviously agrees with you.'

He had to lean across my belly to give me a kiss.

'That's more than I can say for you,' I responded. 'You look awful. You've great bags under your eyes. I don't believe you've slept properly since I left.'

'You're not wrong,' he said. 'We've all been working like crazy men, but I decided to back off for a while.'

'Is it still the anarchists that you're working on?' I asked.

He gave me a warning frown as his mother came out of the kitchen and rushed to embrace him. 'My poor boy,' she exclaimed. 'Look at you. Worn to a frazzle. They are overworking you again. You'll be for an early grave if you don't quit.'

'Thanks, Mother. Nice to see you,' Daniel said, with a grin to me.

She slipped her arm through his. 'I've sherry waiting for you in the parlor and then no doubt you can smell the chicken roasting in the oven for lunch. Your wife went into Tarrytown specially to get it from that good butcher.'

'Lovely. Thank you,' he said and allowed himself to be led through to the parlor, seated in the best armchair, and handed a glass of sherry. I sat opposite him.

'I'll leave you two then,' Mrs Sullivan said. 'I have to get back to the kitchen to supervise Martha.'

'Nonsense, Mother. Martha is quite capable of cooking a chicken by herself,' Daniel said. 'She's been doing it since I was a boy without spoiling it once. Now sit and have a sherry with us. You can tell me all the local gossip.'

Mrs Sullivan sat reluctantly and poured herself a sherry. Then she launched into a description of the jam making, the tea party at Letitia Blackstone's, and the trip to Irvington.

'Your wife went to visit an acquaintance while we were there,' she said. 'A Mrs Mainwaring. Is she a friend of yours too?'

Daniel looked across at me and frowned. 'Mainwaring. I've heard the name, but I can't place it. How do you know her, Molly?'

Ah. Now I was in a spot. 'She was part of Sid and Gus's Vassar circle,' I said, with the sure conviction that Daniel stayed well clear of them.

'Oh, another Vassar girl. Is she another of those awful suffragists?'

'Surely Molly doesn't mix with those dreadful women?' Mrs Sullivan turned to glare at me.

'What's so awful about wanting the right to vote?' I demanded. 'How can it be right that half the country has no say in how we are governed?'

'But women have no experience outside the home,' Mrs

Sullivan said. 'They are not equipped to make decisions of a political nature. It's up to their husbands to guide them in such matters. I know I always trusted the opinion of Daniel's father and would never have dreamed of crossing him.'

I saw Daniel give me a warning look.

'Times are changing,' I said. 'Women are starting to work outside the home and they'll want their say.'

'Let's hope it's not in my lifetime,' she said.

'So was this Mrs Mainwaring another suffragist?' Daniel asked. 'Was that why you visited her, to attend one of their meetings?'

'Not at all. It was simply a courtesy call, since I was in the area,' I said. 'And as it turned out, I did not find her particularly pleasant or welcoming.'

'I pointed out to Molly that it was not wise to stop by unexpectedly in this heat when people do not look or feel their best,' Mrs Sullivan said.

'And you were right,' I said, lowering my head in a demure fashion that made Daniel smile.

'Mainwaring,' he said again. 'In Irvington? It's beginning to ring a bell now. I believe he was at Princeton with Freddie Parsons. I think I met him at Freddie's place a couple of times. Good-looking chap. Thought a lot of himself and his family connections, I seem to remember.'

'Which reminds me,' Mrs Sullivan said. 'We heard that Arabella Norton is now married and living in Philadelphia. They say she's made a very good match indeed.'

'I'm glad for her,' Daniel said shortly.

I was glad when Bridie appeared to announce that the meal was served and we were able to leave the uncomfortable conversation. The chicken was delicious, the beans from the garden were perfect, and the meal was rounded off with a peach cobbler and coffee. Afterward Mrs Sullivan suggested that I go to lie down.

'I'm not at all tired,' I said, 'and I want to make the most of Daniel being here. I hardly ever get time to talk to him at home, so this is a treat.'

'We'll take a little walk, shall we?' Daniel took my hand.

'I want to come too.' Bridie jumped down from her chair to join us. Mrs Sullivan grabbed her arm to hold her back. 'Let them be alone for a while, child,' she said. 'Your turn will come later. Besides, I need help with clearing the table.'

Bridie gave a mournful look after us.

'Don't let her go out without a parasol,' Mrs Sullivan called after us. 'She'll get sunstroke.'

Daniel grinned as he handed me the parasol. An amused look passed between us as I took it and opened it. 'I never thought I'd see the day when you went out with a parasol,' he muttered as we walked out onto the porch and then down the steps to the garden. 'It's quite the transformation.'

'You'd be amazed at how good I'm being,' I said. 'Sweet, compliant, and only one step away from simpering.'

He laughed. 'That will never happen to you. So you're holding up all right under my mother's ministrations? I must say you're looking very well.'

'She treats me as if I'm made of fine china and might break,' I said, 'I want to be helpful but she won't let me do much. At least I've got Bridie here to keep me company. Hasn't she grown up since she's been with your mother?'

He nodded. 'Far more outgoing and sure of herself. I told you Mother would never treat her as a servant, didn't

I? You watch, she'll be scouting out potential suitors to make a good match for her before long.'

We walked silently over the soft grass.

'I've missed you,' he said. 'I lived alone for so many years, I thought of myself as completely self-sufficient. But now I've become used to finding you there when I come home. It feels so empty without you.'

'Do you want me to come home?' I asked cautiously.

'No, it's better for you to stay out here until the temperature cools down,' he said. 'You're clearly being looked after well and it would be purely selfish of me to want you to give this up.'

'I will, if it makes you happy,' I said.

He squeezed my hand. 'You're a good woman, Molly Murphy. But I want to make sure my son is born fit and healthy.'

'Oh, it's a son, is it?' I asked, my eyes teasing his. 'What if it's a daughter? Are you going to throw her back?'

He laughed. 'If she's anything like you, I'm in for a rough time.' He stood there looking at me. 'I can't tell you how glad I am that you're learning to slow down to a woman's pace and enjoy home and family. I was worried that after all the excitement of being a detective you'd never manage to settle.'

'Of course I miss the excitement,' I said. 'Wouldn't you? But I also have to admit that I ran terrible risks and I'm lucky to be alive today.'

'You certainly are,' he said. 'At one point I was ready to lock you up for your own protection.'

'I might say the same for you. You take terrible risks. I worry about you all the time.'

'I'm a man. Men are designed to take risks.'

I turned my gaze to the magnificent roses that spilled over the far wall, conscious that I was being just a tad hypocritical with my husband and not quite honest either.

We had reached the shade of a massive elm tree at the bottom of the garden. A rough bench had been built around the trunk and we sat on this, looking back at the house. I turned to Daniel.

'You could enjoy the benefit of my expertise if you'd only share your cases with me,' I said in what I hoped was a casual manner.

'Molly, we've been through this. You know I'm not supposed to discuss police business.'

'Surely that doesn't apply to your wife – especially a wife who has been a darned good detective.'

'As it is I'm already ragged by the other fellows about my wife solving my cases for me.'

'There you are then. So it doesn't matter if you discuss them with me.'

Daniel sighed. We sat for a while in silence, listening to the click of a mower in a distant garden.

'I'll tell you one thing,' he said. 'I think your brother has left the city. We've not found a trace of him anywhere, and none of my usual sources of information in the Lower East Side has seen him.'

'That's good news,' I said. 'I was so worried he'd be caught.'

'Of course you were. I understand that. It can't have been easy feeling that you were trapped in the middle. That was precisely why I wanted you safely out of the city.'

We fell silent again while I considered things. 'We don't know for sure that he was sent here to make contact with the anarchist group, do we?'

'We don't.'

'Have you managed to find them yet?'

'The anarchists?' He shook his head. 'Not yet. All that we have is the vaguest of hints – intercepted messages between Europe and America that mean nothing to any of us. And between you and me, I've backed off from trying too hard. After I found out that John Wilkie had approached my wife to work behind my back, I decided he could do his own searching without the help of my informants.'

'So you're off that case then?'

'Not officially. But let's just say that it's no longer my main priority.'

'I'm glad,' I said. 'Anarchists are known to be ruthless. I don't want to find that our house has been blown to pieces with a bomb.'

He smiled. 'I don't think that's likely to happen. They only blow up important people – people whose death can bring a country to its knees.'

'So you don't know which country they are aiming at?'

He shook his head. 'Although we have reason to believe it's either England or America. Apart from that, as I say, it's all rumor.'

'What about those kidnapped babies?' I asked, daring to forge ahead now he had become so talkative. 'Have there been any more of them?'

'Not since you left. Not since that awful mix-up when they returned the wrong baby. You heard about that, didn't you?'

'I did.'

'Well, they are lying low at the moment. I think they realize that our scrutiny is on them.'

'Did you ever find out where the other baby came from? The one the woman claimed wasn't hers?'

'We did. From the Foundling Hospital. It was one of theirs, taken from its bed.'

'What do you think happened to the real baby then?'

He looked grim. 'We think they somehow let the real baby die, but they were given the ransom money and felt they had to return a baby or face possible murder charges. So they grabbed the first baby they could set their hands on without it being noticed immediately. The one they took was in the crib nearest to the door.'

'How horrible.' In spite of the heat I shivered. 'I really feel for that poor woman. She has gone through a double agony now.'

'I know. It's despicable. I only hope we manage to catch them. We've little chance if they don't choose to strike again.'

'I did offer my services,' I reminded him. 'I would have been the ideal person to watch out for potential kidnappers. I'd have blended in and they'd never have suspected.'

He turned to put his hands on my shoulders. 'Molly Murphy, when are you ever going to learn that your detective days are over? You are never going to tail anybody again. You are going to be the perfect wife and mother.' There was a long pause. 'Aren't you?'

'Yes, Daniel,' I said, so sweetly that he burst out laughing, wrapped his arms around me, and kissed me fervently on the mouth.

'God, I've missed you,' he whispered.

His lips were warm against mine and I found myself responding to his kiss.

'I've missed you too,' I said and meant it.

Chapter 16

Daniel had planned to stay for at least a couple of days, but on Monday morning he received a wire summoning him back to New York as quickly as possible. His mouth was set in a hard line when he burst into the bedroom as I sat at the dressing table, brushing my hair, still in my robe.

'I have to go back to the city,' he said.

'Bad news?'

'Not good. They intercepted a crate of explosives on a ship bound for England.'

'Linked to your anarchist group, I suppose?'

'I know nothing more yet, but I have to go back. The ship is being held in port.' He bent to kiss the top of my head. 'Good-bye my love. Take care of yourself, won't you?'

'I will, but more to the point, you take care of yourself,' I called after him, but I could already hear his feet running down the stairs. I felt sick and hollow inside. He was only going to the city twenty miles away, but the way he had said, 'Take care of yourself,' had made it sound like a final farewell. I almost got up to run after him, to give him one final kiss.

Thank the Lord that Liam was no longer in the city, I thought, because a crate of explosives bound for England sounded like something the Irish Republicans might try. I finished dressing and came down to breakfast.

'Poor Daniel. They never give him a minute's peace.' Mrs Sullivan looked up from her boiled egg. Then she saw my face. 'Cheer up, my dear. I know you miss him but you're doing the right thing for the baby. And here's something to cheer you – a postcard from your friends.'

I took it from her. It was a pretty view of the Tarrytown lighthouse. On the back was scrawled in Sid's black jagged script:

We've arrived. Quite charming. Come and pay us a visit as soon as possible.

I looked up. 'My friends are already staying at an inn in Tarrytown. They want me to come out to visit them as soon as possible.'

I had expected a lecture on not tiring myself with too much jaunting around, but she said, 'Of course. What a good idea. That will help you get over the disappointment of Daniel's hasty departure, won't it?'

This was working all too well. I decided to test the waters one stage deeper. 'I thought I might stay at the inn with them for a night or two, if that's all right with you. I do so enjoy the cool breezes on the river, and they suggest going to look at some of the mansions together, which I have been wanting to do.'

'I've nothing planned for the rest of the week. I was

hoping we'd have Daniel here,' she said. 'You go and enjoy the company of other young people. I'm sure it's not much fun being stuck with a doddering old lady like me.'

I couldn't quite tell whether she was being kind or admonishing me for choosing my friends over her. I took it as the former and went around the table to kiss her on the cheek. 'You know I enjoy being here,' I said, 'but I'm used to being on the go all the time and I find it hard to sit around doing nothing.'

'Just you make sure that you don't tire yourself out,' she said. 'If those friends want to take you off on jaunts all the time, you tell them no.'

I smiled. 'I will. But don't worry. They are very considerate, and they like nothing better than to sit writing and painting. I may take my own sketchbook with me. This will be my last chance to improve my painting skills, I fear.'

I ate a hearty breakfast and then I went upstairs to pack.

'Can I come with you?' Bridie asked as I crossed the hall. 'I want to go back to the river.' She stood there looking so plaintive that my heart went out to her. Of course she wanted to be with me and she had had such a good time at the river. But how could I possibly do any investigating into Maureen if I had a child with me?

'I don't think Molly will want to be bothered with looking after you,' Mrs Sullivan said, and I saw Bridie's face fall even more.

My good nature won out. 'Of course it would be no bother to have her with me,' I said. 'If I take a room at the inn, there's no reason a little person like Bridie can't share it. If you can spare her for a couple of days, that is?'

Mrs Sullivan put an arm around Bridie. 'There now.

See how lucky you are that you've such kind people around you. Go upstairs and pack yourself some clean undergarments and hose. And put on the fresh white pinafore too. We don't want you going away looking like a ragamuffin.'

Bridie bounded up the stairs with such glee that I was glad of my decision, however inconvenient it was going to be for me. An hour later we were ready with a carpetbag packed.

'I want to go swimming, but I don't have any kind of bathing costume,' Bridie said. 'The boys were swimming in their underpants. What can I swim in?'

Mrs Sullivan looked appalled. 'Young ladies do not swim in the river, Bridget,' she said using her proper name. 'What ever were you thinking?'

'Then when can I swim?' Bridie asked. 'It looks as if it would be fun. The boys were having fun. They were squealing and laughing when they jumped off the dock.'

Mrs Sullivan's lips pursed. 'The only time we are permitted to swim is at the seashore, when there is a proper bathing machine and we do not have to risk exposing our legs.' She gave us a frosty stare. 'Remember what I told you, that a lady never shows even an ankle. It is not seemly.'

'No, Mrs Sullivan,' Bridie said. She looked at me and I winked.

'And make sure you wear your sun hat at all times, Bridget,' Mrs Sullivan called after us as we went toward the trap. 'If you don't you'll get freckles and no man would want to marry a woman with a freckled face.'

As we climbed into the trap together I whispered, 'We'll see if we can find you a bathing costume in Tarrytown.

Maybe they have one at the dry goods store. Only you have to promise not to tell Mrs Sullivan.'

She gave me a wide-eyed smile. 'I promise,' she whispered.

This time the journey seemed to take forever, although it was only a mile or so. The mare plodded along slowly until Bridie and I were both bursting with anticipation. And not just because I had escaped from my mother-in-law's scrutiny and was about to see my dear friends, but because I finally would have a chance to find out exactly what happened to Maureen O'Byrne. Jonah drew up outside The Lighthouse Inn and we went into the cool reception area, where the smells of a recent breakfast – coffee and bacon – mingled with that of furniture polish and fresh flowers. Jonah carried in our bags and the stout innkeeper came bustling out of the kitchen when I rang the bell, wiping her hands on her apron.

'Are Miss Walcott and Miss Goldfarb available?' I asked.

'They went out about half an hour ago, ma'am,' the lady innkeeper replied.

'Do you have any idea where they might have gone? I'm their friend and have come to meet them.'

She glanced out of the glass-paneled front door. 'They took their sketchbooks with them and I think I heard them say that they were going to paint by the river.'

'Then we'll go and see if we can locate them in a minute,' I said. 'But before we go, I wondered if you might have a room for the two of us. We'd like to stay here for a few days so I can enjoy the company of my friends.'

She looked worried. 'Oh dear. I'm afraid we're rather full at the moment,' she said.

I reminded her that my two friends from New York were staying with her at my recommendation and I had hoped to give them a surprise and join them. Her face softened. 'Well then,' she said. 'If you don't mind a small room and two flights of stairs I've a single room in the attic and I could probably squeeze a cot in for the young lady.'

She led us up two steep flights of uncarpeted wood stairs that twisted and turned until we came out to a narrow landing. She was breathing as hard as I was as she opened a door.

'Mercy but it's a climb, isn't it?' she said. 'Are you sure you'll be able to manage it?'

The room was indeed small with a sloping attic ceiling, but it was charming, and the open window caught the breeze from the river. The gauze curtains billowed out, revealing a superb view of sparkling water and the New Jersey shore on the far side. It was simply furnished with a single bed with a handmade quilt on it, a writing desk in the window, a washing stand with a flowery china basin and jug, and a corner closet. But it was painted pale yellow and the wallpaper had blue irises on a yellow background. An all around cheerful room.

'It will do just fine,' I said. 'I'll take it. I'm not sure how long I'm staying yet.'

She named a very reasonable price and started to relate times of meals and house rules, then left us to spruce up before we went to find Sid and Gus. After asking a policeman and then a stallkeeper if they had seen two ladies, one of them with black-bobbed hair, carrying with them sketching equipment we found them easily enough, down at the river, at an area of green grass on the other side of the railroad tracks. Gus had set up an easel in the shade of a willow tree and was sketching Sid, who posed on a rock at the water's edge, looking like a sleek, dark Lorelei. Gus cried out to Sid as she spotted us approaching and Sid almost fell into the water in her haste to join us.

'Well, here you are at last,' she said giving first Bridie and then me warm hugs. 'We wondered when we were going to see you. We hoped you'd be here on Friday to welcome us. We didn't like to call upon your mother-in-law without an invitation, knowing what a stickler she is for proper manners.'

'I couldn't come sooner. Daniel was visiting this weekend,' I said. 'In fact I was afraid I'd be stuck at the house even longer, but then he was summoned back to New York at the crack of dawn today.'

Gus gave me a wry smile. 'That doesn't sound like the devoted wife – couldn't wait for her husband to leave?'

'Of course I enjoyed seeing him,' I said, 'but it's a relief to get away from my mother-in-law for a while.'

'That bad, is it?' Sid asked.

I was conscious of Bridie standing beside me, shyly hanging on to my skirt. 'To be fair to Mrs Sullivan, she is looking after me admirably. Spoiling me, in fact. But she won't let me do anything and I'm chafing to get back to work.'

'Get back to work?' Gus said. 'Molly, dear, what kind of work are you talking about? You're not still trying to find your brother, are you?'

'No, I'm relieved to say that Daniel thinks he's left the city,' I said. I glanced down at Bridie. 'If you like you may take off your shoes and hose and play at the edge of the water,' I said. 'And you'd better take off your clean pinafore too. We don't want that to get dirty.'

I helped her out of them and she ran off delightedly, picking her way barefoot among the rocks. I turned back to my friends. 'I didn't want to mention this in Bridie's hearing, but remember the other matter – the letter I showed you from the people in Ireland?'

'And you asked if we knew anyone called Mainwaring,' Gus looked at Sid for confirmation.

'I've located the Mainwarings,' I said. 'They live out here, in Irvington.'

'In Irvington, fancy that,' Sid said. 'And was your Irish lass working for them?'

'She was, until she got herself into trouble,' I said.

'That sort of trouble?' Sid asked.

I nodded. 'Yes, that sort of trouble. So Mrs Mainwaring sent her to a local convent . . .'

'Isn't that a case of closing the stable door after the horse has bolted?' Sid said.

I had to laugh. 'You didn't let me finish. This convent takes in unmarried mothers and lets them stay until they have had their babies, then the nuns find adoptive families for the infants and the young women are able to come back into society.'

'Admirable,' Sid said.

Bridie gave a squeal as a big ship passed and its wash created a wave that splashed around the rocks.

'Careful,' I warned, noting that the hem of her skirt was now all wet. We watched her as she turned to give us an apologetic grin.

'But what if they want to keep their babies?' Gus said. 'I know that I should find it hard to give up a child.'

'Gus, dear, you have money. That alters everything. Most of them would have nowhere to go with a child,'

Sid said. 'They'd be outcasts. Shunned by society, denied employment. And think of the stigma on the child to be known as a bastard all its life.'

Gus sighed. 'I suppose that's true,' she said. 'It seems so unfair, doesn't it? The man in question gets on with his life and the woman is ruined. When will our society ever accept equality and fairness for women?'

'Not until we have the vote,' Sid said. 'But Molly hasn't finished her story yet. So you found the poor girl hiding her shame with the nuns, did you?'

'That's just it,' I said. 'This is where the plot thickens. I found that she had indeed been with the nuns and given birth to a child. She was supposed to return to the service of Mrs Mainwaring who had generously said she'd have her back, but she never showed up. And the nuns said she ran off one morning without saying good-bye.'

'Perhaps she didn't want to return to a place where they knew of her downfall,' Gus said. 'She had unhappy memories. So she went to try her luck in the big city where nobody knew her.'

'Either that or the child's father showed up and whisked her away,' I suggested.

'Do we have any idea who the child's father might have been?'

I shook my head. 'She wouldn't tell Mrs Mainwaring or the nuns. But they seemed to think that he couldn't or wouldn't marry her.'

'So she escaped from the nuns as soon as possible, did she?' Sid said. 'A girl after my own heart. I wouldn't want to be cooped up with a lot of old women.'

'You'll find it hard to track her down now, Molly,' Gus

said. 'My bet is that she went back to New York and got a job there.'

'I hope it's as simple as that,' I said, 'because there is something worrying about her disappearance. One of the other girls who is staying at the convent said that Maureen left some prized possessions behind – a statue of Our Lady carved by her grandfather, and her tortoise-shell hairbrush. So now I'm intrigued. What would make her rush off in such a hurry that she left her hairbrush behind, or her prized statue?'

'She saw a chance to escape and took it?' Gus suggested.

'But she was due to leave the convent any day. She had no need to escape.'

'Maybe she wanted to get away before the Mainwarings came to collect her and she was taken back to them,' Gus suggested.

'She could always have run away from them at her leisure.'

'That is a mystery,' Sid said, 'but I can't for the life of me see how you'd solve it.'

'There are a couple of avenues I'd like to pursue, now that I'm here,' I said. 'The girl I spoke with mentioned a friend Maureen had had while she was at the convent. This girl has left the convent and gone home to Cortland, so I understand. I thought Maureen might have confided her plans to another girl there. If you are planning some-thing daring you usually like to sound out your idea to someone else, don't you?'

'It depends if she was the secretive type or not,' Sid said. 'And if she was worried that the other person might spill the beans to one of the nuns.'

'There aren't any other girls at the convent who were close to Maureen then?' Gus asked.

'The nuns I spoke with weren't entirely welcoming and seemed reluctant to let me speak to any of the girls. I was told there were no girls still there who knew Maureen. They don't stay long. The nuns turf them out as soon as they are recovered from the birth. They only have a certain number of beds and more girls waiting for them than they can ever accommodate.'

'I'm sure of that,' Sid said. 'A place like that would even be in demand for girls from good families who behave foolishly and find themselves pregnant. And their families would probably pay well for the privilege.'

'I don't think good families would send their daughters to that convent,' I said. 'It looked awfully bleak and forbidding.'

'So your plan is to go to Cortland and speak with the one girl who did know Maureen?' Sid asked.

'It is.'

'Where exactly is Cortland? The name is familiar but I can't quite place it.'

'You remember,' Sid said. 'It's the stop before Peekskill on the train, isn't it? We used to count the stations because we couldn't wait to get back to Vassar.'

'Oh, yes,' Gus said. 'You're right, as usual. So not too far then. Only half an hour by train at the most.'

'Then we'll come with you, Molly,' Sid said. 'We love any excuse for a little jaunt.'

Oh, dear. Much as I loved my friends, having them along when I was trying to do my work was always a liability. They had never had to work and were inclined to treat any assignment as a big game. But I couldn't say no. Besides, when Bridie related our escapades to Mrs Sullivan a trip up the river together would sound harmless

– and I could claim the young woman we went to visit was a friend of my friends.

'Wonderful,' I said. 'I'd enjoy the company.'

'We can check on train times when we go home for lunch,' Gus said. 'How long do you have, Molly? Do you have to get back to your mother-in-law's by nightfall?'

'No, I've taken a room at the inn where you are staying. I told Mrs Sullivan that I'd be joining you for a few days. So I'm free to do what I want.'

'Isn't that perfect, Sid?' Gus said. 'We have a chance to join Molly in another of her escapades. And we thought that when she got married she'd turn into a boring and respectable housewife.'

'I can't say I ever really thought that,' Sid said.

They both looked at me and laughed. And I felt a wave of happiness run through me, too.

Chapter 17

The next morning, after a hearty breakfast of sausage and flapjacks at the inn, we set off early for the train station. Bridie was excited at the thought of going on a train. She tried to restrain herself in the presence of two strange ladies, but was dancing around like a colt at the start of a horse race. Overnight, I had lain awake in my unfamiliar single bed, listening to the sounds of the river while thoughts raced through my head. An idea had come to me which I subsequently mentioned to Sid and Gus as we walked through the busy early morning streets.

'I have Maureen's photograph with me. I should show it around at the station. Maybe someone might have remembered her catching a train.'

'You could show it around town too,' Sid suggested. 'She could have found someone to give her a ride. Where exactly is the convent?'

'It must be more than a mile from here, on the far northern fringe of the town. Up on a hill.'

'So it would be a long walk down into town, especially for one who had recently given birth,' Sid said.

'And I expect it's quite a lonely road, isn't it? Not much traffic?'

'It was quite lonely,' I said. 'Certainly no buildings nearby and not much sign of houses beyond.'

'Then probably any passing cart would have offered her a ride down the hill,' Sid said. 'We'll have to find out who might go up and down that hill into town.'

'Splendid idea, Sid,' Gus said. 'But Molly isn't up to walking for miles at the moment. We should look into renting a little horse and buggy of some sort. Then we can go around the neighborhood at will.'

'You know how to drive a horse and buggy, do you?' I asked.

'Of course. Doesn't everyone?' Gus looked surprised. 'We always had our own little pony and cart to drive around the estate when I was growing up.'

'You led a very privileged life, dearest,' Sid said.

The station with its fretwork-carved roof appeared ahead of us, with the river beyond – early morning mist was curling over the river's surface and hiding the far bank. The air was delightfully cool. After we had bought our tickets I showed Maureen's portrait to the man in the ticket booth and asked if he might have seen her.

'When was this?' he asked.

'I think it must have been two months ago.'

He looked at me as if I was mad. 'My dear young lady, do you know how many day-trippers come out this way during the summer? Trainloads of them. If I remembered any particular young lady she'd have had to be a corker or else have something wrong with her. This one looks nice enough, but I see a lot of pretty young ladies every day.' He looked at Sid, with her cropped black hair and black silk jacket. 'I'd remember you, miss,' he said. 'Would the young lady in the photograph have been wearing something out of the ordinary?'

'I don't think so,' I said. 'She had been staying at the convent with the nuns. I expect she would have been wearing something demure and suitable.'

'With the nuns. One of those girls, huh?' He gave us a knowing look. 'I'd have remembered her when she arrived then, but not when she departed.'

A discreet cough behind us hinted that someone else was now waiting in line. We thanked him and moved on. I tried my picture again with the porter and the man who blew the whistle, but got no reaction from either of them.

'You wait until later in the day,' the porter said. 'This platform will be filled with young ladies, come up for the day from the city.'

'But this would have been early in the morning,' I said. 'One of the first trains.'

He stared at the photograph again then shook his head. 'Doesn't ring a bell. But then my wife always tells me I'm an unobservant kind of guy. I never even notice if she's got a new hat.'

We heard the sound of puffing and the train approached, sending up a plume of dark smoke. Sid helped me up the high step into the compartment and the others clambered in beside me. Then with a lurch we set off, the puffing slow to start with but rapidly gathering momentum. Mist drifted across the track from time to time. Ships appeared and were swallowed into mist and as we traveled we watched it curl upward, as the sun's heat warmed the air.

Sid and Gus kept Bridie informed as we proceeded northward. She looked fearfully at the great stone wall of the prison at Ossining and asked if the convicts ever escaped. Then the train came to a halt in Cortland. We were the only people to disembark, and we walked through a deserted station forecourt. This was a sleepy country town with only a few shops and cottages to be seen. We went into the nearest store, a pharmacy, and asked if they knew where the Robbins family lived. There was a young girl at the counter but an older man came forward to speak with us.

'You mean old Josiah Robbins?' he asked.

'We're looking for a Miss Emily Robbins,' I said.

'That would be his granddaughter. She's back from her travels now, so we hear.'

'And where would we find her?'

'They all live out on the family estate. About two miles from town. A fine house, it is. Honniton, that's the name of it. But we call it the Ice Palace around here. Old Man Robbins had it built about thirty years ago. He made his money from ice, you know. Owned the ice lease for this stretch of river. Who'd have thought that a man could get rich from selling frozen water, eh?' He shook his head.

We asked about how we might find transportation out to their house and were told there was a livery stable in town where we might find someone willing to drive us. We went straight there and rented what looked like a rather rickety buggy. Gus assured me that she would be able to drive it splendidly and Sid looked confident in her abilities, so I hoisted Bridie up to join them and we set off. I need not have worried. The tired old nag was not capable of going beyond a walking pace and it took us a good hour to cover the ground to the Robbins estate. It was indeed a fine-looking house, a veritable Hudson mansion, built in the manner of a French château set amid manicured lawns, and I wondered at people like this sending their daughter off to the grim convent. They must have wanted to punish her very badly.

A servant came out at the sound of our approach and led the horse away while we went inside to a cool front hall with marble floor. A maid went off to summon her mistress and almost immediately we heard the tapping of heels on the marble floor and a thin woman in a severe gray dress came out to meet us.

'May I help you?' she asked, taking in the cut of our clothes and no doubt Sid's cropped hair.

'I'm sorry to intrude but we were hoping to find Miss Emily Robbins here,' I said. 'Is she at home?'

'She is,' the woman replied, 'but I'm afraid she is occupied with another visitor at the moment. Her fiancé, Mr Clifton, is here and they are going through wedding plans together.'

'Her fiancé, how lovely,' I said. 'I hadn't realized that she had become engaged.'

'Are you friends of hers?' the woman asked. 'I don't recall meeting you before.'

'You must be her mother. We are friends of a friend, who recommended that we give our best wishes to Emily as we were making a tour of this area,' I said, keeping as close to the truth as possible.

'So you're not from these parts then?' Mrs Robbins asked.

'We live in New York City,' I said. 'I am currently staying with a family member in Elmsford.'

'And your connection with Emily?'

I was tempted to say that we met her abroad recently,

knowing of the lie they had perpetrated about her. I wondered how she would handle that. But she saved me from having to come up with a lie by adding. 'From school, I presume.'

'That's right,' I said. 'From school.'

At that moment there was the sound of feet on the marble floor and two people came down the long corridor toward us. One was a pretty, young dark-haired girl; the other a ruddy-faced, robust middle-aged man. When Emily's mother had mentioned her engagement I had hoped that she might have been allowed to marry the father of her child. But I hadn't expected this old and unattractive man. Surely he couldn't be the one?

As he bent to give her a kiss on the cheek I watched her flinch and knew that he wasn't. I guessed she was being rushed into marriage for respectability's sake and to get her away from the house where her family found her presence repugnant.

'I'll come for you in the morning then,' the ruddy man said. 'And you can take a look at the furnishings for yourself. We can change the wallpaper if it's not to your taste.'

Emily nodded, looking at us with interest.

'How kind you are, Mr Clifton,' Emily's mother said. 'Emily, where are your manners. Thank your fiancé for his kindness.'

'Thank you, sir,' Emily muttered.

'And look here, Emily, my dear, you have visitors,' her mother said. 'Apparently old school friends.'

I expected her to say she'd never seen us before in her life. I said quickly, 'We weren't exactly friends at school, but we shared a friendship in common with Maureen.'

'Maureen?' she asked, her eyes darting from one face to another.

'Your friend Maureen. From school. She asked us to pay a call on you, on her behalf.'

I saw a flicker in her eyes and she said. 'Of course, I remember now. Maureen, from school.' She emphasized the last word. 'And I do remember you now. You were all in the senior class when I first arrived and you were so kind to me. How nice of you to look me up again.'

'I'll be off then, Emily, my dear. Good-bye. Until tomorrow,' her fiancé said.

'Good-bye, Mr Clifton,' she said.

'Don't be ridiculous. Call him John,' her mother admonished.

'Good-bye John,' Emily called after him in a mechanical voice. 'Thank you for coming over.'

Chapter 18

As Emily's fiancé went down the front steps she turned back to us. 'Would you care to take a walk around the grounds? We have a pretty little lake and I know your young charge will like to see the ducklings.'

She didn't wait for her mother to reply before she ushered us back to the front door and out into the sunshine. As soon as we were well clear of the house she took my arm. 'You have news of Maureen?' she asked. 'I've been waiting to hear from her. She promised she would write. Is she all right? Where did she go?'

I looked at her hopeful face and felt terrible. 'I'm sorry to disappoint you, but I've no news of her. That's why I'm here.' Then I added hastily because I saw the agitation in her face, 'My name is Molly Sullivan. I was asked by her family in Ireland to trace her and I'm trying to find out where she went when she left the convent.'

'Oh.' She looked so horribly disappointed. 'Then you don't know anything about her. I so hoped that you had come with a message from her. I don't understand why she hasn't tried to get in touch with me, unless Mama has been intercepting all my mail – which I wouldn't put past her.'

Our feet crunched on the gravel as we walked along a well-raked path between rose beds; Emily and I in front, and the others following at a respectful distance behind.

'I went to inquire at the convent but they couldn't tell me where she had gone. Only that she had run off without saying good-bye. However, I gathered that you were her friend. So I wondered if she perhaps had a secret plan and might have shared it with you.'

Emily shook her head. 'I thought she was going back to those people. What was their name now?'

'The Mainwarings,' I said.

She nodded. 'That's right. Mainwaring. She didn't want to. She said she hated it there, but it was better than nothing. And in fact Mrs Mainwaring came to the convent the day before Maureen ran off. I know it was she because one of the sisters mentioned her name.'

'But she didn't leave with Maureen at that time?'

'No. I don't believe Maureen even saw her. She came to see the sisters. I do know Maureen was furious afterward and said Mrs Mainwaring couldn't be trusted.'

'Did she say why?'

Emily shook her head. 'You have to understand that we had almost no time to ourselves. Everything we did was monitored by the sisters. We weren't allowed to talk and Sister Angelique was always snooping. It was like being in jail.'

'I know a jail,' Bridie chimed in brightly. 'It's called Sing Sing. Were you there?'

'No, Bridie,' Gus said firmly.

I realized that there were aspects of this conversation

that Bridie should probably not overhear, now that she was old enough to understand. 'Now why don't you go and see if you can find the ducklings,' I suggested.

'I think I can see them over there.' Bridie skipped off happily.

I gave Emily an apologetic smile. 'I didn't want her to overhear,' I said. 'So you have no idea why Maureen ran off suddenly?'

'I was as surprised as anybody. I looked for her at breakfast that morning and I asked if she was not feeling well. Sister Jerome sent someone back to our dormitory and she had gone. Sister was furious.'

'Had anything happened that would have made her run away like that? Apart from not wanting to go back to the Mairwarings. Had she perhaps received a letter?'

'Nothing that I know of. We were both due to leave that week and we were both dreading it in a way. We couldn't wait to be out of that place, but we really didn't want to return to our previous situations. She promised she would come and see me and we joked about running off together and opening a tea shop in a small town, and then coming back to rescue our babies. She really loved her baby and she was furious at having to give it up.'

'Do you know who adopted the baby? Maybe she went there.'

'We were never told. Sister said it was better that we didn't know; better to make a clean break. One moment our baby was with us, the next it had vanished.'

'So nothing happened just before she ran off? Nothing at all you can think of?'

She paused, staring out over the lake on which swans were swimming. 'There was one thing,' she said carefully.

'She had an awful row with somebody the day before she left. I heard her shouting. She said, "I've made up my mind. You can't make me do it and I won't. I won't go through with it. You can't make me. It's cruel." Then a door opened and she came running out. I tried to stop her and ask her what was wrong, but she just pushed past me and ran away.'

'Was this row while Mrs Mainwaring was there?'

'I'm not sure. It might have been.'

'And you didn't know who she was arguing with or what the argument was about?'

'I never got the chance to speak to her again,' Emily said. 'The next morning she had run away.'

'Oh, dear,' I said. 'I had hoped that there was a happier reason – that the father of the child had come for her and they had run off together.'

'No. It wouldn't have been that,' she said. 'I know she wanted nothing to do with him. If any of us had had any hope, any other possibility, we'd never have gone to the convent. It is a place of last resort for those who have nowhere else to go.'

'You don't think she would have tried to go back to her family in Ireland then?'

She shook her head firmly. 'She always said she could never go home. She was too ashamed.'

'Can you think of anyone else she might have confided in? Was she close to any other girl there?'

Emily sighed. 'She was rather a reserved person – kept her thoughts to herself. She never said much about her home or family. Well, none of us did. It was as if we were afraid to get close to anyone, or to trust anyone. We never knew which of the girls might be Sister's spies.'

I was startled at this. 'Sister Jerome, you mean? She treated you cruelly?'

'I meant Sister Angelique.'

'Who was she?' I asked.

'Sister Jerome's assistant. She was brought across to us when Sister Francine died and Sister Jerome was training her. Sister Jerome was cold and strict, but at least you knew where you were with her. Sister Angelique was just downright mean and reported back to Jerome. She had her favorites, and she could be quite charming. But if she didn't take to you – watch out. She was spiteful in small ways. If a girl was afraid of mice and rats, she'd make her work down in the cellar, which was full of them. She'd withhold food as punishment. She'd stick one girl with washing the dirty diapers day after day. And she'd hand out favors to those who were compliant.'

'It sounds like a horrible boarding school,' I said.

'Not like my school,' she answered. 'I loved my time there. I was never happier.'

'So there is no other girl you can think of who might know where Maureen went?'

She shook her head. 'I can't think of anyone she would have confided in. I was really her only friend. She was my only friend.' She had been staring out at the lake, but looked up to meet my eye. 'Look, I wish I could help you more. I want to find her as much as you do – more than you do. She was good to me when I was in that hateful place and went through . . .' She glanced down at my own round shape. 'Well, you know,' she said. 'You can imagine.'

'I'm sure it must have been awful for you.'

We had reached the shore of the lake. Sid and Gus

came up beside us. Emily turned away and stared across the water again.

'It seems that some nightmares never end,' she said. 'Some people are destined for happiness while others aren't.'

'Your fiancé?' Sid said. 'I take it he was not your choice.'

'Would you marry a man like that if you had a choice?' Emily demanded fiercely. 'You saw him. He's repulsive and old. And he paws me with those big meaty hands. It's almost more than I can bear.'

'Then refuse to marry him,' Gus said. 'They can't force you to marry against your will.'

'Unfortunately they can,' Emily said. 'My mother still hasn't forgiven me for disgracing her, and they've made it quite clear that I am no longer welcome in the family home. It is to be a quick marriage to Mr Clifton, whose lands adjoin ours and thus is advantageous to us, or I am to be cast out, alone with no money. I've nowhere to go. No money and no skills. So actually it's a choice between life and death.'

'I'm sorry,' I said.

She pressed her lips together as she nodded. 'My only consolation is that he's old. He can't live forever, can he? But then who knows how long I will live? I almost died when I had the baby. There is no guarantee I'd survive a second delivery.'

'Is there no chance of being reconciled with the baby's father?' Gus asked gently.

Emily shook her head. 'He went away.'

'And you haven't tried to get in contact with him again? You wouldn't want to see him again?'

'Of course I'd want to,' Emily snapped. 'It's impossible, that's all.'

'I'm sorry,' Gus said gently. 'We have no right to pry. I just hate to see a woman being treated so unjustly.'

'He said he couldn't marry me.' Emily squeezed her eyes shut as if she was trying to hold back tears. 'He was a young English painter. He came to paint the river and my grandfather saw him and thought he was pretty good. So he let him stay in one of the outbuildings on the estate while he worked. We met and fell in love. But he had no money. He said it was for the best that he went away. I didn't know I was with child until he had gone.' She paused. 'It wouldn't have been any use anyway. He couldn't have supported us. Not like Mr Clifton with his fine big house.'

Sid glanced at Gus. 'Emily, listen to me,' she said. 'If you really don't want to marry this man, maybe we can help you.'

'How can you help me?' Emily asked angrily. 'Why should you want to help me? You don't know me from Eve.'

'That's an easy question to answer. We are passionate about the rights of women. It angers us to see someone like you treated so unfairly.'

'You're very kind.' Emily managed a weak smile. 'But I really don't see what you could do. My mother won't change her mind. I've nowhere else to go.'

'Listen, Emily,' Sid said. 'We live in the city. We have sufficient money to live our lives as we choose and we have friends who are also independent women. I'm sure we could find you a place to stay and some kind of employment.'

There was a flicker of hope in her eyes that was extinguished in a second. 'That sounds wonderful, but it would be no good. They keep me a virtual prisoner here. I'm allowed to meet no one. I'm surprised my mother allowed me to talk with you. She only did so because Mr Clifton was here and she couldn't make a scene. I'm sure she has sent a spy out to follow me around the grounds. You can bet there is someone watching us at this moment.'

'Where there's a will, there's a way,' Sid said. 'Slip out in the middle of the night when everyone is asleep. Your friend Maureen did it, didn't she? Nobody saw her leave an enclosed convent.'

Emily nodded at this. 'I suppose.'

Sid fished into her handbag. 'I'll give you my card. We were planning to stay a couple of weeks on the river, but we can cut our stay short if necessary.'

'Don't cut short your vacation on my account,' Emily said. 'I'm sure I could put up with things for another two weeks.'

'In the meantime we will write to friends, to see if any of the women we know needs a private secretary or companion,' Gus said. 'And of course you can stay at our house until you have found a situation.'

Emily looked from one face to the next. 'I can't believe you'd do this for a perfect stranger,' she said.

'We all belong to the same sisterhood,' Sid said. 'We see it as our duty to help a sister in distress and I can't think of a bigger distress than marrying Mr Clifton.'

We had to laugh at this, and Emily joined in.

'We'll look for you in two weeks then,' Sid said, 'and may I suggest that you act as if you are learning to accept your coming marriage. If you begin to show enthusiasm for your upcoming role as a bride, then they will not watch you so closely.'

'You're right,' Emily said. 'I'll try to be nice to Mr Clifton, however repugnant that is to me.' She looked up and turned back to us. 'My mother is approaching. I knew she couldn't leave us alone for long.'

'There was one more thing,' I said hastily, drawing Emily close to me so that nobody else heard what I was saying. 'Do you remember that Maureen had a little carved statue?'

'I do.'

'Then would it surprise you to know she left it behind when she ran off?'

'She left it behind?' Emily looked up warily as her mother approached us.

'It was found in a wastebasket,' I said.

Emily nodded. 'Then my guess would be Sister Angelique. Maureen stood up to her, you see. Stealing her statue and hiding it in a wastebasket would be just the kind of mean-spirited thing she might do. So no, it wouldn't surprise me at all.'

'Ah, there you are, ladies,' Emily's mother called to us. 'Emily, my dear. Don't forget we have the dressmaker coming.'

Emily gave her a convincing smile. 'Of course, Mama.'

Chapter 19

We took our leave and retrieved Bridie from the ducklings. I noticed that Emily's mother had not offered us any refreshment and was clearly anxious to be rid of us.

'I'm sorry my daughter is busy and doesn't have time to be sociable at the moment. Weddings are hectic occasions, aren't they?' she said. 'It was kind of you to visit my daughter and to bring news of a friend. I hope it hasn't taken you too far out of your way.'

'Not at all,' I said. 'We were glad to meet up with an old school friend again, and the journey here was most refreshing after the heat of New York.'

'Thank you so much for coming,' Emily said, taking my hand. 'I do hope you might come and visit me again when I am married and installed in my own home.'

I must say she did it surprisingly well, making me think that we didn't really know her and wonder about the wisdom of Sid and Gus inviting her into their home. They chatted with great animation about this all the way back to the station – whom they might approach to find a position for Emily, whether she could stay with this friend or that friend, or whether they would keep her to themselves. I was pleased that they were prepared to put themselves out to rescue Emily, but annoyed at the same time that they had taken the conversation away from the very reason we had gone there. They had clearly lost interest in my original quest.

As they talked, I tried to go over in my mind what facts Emily had shared with me. They seemed to be lamentably few. Maureen did not want to return to the Mainwarings but felt she had no choice. She was angry that Mrs Mainwaring had come to see the sisters, but hadn't spoken to Maureen. She had said that Mrs Mainwaring was not to be trusted. That was interesting. Maureen had had a furious row with someone the day before she left and stormed out of the room, and this row might also have been about Mrs Mainwaring. She had shouted that she couldn't be forced to do something that was cruel. But all of this got me nowhere because Maureen had vanished early the next morning.

Gus sensed that I had been silent for a while. Perhaps she realized they had gone off on a tangent. She turned to me. 'So, Molly, did you learn anything that might be of use?'

'Nothing much, I'm afraid.'

'So it seems that Maureen is lost, vanished without a trace.'

'I'm not going to give up so easily,' I said. 'We now know that she had a shouting match with somebody the evening before she ran away. We know she was angry with Mrs Mainwaring for coming to the convent and said she couldn't be trusted.'

'But neither of those sheds light on where she might have gone,' Sid said.

'We know she wasn't seen at the station,' I said, 'Or at least she wasn't remembered at the station.'

'That could be easily explained,' Sid said. 'If she'd just run away from a convent, after having a child, she would be dressed in drab clothing, wouldn't she? Men do not remember unappealing women.'

'That's true,' I agreed. 'So it is possible she did take the train to New York, in which case we've probably lost her. And I'm afraid with no money her chances won't be good there.'

'You did your best, Molly.' Gus touched my hand gently. 'You did more than required. I think you should admit that the quest is out of your hands. Write to her family, give them the Mainwarings' address, and let them take it from there.'

'I feel there is more I could do, before I give up completely,' I said. 'I could show her photograph around the town. Maybe, as you suggested, someone gave her a lift in a wagon or carriage. And I think I'll go back to the convent and speak to Katy again. She might have more to tell me. She was called inside while she was telling me about Maureen leaving her little statue behind. I've a good excuse to go back to speak to her, because I want to hire her as my maid when she has delivered her child. I can say that I want to interview her in private.'

'Hire her as a maid?' Sid said. 'Molly, what exactly do you know about this person?'

'I met her when I was at the convent the other day. She seemed like a pleasant girl.'

Sid and Gus exchanged a look. 'Molly, dear,' Gus said.

'You know nothing about her really, and inviting someone like that into your home is a big risk. She'll be helping out with your baby.'

'Oh, I like that.' I gave a short laugh. 'You meet a girl and two seconds later you invite her to stay with you in New York, promise to find her employment, and take care of her.'

'Well, anyone could see she was a well-brought-up young woman who has been wronged,' Sid said. 'This Katy has already proved she is not able to make good decisions and lets her heart lead her head. You need someone solid and sensible to be your servant.'

'Jesus, Mary, and Joseph,' I said angrily. 'You two are the end. You profess equality and tolerance and yet you're actually judging on the basis of class. Emily is all right because she comes from a fine house, therefore she is reliable. Katy, whom you haven't even met, is not, because clearly she doesn't come from a fine house.'

'Keep your hair on, Molly,' Sid said with a smile. 'We didn't wish to imply that at all. The two situations are different. We plan to give Emily some introductions, but it will be up to her future employer to decide whether to hire her or not. We may even put her up in our house for a few days, because even you have to agree that she is not a potential ax murderer. But you are planning to bring this girl to live in your home with you and to help take care of your baby. Do you know if she's got a nasty temper? What if she hits the child when you are not there? Is she too influenced by the opposite sex? Might she make a play for Daniel?'

'I see your point,' I said, 'but I could say that about any potential servant I hired.'

'If you hired from a reputable agency, the girl would come with references.'

'Obviously I will ask the sisters for a reference, and she would be on probation until I've seen whether we get along well. But I have to tell you that I took to her right away. A pleasant, unsophisticated, open sort of girl.'

'I'm sure she'll be just fine, Molly,' Gus said in soothing fashion. 'We're just warning you to proceed with caution, that's all.'

'I know,' Sid said. 'Why don't we come with you to observe when you interview her? And we can see whether she is good with children or not by the way she gets along with Bridie.'

'I'm sure everyone in the world would get along with this sweet young lady.' Gus ruffled Bridie's hair and Bridie gave her a beaming smile.

We were coming into the station yard. I helped Bridie down from the trap and waited until she ran on ahead before I said in a low voice, 'I'm not sure it's such a good idea to take Bridie to a place like that. There might be difficult questions to answer about what the young women are doing there?'

'Simple. They go there to have their babies. It's like a hospital,' Sid said easily. 'And you have to admit that three heads are better than one. Besides, I don't know about you, Gus, but I'm dying to see inside that convent. It sounds deliciously Gothic.'

'I wonder if families can still pay to have their daughters locked away in cells,' Gus said. 'To keep them from the wicked world.'

'Or to claim their inheritance,' Sid added. They were both chuckling merrily now.

'Who is going to be locked away?' Bridie asked, turning up at my side unexpectedly.

'Nobody, my sweet,' I said, giving a warning frown to the other two. 'The ladies were just joking.'

'Yes, we were just joking,' Gus said. 'Just having fun.'

Just joking. I tried to agree with this, but I felt a chill go through me. Presumably Emily's family had paid to have her shut away there. Sid and Gus weren't so far off the truth. And I found myself wondering yet again whether Maureen had actually left the convent at all.

That's ridiculous, I thought. No nuns would force a girl to join them against her will. Those are the sort of rumors that Protestants like to spread, but we Catholics know that most sisters only go into the convent because they have a calling, and are devoted servants of God – brides of Christ, they call themselves. And the sisters in this convent were doing a wonderful job, taking in girls who had nowhere else to go. Of course it would be right that those who could afford to pay did so. How else could the nuns afford to look after all of them?

Sid interrupted my thoughts. 'So you are going to let us come with you, aren't you, Molly?' she asked.

I managed a smile. 'Of course,' I said.

We arrived back at the inn just as lunch was being cleared away. The innkeeper scolded us for our tardiness, but she then was kind enough to make us sandwiches, which we ate in the shade on the porch.

'Should we go to the convent this afternoon?' Gus asked. 'Or would it be better to write to them, asking to set up an appointment to interview your Katy?'

The day had become hot and humid and I was feeling decidedly languid after our morning's escapades.

An afternoon nap seemed like a good idea, but I didn't want to show my friends signs of my frailty. Besides, I was anxious to see Katy again and find out if she knew any other details that could throw light on Maureen's disappearance.

'Oh, I think we can just turn up on the doorstep,' I said. 'If I write to them they may not respond right away and Katy might well go into labor before I have a chance to see her.'

'Very well,' Sid said. 'We should look into hiring some kind of vehicle, as I suggested, Gus. I certainly don't feel like walking a mile or two in this heat, and uphill too. And Molly certainly shouldn't.'

We asked at the inn about vehicles for hire and were told that we'd be likely to find a cab at the station. Gus conceded that she had had enough of being the driver for one day and was content to let someone else drive us up the hill.

'Tomorrow I'll look into hiring a buggy for us at the livery stable,' she said, 'but in this heat let someone else sit up front and crack the whip.'

I was still having misgivings about taking Bridie with us to such an inhospitable-looking place, and she solved the problem by saying she didn't feel well and wanted to take a nap. The innkeeper promised to check in on her, so I left her lying on her cot.

We found a horse and cab standing in the shade of some trees near the station, and climbed aboard. It was a tight squeeze with three of us in the passenger seat and we were hot and uncomfortable by the time we turned into that narrow lane between the fir trees. I had been fighting off sleep until Sid suddenly exclaimed, 'There it is. Look,

Gus. It *is* deliciously Gothic – like something out of the Middle Ages. How long has this convent been here?'

'It used to be the old fever hospital, so I was told,' I said. 'It had been abandoned for some time when the nuns came down from Quebec and took it over during the last century.'

'They obviously looked for the most uncomfortable building in New York State,' Sid said. 'To make it easy to do penance every day. And avoid purgatory.'

She and Gus exchanged a chuckle.

I felt the hackles of my Catholic roots rise, but I'm afraid I had to agree with them. It was the most uncomfortable-looking building in New York State. We climbed down, stiff and sweating after the trip, and attempted to straighten out the creases in our dresses and mop our perspiring brows. I tucked flyaway strands of sweaty hair under my hat and adjusted the little veil so that I looked prim and proper. I realized that the nuns would also have to approve of me as a potential employer for Katy, and my friends, however much I was fond of them, were a trifle bohemian in the way they dressed.

Sid strode up to that massive front door and gained great pleasure from hammering on it with the iron knocker.

'One now expects it to open and Frankenstein's assistant to lure one inside,' she said. 'If an aged nun with a hunchback says, "Come inside, young mistress," I don't think I'll go.'

We waited for a while, the sun beating down upon our backs and heat radiating from that blank stone wall. Sid knocked again. 'Perhaps they are all at prayer,' she said. 'Or at tea.'

Then slowly the door opened, with a deep creaking

noise. A young woman stood there, a pale creature, dressed in a simple black dress with a deep white collar. Her hair was pulled back severely from her face into a braid down her back and there was no bulge under her pinafore.

'*Pax vobiscum*,' she said.

'Oh, hello.' I stepped forward and held out my hand. 'I wondered if we might have a word with Katy. I spoke with her the other day and have decided that I'd like to offer her domestic employment in my household when she is ready to leave.'

'With Katy?' For a moment I wondered if she was simple-minded.

'Yes, you have a young woman here called Katy, don't you? She was minding the door last time I came.'

I saw a spasm of pain cross her face. 'Oh, ma'am. I'm sorry to tell you that Katy is dead.'

'Dead? Oh, no. Did the baby come early then? Did she die in childbirth?'

She shook her head as if trying to shake out a bad memory. 'No, ma'am. She fell down a flight of steps and broke her neck. The poor baby died too, God rest its little soul.'

Chapter 20

We stood staring at her, frozen like a group of statues, our shadows black and rigid on the ground in that bright sun.

'I'm so sorry,' I said. 'She seemed like such a nice cheerful girl.'

'Oh, she was, ma'am,' the girl said. 'I understand that everyone here was very fond of her. They were most upset about it.' She paused. 'Would you like to come in? I'm not supposed to keep you standing on the doorstep. I can fetch one of the sisters.'

I was trying to make my brain work, but it refused to. 'No, thank you,' I said. 'There is little point now that Katy is no longer with you.'

'You might want to consider one of the other girls for service in your house,' she said. 'They are always looking for good situations and kind people who will take them in, knowing their past.'

I hesitated, wondering if she was trying to convince me to hire her. 'Are you about ready to leave here yourself then?'

She smiled for the first time. 'Oh, no, ma'am. I'm about to enter the order. I'm a novice here.'

'You're going to be a nun here?' Sid asked before I could stop her. 'To shut yourself away before you know anything of life?'

The girl smiled again, such a sweet smile. 'Oh, yes. It's what I've wanted for a long time. I know I have a calling.'

'You've been here for a while?' I asked.

'Almost a year now,' she answered.

'Then you will remember a girl called Maureen O'Byrne who left abruptly a couple of months ago?'

'Was she one of the young mothers?'

'She was. An Irish girl. Light hair.'

She was still smiling sweetly as she shook her head. 'We novices don't come in contact with the young women who stay here. Mother doesn't think it's wise for us to see that other side of life. She thinks we'll fall in love with the babies and not want to stay.'

'And you don't think you would?' Sid asked.

'Oh, no,' she said. 'I saw what you'd call normal life did to my mother. One baby after another and her growing weaker and weaker until she was just a shadow of the person I remembered. That's not for me, thank you.'

'But isn't what you're doing running away not running toward?' Sid demanded. I could tell she was all ready to talk this girl out of her decision.

'We should be going, then,' I said hastily. 'I wish you well.'

'Thank you.' She paused, taking in our faces. 'You are probably the last outsiders I will be able to chat with like this. I go into retreat tomorrow before I take my first vows.' She glanced back into the darkness. 'I should probably go back inside.'

The big door closed with finality. I turned to walk away.

Sid caught up with me. 'Why did you say you didn't want to go in and see one of the sisters, Molly? You know we were dying to look around inside.'

'I'm sorry,' I said. 'I wasn't thinking. After I heard the news about Katy I was so upset all I wanted to do was to get away. Besides, you wouldn't have seen much. They take you into a little parlor opposite the front door and you have to talk to the nuns through a carved wooden grille in the wall. It's so dark that all you see is a vague shape.'

'I would still have wanted to see that,' Sid said. 'Wouldn't you, Gus?'

'I could see no reason to talk to one of the sisters,' I said. 'It would obviously have been painful for them to speak about Katy and they might have tried to foist another girl onto me when I am not really in a position to take one now.'

We summoned the cabby who had been waiting in the deep shade of the fir trees.

'You really must have developed an instant bond with this girl, Molly,' Gus said. 'You seem deeply affected by this news.'

'I am affected by it,' I said. 'She was so young, so fresh-faced and cheerful, and it seems like such a horrible, senseless end to her life.'

'I suppose one can understand how it happened,' Sid said. 'If the place is as old and crumbling inside as it looks from the exterior then there are bound to be dark and broken staircases, aren't there?'

I nodded, trying to make myself agree with this, but I couldn't. I sat staring out straight ahead of me.

'And if she was in the late stages of pregnancy she could

hardly see where she was putting her feet on the steps,' Gus added. 'And I'm sure one's balance is off-kilter. One small stumble and she fell.'

'I suppose so,' I said. 'But I can't help thinking—' I left the rest of the sentence hanging in the humid air.

'You can't help thinking what?' Sid demanded.

'Katy fell to her death right after she had told me her suspicions about Maureen. Maybe she remembered some other details. Maybe she confided her suspicions to someone else.'

'Are you trying to say you think that foul play was involved?' Gus asked. 'That somebody deliberately pushed Katy down the stairs to stop her from talking?' She looked at me and a smile spread across her face. 'Molly, you have spent too much time investigating crime. This is a convent. In spite of the way Sid and I were joking about it, I'm sure the inhabitants are nice, normal, and gentle women who do not make a practice of pushing people down stairs.'

'A tragic accident, Molly,' Sid reiterated. 'Accidents happen. Nothing sinister about it. Just coincidental that she spoke to you before she died.'

I sat there silently. Then I dared to voice the thought that had crept into my mind. 'I can't help wondering now whether something bad happened to Maureen. Perhaps she didn't run away at all. And Katy figured it out and . . .'

Gus put her hand over mine. 'Molly, my dearest. I'm afraid your current delicate condition is making you over-emotional. You're reading too much into this. Maureen took her chance to run away while everyone was at breakfast, but she didn't have time to go back for her possessions. And poor Katy fell. Please accept those things and let this be. I'm sure it's not good for you to be thinking such worrying thoughts at this time. You should be thinking calm and happy thoughts for the baby's sake.'

'Yes,' I said. 'You are right. I should let it go. There isn't anything I can do anyway.'

And I tried to think those happy thoughts as we arrived back at Tarrytown Station.

Bridie was awake and feeling better enough to go in search of an ice cream, and we spent a pleasant evening sitting on the porch of the inn, watching the commerce on the river, and the sun setting on the far shore. I resolved to stop worrying about Maureen and Katy, and to accept that I could do nothing more and that my duty was now to my unborn child. I would do what I supposedly came to do, enjoy my time on the river with my friends.

But that night I had a dream. I dreamed that I was standing in some kind of dark place; a place of whispering wind, or was it voices? All I could make out were vague archways. I looked around, trying to work out where I was, when I noticed a figure standing before me in the darkness. I could see that it was a young woman. As I moved toward her she half turned toward me and said, in a very Irish voice, 'Katy, it was good of you to come and find me.'

And I saw there was another girl standing in the shadows and they were suddenly aware of my presence and turned to look at me.

I woke up with a jolt and sat up in bed, my heart pounding. We Irish have great faith in dreams and the second sight. If ever there was a clear message from the beyond then that was it. Katy had been on the right track after all. That voice had to belong to Maureen. Katy had found out what really happened to her and where she had gone. And presumably she had come to me in a dream because she wanted me to know the truth too. Sleep was now impossible. I got up and went to sit in the open window, feeling the cool breeze from the river gently caressing my skin.

'I wish you'd been more specific,' I muttered. Katy obviously hadn't left the convent, so she must have uncovered another clue to Maureen's whereabouts within the confines of those walls. And therefore in a place inaccessible to me. Yet they had come to me in a dream, which meant they still wanted my help.

Bridie slept, her light hair spilling over the pillow. I looked down at her fondly, then went back to the task in hand. Maureen had come to me. Katy was dead so I wasn't going to get any more clues from her. But Maureen thought I had enough knowledge to come to the truth. And having had this dream, I was now sure that it wasn't as simple as just running off to New York. Something bad had happened to Maureen O'Byrne and she wanted me to uncover the truth.

I went over everything I had heard and seen and I realized that I kept coming back to the Mainwarings. Something didn't add up with them. Mrs Mainwaring was described by the sisters as generous enough to want Maureen back. And yet she hadn't come across to me as a warm-hearted woman. To her, servants would be ten a penny, to hire or discard at whim. Maureen had stated that she had to go back; she had no choice. And yet she surely had plenty of choice. She was under no obligation to return to a place where she wasn't happy. Now she was no longer encumbered with a baby she could easily do what Sid and Gus had suggested and start afresh in New

York City. Mrs Mainwaring wouldn't give her a reference, of course, but she could claim to be freshly arrived from Ireland and start with a household where references weren't so important.

And another thing: why was she so angry that Mrs Mainwaring had come to see the sisters the day before she ran away? And what had brought about that final explosion in which she had yelled, 'You can't make me. It's cruel.' What could have been so cruel that she chose to sneak away and be gone by the next morning? Was it possible it had something to do with murdering her own child? No, I was letting my imagination run away with me. Surely nobody would ever try to force her to do that.

Was it then to do with joining the order? Were they forcing her to enter the novitiate against her will? Obviously not, since the young novice had never come across her or even knew her name. Besides, I had been raised to respect nuns. I didn't believe any of the rumors that the Protestants circulated. What would be the point of gaining recruits to the convent against their will?

You can't make me. It's cruel. I tossed those words around in my mind. I remembered what Emily had said about Sister Angelique being mean and spiteful and not liking Maureen because Maureen had stood up to her. Might the words have been as simple as Sister making her throw away her little statue to show she was renouncing earthly goods? But if that was all, would it have driven her to run away?

Gray light of dawn lit the sky and still I was no nearer to any enlightenment. But I knew I had to visit the Mainwarings again. I had to find out why Maureen thought she had to return there.

Chapter 21

I went back to bed but I don't think I did more than doze for the rest of the night. When I came down to breakfast in the morning Sid and Gus were already tucking into ham and eggs. Gus looked at me critically.

'Molly, you look terrible. You've bags under your eyes and you're quite pasty-faced. All this rushing around has not been good for you.'

'No, Molly,' Sid said firmly. 'Gus and I have been talking and we think this whole business with Maureen has overly upset you. We've decided that the best thing would be to take you back to your mother-in-law's today and let her look after you. If you're trapped with her in the country, you won't have any more mad urges to solve problems.'

I shook my head violently.

'I know you're not entirely thrilled with your mother-in-law,' Sid continued hastily, 'but for the sake of the baby we've got to find a way to make you rest.'

'I can't,' I cut into her words. 'You don't understand, I have to see this through now. I had a dream last night. It was Maureen who came to me. I know she wants me to find out the truth.'

Gus smiled. 'You Irish and your dreams. Molly, dear, I've been to lectures on the subject. Professor Freud has been studying dream psychology in Vienna and he says that all dreams come from our own emotional state. You are worried about Maureen, you are upset about Katy, ergo you dream about them. They are lurking in your subconscious at night. It's perfectly normal and it doesn't mean that you're getting a communication from the beyond.'

'I believe it does,' I said. 'You can say what you like but I've had dreams before that really were communications "from the beyond," as you put it. And everyone in Ireland can tell you stories of dreams like that.'

'Professor Freud would disagree,' Gus said. 'But I thought we came to the conclusion last night that there was nothing more we could do to look for Maureen. And you'd certainly never be able to prove that somebody pushed Katy down those stairs.'

'There is one thing I can do and I will do,' I said. 'And that is to go back to the Mainwarings' house and talk to the servants.'

'And why would you want to do that?' Sid asked suspiciously. 'I thought we ascertained that Maureen never returned to them, even though they expected her to.'

'So Mrs Mainwaring said,' I said, surprised at the words that came out of my mouth. 'I only have her word for it.'

'What reason would she have for denying it?'

I shrugged. 'Maybe she changed her mind about having a fallen woman in a house where there was her own young child, but she didn't want to appear ungracious and lose respect in the eyes of the sisters. Besides,' I added, 'there is something that doesn't quite add up about that place.'

Gus wagged a finger at me. 'Are you sure you're not being Irish and fey again? Just because this Mainwaring woman wasn't open and welcoming to you, doesn't mean she has anything to hide. She probably saw from your dress that you were not a person of consequence and therefore not worth the effort.' She reached across and touched my hand. 'I'm sorry, I didn't wish to offend.'

'No offense taken,' I said. 'I'm sure you're quite right about that. She was a person to whom such things matter. Rather shallow and maybe vindictive, I thought. That's why welcoming a disgraced servant back didn't quite add up.'

'I see what you mean,' Sid nodded.

'So that's why I need to go back there and talk to the servants. Servants always know what is going on. They'll be able to tell me things about Maureen.'

'What sort of things?' Sid asked.

'Why she said she had no choice about going back there when she clearly didn't want to. Why she was angry with Mrs Mainwaring for coming to the convent. Why I have such a strange feeling that something is not right there.'

'You are a very stubborn woman, do you know that?' Sid said. 'I pity Daniel, having to deal with you. I'm sure he sent you to his mother so that you couldn't rush all over town, and now here you are doing exactly what he wanted to avoid.'

'I can't help it,' I said. 'And I'm not an invalid. I'm having a baby. And I feel fine. Women all over the world get on with their lives while they are pregnant. Anyway, I've made up my mind. I'm going back to the Mainwarings today.'

Gus looked at Sid and sighed. 'Impossible,' she said. 'I can see we'll just have to kidnap her and lock her up.'

'I don't try to stop you when you go on your suffragist marches, do I?' I reminded.

'We are not with child, Molly. If one of us were then I'm sure the other would make sure she did not do anything too strenuous.'

'Going to Irvington on the train cannot count as too strenuous,' I said, 'and I'm sure you agree that the servants there may be able to shed light on Maureen's character and why she felt she had to go back there if she was unhappy.' I gave them an appealing look. 'One of them might also know where Maureen has run off to. Servants confide in each other, you know.'

'Very well,' Gus said at last. 'I don't suppose there can be any harm in your going to someone's house, as long as you don't walk out in the sun and make yourself exhausted.' She looked across at Sid. 'Make sure you take a cab. There is bound to be one at the station.'

'I suppose we had better go with her to make sure she doesn't do anything too risky and outlandish.' Sid looked at Gus for confirmation.

'You've been very kind,' I said. 'You've already given up one full day of your holiday on the river. I can't ask you to again. Besides, it might look suspicious if a whole bevy of women descends on the servants' entrance at once.' I looked across at Bridie who was already tucking into her eggs with gusto at the other end of the table. 'But I would ask a favor and leave Bridie with you today. I don't want to show up with a child in tow. And I'm sure she doesn't enjoy traipsing around all over the place with me.'

'Of course. We'd be delighted,' Gus said. 'What would you like to do, Bridie?'

'Go swimming,' Bridie said quickly.

'Bridie, remember what Mrs Sullivan said,' I reminded her. 'She said that ladies only swim where there are bathing machines and when they have proper swimming attire.'

'Fiddle faddle,' Sid said, warming to the task now. 'We'll take you swimming, Bridie. We'll go and find you a costume. I'm sure there will be bathing suits for children in a local store.'

Bridie looked at me with a half-guilty smile. 'You won't tell Mrs Sullivan, will you?' she asked.

'My lips are sealed,' I replied.

So we set off, the others in search of swimming attire and the right place for a safe swim, and I to the station where a train soon arrived to take me to Irvington. There was no cab in sight when I arrived. I had remembered that the Mainwarings' house was only a short way up the hill, and, the day still being cool and fresh, I set off. I hadn't realized that a short carriage ride is not the same as a short walk, or that the hill was so steep. I was huffing and puffing like a steam train by the time I reached those impressive wrought-iron gates and I had to sit for a while before I dared go inside. I had dressed simply today in a plain muslin with a little cape, as I wanted the servants not to be sure of my rank, and thus willing to chat with me. But the muslin I had chosen now clung to my back like a damp rag. I was sure I looked a sight. I took out the small mirror I carried in my purse and surveyed the damage. My hair was plastered to my forehead beneath my straw hat, and my face was as red as a beetroot. Thank heavens I wasn't coming to call on Mrs Mainwaring herself. I'd have to make sure I slipped through grounds and arrived at the servants' entrance unseen or I would find myself summarily ejected.

I discovered a small gate in the wall and slipped in through it, glad I hadn't had to draw attention to myself by opening those impressive wrought-iron affairs. I hadn't gone far when I heard the sound of footsteps on the path. There was the nursemaid coming toward me, in a crisply starched gray-and-white uniform, pushing the baby carriage. She nodded to me, looking unsure as to who I might be and what I was doing there.

'If you've come to see the mistress, I'm afraid she's out,' she said. I could see her analyzing my outfit and noticing my sweaty and unkempt appearance.

'No, I've come to talk with the servants,' I said. 'About a young woman who worked here until recently. Maureen O'Byrne. Did you know her?'

'No, I didn't, I'm afraid,' she said. 'I haven't been here long. I was only hired after the baby came.'

I had drawn level with her now and looked into the carriage. A beautiful child, probably two or three months old, lay asleep on a pale-blue, silk pillow. He had a little fuzz of red-gold hair and long dark lashes curled across his cheeks.

'What a lovely baby,' I said. 'It's a boy, is it?'

'That's right. A little boy, ma'am.'

'Is it their first?' I asked, thinking that Mrs Mainwaring was no longer in the first flush of youth.

'It is. The master's pleased to have an heir at last, I can tell you.'

'And Mrs Mainwaring? She must be pleased too, after waiting so long.'

The nursemaid gave me a sideways look. 'She's not exactly the motherly kind, if you know what I mean. Ladies from her class, they're not raised to take much interest in their children, are they? Thank heavens for people like us, or the little mites would get no love and affection at all.'

I noted she had decided that I was not the same rank as the Mainwarings. I was 'people like us.' That would be useful when it came to chatting with the other servants.

'I should be getting along. I'm holding you up from your walk,' I said. 'Do I go around to the back of the house to find the servants' entrance?'

'That's right. If you follow that path it will take you through the orchard and you'll see the back door.'

I thanked her and followed the path that skirted the wall, nicely hidden by large shrubs, until it came out to an apple orchard. Beyond the orchard was a stretch of lawn and beyond that some sort of earthwork was going on with a couple of men digging away and another hammering at some wood. I spotted the servants' entrance at the back of the building and made for it. A maid was hanging out a line of laundry. She must have been so involved in her task that she didn't hear me coming because she jumped and put her hand to her mouth to cover a scream.

'I'm sorry,' I said. 'I didn't mean to startle you. I've come about Maureen O'Byrne.'

'Maureen? She's not here anymore.' The girl looked around nervously as if she wasn't sure whether she'd get into trouble for talking to me. 'Are you a relative of hers?'

I decided there were times when lying was permissible. This was one of them. 'I am,' I said. 'My name's Molly.

I've come over from Ireland because the family is worried about her.'

'I'm Anna.' She gave me a friendly little nod. 'You heard then, did you?' she paused. 'About what happened to her and why she's not here?'

'About the baby, you mean? I did,' I said. 'I was up at the convent and they said she was supposed to come back here, but that she ran off.'

'That's what we heard too,' the girl said.

'So she never did come back then?'

She shook her head. 'The last we saw of her was when she left here several months ago.'

'How well did you know Maureen?' I asked.

A wistful smile crossed her face. 'We were good pals. A really nice girl. Refined. Kept herself to herself, if you know what I mean. Rather religious, wasn't she? Really cut up about the baby. She said, "I'll be spending centuries in purgatory for this, if I don't go to hell." '

'It must have been hard for her with Mrs Mainwaring having a baby at the same time.' I said. 'Sort of reminding her of what she was giving up.'

She looked at me funnily, embarrassed, almost as if she was in an agony of indecision.

'I suppose that's why she didn't want to come back to have to take care of another woman's child,' I went on.

Her cheeks were bright red now and she shifted from one foot to the other, looking extremely uncomfortable. 'It wasn't exactly as easy as that. That's why she was so torn. She didn't want to be here, in fact she hated Mrs Mainwaring, but she wanted to be near the baby. Well, who wouldn't?' She looked at me, her eyes imploring me to understand. And suddenly I did. And as soon as I realized, I wondered how I could have been so dense.

My hand went up to my mouth. 'It's her child, isn't it? Maureen's. Mrs Mainwaring couldn't have children so they decided to adopt this one.'

She nodded. 'We're not supposed to know about it, but of course we all do. It's the closest he'd ever come to a proper heir, I suppose.'

And then the final piece of the puzzle fell into place and again I wondered how I could not have seen the truth earlier.

'I see now. It was his child. Mr Mainwaring. He was the father.'

She looked around, in case anyone might have overheard us. Then she moved in closer to me, speaking in a low voice. 'That's why she was scared to come back here. She thought he wouldn't keep his hands off her again. Well, you know – Maureen is a pretty girl, isn't she? And Mrs Mainwaring – she hasn't much interest in that sort of thing. She keeps her bedroom door locked most nights. I can tell because I take up her morning coffee, and I have to tap on the door and say, "It's me, Anna, with the coffee, ma'am," before she'll come and open it.'

'I see,' I said.

'And he's that sort of man, isn't he?' she went on. 'Healthy appetite for that kind of thing, you know. He's tried it with other servants in the past and some girls left rather than giving him his way. He tried it with me once, but I slapped his face and made it quite clear that he'd better not touch me. Maureen was so naïve, she didn't realize until too late. And she didn't want to be fired.'

'So she didn't want to come back and yet she wanted to be close to her child. Poor thing. What a tough decision to make.'

Anna nodded. 'Mrs Mainwaring was furious too when she found that Maureen had run off. She's not normally an emotional sort of woman but she was in a right state, I can tell you – stomping about and calling her ungrateful. I suppose she felt that Maureen had put her on the spot when she had to hire another nursemaid at such short notice. Poor Maureen – in the end her religion probably made her see it was better to give up the child rather than risk it happening all over again.' She put a tentative hand on my arm. 'I'm sorry. This has obviously been a shock to you. Were you close to her?'

'Not really,' I said. 'Only a distant cousin, but she was well loved by the family back in Ireland. I only hope I have some way of finding her now. Nobody seems to know where she might have gone. You don't have any idea at all where she might go if she chose to run away? Did she ever talk of going off somewhere? Any friends she might have gone to?'

Anna thought about this, then shook her head. 'She hated New York City. Too much noise and bustle for her after coming from the quiet of the Irish countryside, so I don't think she'd have gone back there.'

'No young man then?'

'Who has a chance to meet a young man when we're stuck at a place like this? There's only the gardeners and the groom and they're old and married.' She met my eye with a look of concern. 'I'm sorry, but I can't think where she might have gone.'

'I see,' I said. 'Look, is there anyone else here she was

close to? Anyone else she might have secretly contacted or confided in?'

'I can't think who that would be,' she said. 'Maureen and I shared a bedroom. I'm the head parlormaid. She was under-parlormaid. Apart from us there's the lady's maid, who's a real snooty old cow, the master's valet, who's not interested in girls, if you get my meaning. And then there's the cook, the scullery maid, and the butler. That's it.'

I tried to think what else I might ask. It was all horribly clear now. Poor little Maureen, at the mercy of the master while his wife was quite happy to turn a blind eye as long as he didn't bother her. No wonder she didn't want to return to the house, especially when her religion was so important to her and she felt that she had committed a sin for something that wasn't in any way her fault. I toyed with the word 'religion.' Anna had stressed it several times. And a new thought came to me.

'Anna, is it possible that she decided to stay in the convent and become a nun?' I asked.

She thought about this. 'Stayed and become a nun?' She frowned, considering something that hadn't occurred to her before. 'I suppose it is possible,' she said. 'I wouldn't put something like that past her. Like I told you, she was very devout. Always on her knees praying and she remembered every kind of saint's day and holy day. And no meat on Fridays. All those kinds of things mattered to her.'

'Then it's possible she didn't leave the convent at all,' I blurted out. It all made sense now. The abandoning of the little statue and her hairbrush. She had renounced her worldly goods when she went into the novitiate. Perhaps she had even taken a new name, which was why the novice at the door didn't know who she was. The only strange thing was why the nuns claimed that she had run away – unless they had promised Mrs Mainwaring she would return to be nursemaid of her child, and she had begged the nuns to hide her. It had been easier to slip Maureen into the convent and then claim that she had run away.

'Thank you, Anna,' I said. 'You've been really helpful. I think I might have a good chance of tracing Maureen now.'

She looked pleased. 'If you do find her, would you give her my best? I was real fond of her and I worry about her.'

'I will,' I said.

She glanced around again. 'I'd best get back to work before someone sees and I get an earful.'

'Thank you,' I said. 'I'm glad I had a chance to talk to you. If I had listened to other people I'd have believed she'd run off to New York.'

'Not Maureen. Never.' We broke apart as one of the workmen came toward us. 'Can you fill up the water jug again for us, miss?' he asked. 'It's hot work today.'

'Of course.' Anne glanced across at me. 'Mrs Mainwaring has taken it into her head that she wants a summer house.' She hesitated as if she might want to say something more, but then added. 'I hope you find Maureen and she's all right. Tell her Anna sends her kind regards.'

Then she went inside to refill the water jug, while I made my way unseen to the front gate and back down the hill to Irvington Station.

Chapter 22

I found myself smiling with satisfaction as I took the train back to Tarrytown. It all made sense now. Maureen had been heard to say, 'You can't make me. It's cruel.' And she'd meant going back to a situation where her child belonged to another woman and where she was at the mercy of a master with lustful ways. I remembered the way he had looked at me, almost undressing me with his eyes, in spite of my condition. Perhaps when she ran off angrily she had gone straight to the mother superior and appealed to her. And that good woman had decided to spirit her away.

It was still early in the day. Sid and Gus would hardly have had time to buy a bathing costume for Bridie and go swimming with her yet. They wouldn't be missing me and wouldn't want me to interrupt their fun. Which meant I had hours of freedom ahead of me. If I went up to the convent, I could ask to speak to the mother superior and nobody else and surely she would tell me the truth – maybe even let me speak to Maureen and give her a message of reassurance from her family.

But what if they brushed me off again, as they had certainly done last time? If those two nuns I had seen before claimed that the mother superior was busy or at prayer again, what then? If I told them I wanted to interview girls for possible future service in my household would they let me in? Let me chat with the girls? Wouldn't they be suspicious that I had returned after questioning them about Maureen – and if there was anything to hide, they'd simply get rid of me as quickly as possible again. And there would be no way I could look into what really happened to poor little Katy.

Then suddenly I came up with a brilliant idea, one so daring that it made my heart beat faster. I actually had a way to get inside the convent and see for myself. I put my hand on my belly. If I arrived on the doorstep as a fallen woman in need, surely they'd take me in. Then I'd have a chance to look around, to speak to Maureen, and when I was ready to leave, I'd simply tell them that I'd changed my mind and I wasn't going to stay.

The only people who had actually seen me clearly before were Katy and the novice, and Katy was now dead and the novice in the solitude of retreat. The nuns had only been shadows behind the grille to me, so presumably they'd only seen a similarly indistinct impression of me in that dark little parlor. And I'd been sitting down when they came in, so they'd never have seen that I too was in the family way. All I had to do was to let down my hair and broaden my Irish accent. Daniel always said that with my hair down I looked no more than fourteen. It was worth a try and the very worst they could do would be to tell me that they had no room for me. In which case I'd let on that I was Maureen's cousin – and we'd see what happened then.

I sat impatiently until the train came to a halt. Outside the station I looked around cautiously, just in case Sid, Gus, and Bridie happened to have chosen that moment to walk from the town to the waterfront. But the station yard was deserted, apart from a horse and buggy standing in the shade, the horse with its head down, half asleep. I went over and asked if they were for hire. The driver also looked sleepy but grudgingly agreed. However, when I asked him to drive me up to the convent, he stared down at my bulging stomach then gave me a pitying nod.

He held out his hand and helped me climb up. 'I'm sure you're doing the right thing, miss,' he said. 'The nuns will take good care of you.'

Once I was seated in the buggy I remembered to remove my wedding ring and tuck it into a pocket at the back of my coin purse. Then I took off my hat and unpinned my hair. It cascaded over my shoulders, blowing out in the wind as the horse got up speed. This had seemed like a brilliant idea in the safety of the train compartment, but when the forbidding wall of the convent came into view, I began to have second thoughts about what I was doing. Was I running a risk going inside those walls? Maureen had vanished. Katy had revealed secrets to me and Katy had died. But then I reassured myself that Maureen's disappearance would now have a simple explanation. And Katy's death would probably turn out to be a sad accident, but an accident nonetheless. It was a convent, after all, I told myself. Full of holy women doing a charitable service.

But I couldn't shake off the thought that Maureen had come to me in a dream with Katy. It was fine for Gus to deny that dreams could come from the beyond. She had never lived in Ireland and had neighbors whose dear departed relatives often came and spoke to them in dreams. That thought made me sit up rigid. Had Maureen been a voice from the beyond? If she was happily at the convent now, why had she come to me in the dream, clearly asking for my help?

The buggy came to a halt. The driver jumped down and offered me his hand to help me from the seat. I almost said, 'I've changed my mind. Drive me back to the town,' but my pride wouldn't let me. The driver refused to take any money either. He gave me a sympathetic smile and a pat on the back. 'It will all work out for the best, you'll see,' he said. 'Good luck to you, miss.'

After that I could hardly ask for him to come and get me again later in the day. I'd have to find my own way down to the town when I came out. I took a deep breath, smoothed down my hair, and walked up to that front door. It was opened by a thin and pale girl, with no bulging belly like mine. In fact she looked distinctly unwell, with dark circles under her eyes.

'Hello,' I said in my best Irish accent that had faded after four years of living with New Yorkers. 'I've come to see the sisters. I'm newly arrived in this country from Ireland and I heard about this place. I've nowhere else to go.'

'Come in,' she said, with a smile of understanding. 'What's your name?'

'It's Molly,' I said, deciding that it's easier to tell the truth than to lie whenever possible.

'I'm Blanche.' She held out her hand and shook mine. She felt as fragile as bone china. And cold too, almost as if she was barely alive.

'Are you a novice?' I asked.

'No. I'm here for the same reason as you,' she said. 'Betrayed by the boy I loved and trusted. I had a baby three weeks ago.'

'Did you? Was it a boy or a girl?'

'A girl,' she said. 'She was stillborn. I had a rough time of it and I'm still trying to get my strength back.'

'I'm sorry,' I said.

She nodded. 'It happens. Not all babies live, do they? Not all mothers live either. It's the curse of Eve, they say.'

On that encouraging note she ushered me into the parlor.

'I'll tell Sister Perpetua you're here,' she said.

'What about the mother superior? I'd rather see her first,' I said.

'Mother's not very well these days, so they say,' she said. 'She's been confined to her room, except for when they take her to chapel. Sister Perpetua is in charge, although Sister Jerome likes to think she is.' She lowered her voice and glanced around as she said this.

'Who is Sister Jerome then?' I asked, remembering that tall gaunt shape with the sharp voice. She'd certainly acted as if she was a person of authority.

'She's the bursar. But recently she's taken over the running of the maternity section. It used to be Sister Francine, but she died recently. Sister Jerome only used to handle the business side of the adoptions but now she's training Sister Angelique to take over as midwife, and frankly neither of them are very good at it. Sister Jerome is far too fastidious and Sister Angelique – well, she just doesn't have a feel for it like Sister Francine did.'

'What happened to Sister Francine?' I asked cautiously.

'What happened? What do you mean?'

'I mean how did she die?'

She frowned. 'She was really old. She just died in her sleep a few weeks ago. Everyone was really sad, both the nuns and the girls. Especially me. I had to have Sister Jerome help deliver my baby, and it got stuck and she had to use forceps. Poor little mite.' She shuddered, then said, 'I shouldn't be scaring you like this. I'm sure you'll be just fine. You stay there and I'll go and find Sister.'

I perched on one of those uncomfortable chairs, this time expecting a face to appear at the grille. I jumped, therefore, when the door opened behind me and Blanche reappeared. 'Sister wants you to come through,' she said. 'Follow me.'

She led me under an arch, down a narrow hallway, and then through another heavy oak door that was now open. She paused to shut the door behind her, pushing the iron bolt into place. It appeared I was inside the convent, whether I liked it or not. We'd only gone a few yards when she tapped on a door and heard a gentle voice say, 'Come in.'

I was ushered into a room even more spartan than the parlor. A small barred window let in a shaft of light. The floor was stone, the chairs plain wood, and on one of them sat a small, delicate figure in a severe black habit.

'Here's the new girl, Sister,' Blanche said.

The elderly nun looked as I would have expected from her voice. The face was ageless, innocent, and the eyes still bright, but I could tell from the hand she held out to me that she was old. 'Thank you, Blanche, dear. You may leave us,' she said. 'I am Sister Perpetua. Mother is indisposed, I'm afraid.' She was still clutching my hand in her bony, withered one. 'Now what is your name, child?'

'It's Molly, Sister,' I said in a voice scarcely more than a whisper. I looked down, avoiding her eye.

'Sit down, Molly. There is no need to be afraid,' she said. 'You are among friends here.'

I pulled up a crude straight-backed chair and sat.

'Now then,' she said. 'I don't have to ask why you are here. I can see that for myself.'

I nodded. I had come up with a story on the train ride from Irvington and it sounded convincing to me. 'I didn't know where else to go,' I said. 'I came over from Ireland to marry Joe. He went on ahead to make some money so that we could marry. But after he left I found out that I . . .' I looked down again. 'You know.'

'He left you with child,' she said severely.

'Oh, he would have married me right away if he'd known,' I said. 'Joe would have done the right thing. He wasn't that sort of man.'

'So you came to America to find him,' she continued.

'I did. I scraped together enough for the fare and when I went to the address Joe had written from, he wasn't there.'

'He'd gone off somewhere?' She was looking at me with great sympathy.

'Yes, but not what you think,' she said. 'It turns out they came around recruiting laborers to go down to Panama and dig the new canal. Good money, they said. And Joe signed up right away.' I put my hand up to my mouth. 'So I don't know if he's alive or dead or where he is,' I said. 'I've no way of getting in touch with him, and no money to go back home. Not that my father would allow me to come back. Terrible strict he is on matters like this.'

'I'm sorry, my dear,' she said gently. 'I hear stories like yours all the time. And I wish we could help you, but we have our full complement of young women at the moment. And a waiting list too. Girls write to us from all over several months before they need to come and we have to turn so many away.'

'You mean I can't stay?' I asked, hoping there was enough desperation in my voice. 'Where else would I go?'

'I can write to other convents on your behalf,' she said. 'There is no other order around here that devotes itself to our mission of charity, but sometimes there is a spare bed to be had and the good sisters will welcome a stranger in time of need. I can't guarantee anything, of course. There is so much need these days. So much suffering.'

I wondered what I should do next. In a way I felt profoundly relieved that I wasn't going to be admitted and I could go back to join Sid and Gus and Bridie at the riverside, where we'd laugh and eat ice creams and enjoy ourselves. They were right. I really had done all that could be expected for a girl I had never met.

I got to my feet. 'Thank you, anyway,' I said. 'I'd better go, then.'

'I hate to do this,' she said, 'but if I took you in, it wouldn't be fair to a girl who has waited months to come here and whose confinement is imminent, would it?'

'I suppose not.'

'When is your baby due, my dear?' she asked.

'Another month,' I said, stretching the truth a little.

'Then we've still a little time. I expect Sister Jerome can come up with some money to keep you going, and, as I said, I'll write letters for you. We'll need a forwarding address.'

'I've nowhere,' I said. 'I stayed at a cheap lady's boardinghouse when I arrived. Just next to the docks.'

'And how did you hear about us?'

Ah. I hadn't thought that one through. 'When I heard that Joe had gone I was distraught,' I said. 'A pair of nuns saw me crying in the street and asked what was wrong. They told me about this place.'

'Did they? God bless them. Yes, they'd be from the Foundling Hospital. Sometimes one of our babies has to go to them, when we can't find a family right away to adopt the little dear. They do wonderful work. So many abandoned babies in the city. So much sin.'

I lingered, my hand on the doorknob. 'I shouldn't detain you any longer then.'

At that moment the doorknob was wrenched from my hand. I almost lost my balance and stepped hastily out of the way as another nun came barging into the room. She was very tall and thin, with high cheekbones and a beak-like nose and her head jerked in a bird-like fashion as she looked around. The impression was of a large black crow and it came to me that I'd seen her before.

'Blanche tells me an Irish girl has shown up on the doorstep,' she said. I recognized the strident tones of Sister Jerome. The bird-like gaze scanned until it focused on me, standing to one side of the door. 'And here she is,' she added. 'With hair as red as the morning sunrise.'

'I've just been telling her that I'm afraid we have unfortunately no room for her, and a long waiting list too,' Sister Perpetua said.

Sister Jerome was looking me over. 'Well, we certainly can't send her away in this condition,' she said. 'It wouldn't be right or charitable.'

'But you yourself said that we've no more beds,' Sister Perpetua reminded her.

'We'll just have to make room,' she said. 'A couple of the girls are malingering, claiming they are not well enough to leave when I know perfectly well that they're simply afraid of going back into the world again.' She looked back at the door. 'That girl Blanche is one of them. It's high time she was gone.'

Sister Perpetua looked worried. 'Really Sister, I don't think we should force anyone to leave before she is ready. Blanche has been through a most difficult time. Giving birth to a stillborn child must be a devastating experience for a girl who has carried that baby for nine months. Healing has to be in the heart as well as the body.'

'Nonsense,' Sister Jerome said. 'They'll be going back into a tough world. We're not helping them by shielding them and spoon-feeding them for too long. I know you mean well, Sister, but you're too soft-hearted. The girls and the babies are my province, so you just leave it to me. And I say we'll find a place for this new arrival somehow. What's your name, young woman?'

'It's Molly, Sister.' I looked down and didn't meet her eye. There was something formidable about this nun. I felt distinctly uneasy in her presence. Why was she so keen to turf out other girls to make room for me? She hadn't come across as the compassionate kind.

'Well, come along, Molly. No sense in dilly-dallying.'

I was now feeling distinctly uneasy. It was one thing to have gained a way to snoop around, but another to be responsible for turfing girls out of their beds.

'Oh, listen, Sister.' I held up my hand. 'I don't want anyone to be moved because of me. I'd feel terrible. Maybe I should just go.'

'Don't be silly. We'll make room somehow. I daresay

it will have to be a cot squeezed in between the beds for tonight, but we'll sort things out tomorrow.'

Sister Perpetua had half risen to her feet. 'With all due respect I think you should talk to Mother first before you expel any of our girls until she feels strong enough to leave.'

'May I remind you that Mother has placed the running of our maternity ward in my hands, Sister,' Sister Jerome said firmly. 'And in her delicate state of health it would be most selfish of us to cause her any worry or distress. I assure you I will pray fervently before I make any decision about any of the girls in my care. Come, Molly. I'll show you where you'll be sleeping, and find you some clothing that is more suitable for hard work than what you're wearing.' She held the door open for me to pass through. 'Sister.' Sister Jerome gave a hint of a bow and closed the door behind us.

Chapter 23

Sister Jerome led me down a long hallway with a polished stone floor and vaulted roof. On one side were closed doors, on the other the arches of a cloister opened onto a quadrangle. It was a pleasant spot – with the sun spilling in, benches under shade trees, a statue of Our Lady in one corner, and a fountain splashing in the middle – but I decided it would be horribly cold in winter with the wind whistling in. Before I could comment on it Sister Jerome turned back to me. 'Come along,' she said sharply. 'It is not fitting for you to be here. This corridor is actually the province of the sisters. It houses our offices, our refectory, and common room. Our cells are upstairs. Outsiders are not permitted here at any time, is that clear?'

I nodded. 'Yes, Sister,' I muttered, hoping to sound suitably humble and penitent.

She paused as we had reached the end of the cloisters. She opened the door before us and we stepped from daylight into darkness. As my eyes grew accustomed to the gloom I could see that we were in a square area such as one would find in a corner tower of an old castle. To my right a spiral stone stair ascended and to my left a similar stone stairway went down into blackness.

Really, I wondered, what possessed people in the New World to build something so hopelessly outdated and uncomfortable, and then what inspired the sisters to select it for their home in America? It must have had something to do with suffering and penance. I grinned to myself. We took neither the staircase up nor down, but went straight ahead to an arched doorway in the rough stone wall.

'Now I'm going to give you a look at the chapel,' Sister said and opened the door. I stepped inside and found myself in a high and narrow chapel. Its lofty, vaulted ceiling melted into darkness. Tall, narrow windows of colored glass threw strips of light onto the stone floor and the single wooden kneelers dotted around before me. Each kneeler had a hassock worked in crewelwork with religious symbols – a lamb, a lily, a cross. There were around twenty of them, indicating that the convent currently housed that number of nuns. The smell of incense hung heavy in the air, mingled with the smells of furniture polish and damp.

'This is the sisters' chapel,' she said in a whisper, although we were the only people present. 'No outsiders are permitted here, not even the priest who comes to say daily mass. I only show you to satisfy your curiosity. You girls sit on the other side of the screen and enter from your own part of the building. Our two worlds meet as little as possible. I am the only bridge between them.'

I saw now why the chapel had seemed so narrow. It was divided in half by a wall in which there was a carved wooden screen. Through that screen I could make out rows of pews. Both sides faced the high altar with its tall polished candlesticks and an alarmingly real-looking crucifix.

'You may come to the chapel to pray whenever you have a spare moment,' Sister said, ushering me out again. 'We hope that will be frequently. We expect the girls to atone for their sins while they are here, and contemplation of the Blessed Sacrament is the best way to do that.'

Now she led me past the upward stair and opened a door in the far wall, inserting a key that hung from her belt. 'We pass now from the sisters' sanctuary to your quarters,' she said, turning to lock the door again behind her. She led me down a small dark hall, vaulted like the first one I had entered. 'This is the entrance to your side of the chapel. Mass is at eight. Then we have laundry room and supplies,' she said, 'and ahead of us the maternity wing. We like to keep the mothers and babies separate. It is important that you girls have as little as possible to do with babies. It makes the separation easier in the end. Now here is where you will be spending most of your time.' She opened a door and I stepped through to a very different hallway. This one was light and bright. Windows down the whole length opened onto a kitchen garden and orchard, enclosed by a high brick wall.

She set off down the hallway, her shoes making almost no sound on the stone floor so that she appeared to glide with no effort at all, like a ship sailing over a calm ocean. She looked back at me and I quickened my pace to catch up with her. 'Here is your kitchen.' She nodded at a closed door but did not open it, 'And this is where you will take your meals.' She opened a door to reveal long scrubbed tables, set with simple metal plates and forks beside them. A smell of boiled cabbage lingered in the air. She closed the door again. 'Mealtimes are posted on the wall of your dormitory. Make sure you arrive promptly. Tardiness is not permitted. And now here,' and she opened the next door along the hall, 'is your common room. The girls gather here in the evenings to do their sewing and mending while they are allowed a brief time to chat together. There is no place for idle hands or frivolity here.' The room housed one decrepit sofa and several wooden chairs. There was a fireplace at one end and a bookshelf containing a few volumes, all of which looked like religious titles.

The memory of my mother's quote flashed back into my head. *Satan finds work for idle hands to do.* Clearly they were making sure that Satan could not find a chink through which to enter this sanctuary.

'All the girls are expected to do their share of the labor, in return for our kindness in taking you in,' Sister said, shutting the door behind us. 'They will all be hard at work now. You'll find yourself working in the laundry, the kitchen, or out in the garden, depending on your physical state. You look like a good strong girl. From a farm, were you?'

'Yes, Sister. We lived on an estate owned by an English family. My father worked in the fields for them.'

'And how did he feel about that?' she asked. 'Working for the enemy indeed.'

'I don't know how he felt,' I said. 'We never discussed it. As far as I know our family had always lived in that cottage. That was just the way things were in Ireland. Most people owned no land of their own.'

'Do you think that's right?' she demanded. 'Do you think we should be subjected to the tyranny of overlords?'

'Of course I don't. And my own brother is working for the Republican Brotherhood, putting his own life in danger for the cause.'

'Is he? God love him,' she said. 'I took to you from the moment I saw you. We're going to get along just fine, Molly, I can tell.'

'So are you from Ireland, Sister?' I asked because her accent sounded American.

'I count myself as Irish although I wasn't born there. My family came here during the great famine and I was born two years later. Thrown out of their cottage, they were, and do you know, the landowner had his men tear down the cottage, stone by stone, so that they could never return. They were already starving to death and yet the landowner saw fit to destroy the home before my parents could get out all their possessions. My mother said it broke her heart to see her china teapot smashed. She begged them for just a minute or two, but they didn't care. They just pushed her out of the way. That's how they treated us in our own country.'

'I know,' I said. 'There have been some terrible wrongs. My little brother was sold into servitude by the landowners, after our father died and there was no one to look after him.'

'Terrible.' She shook her head. 'We must do all we can to right these wrongs, Molly. Of course all I'm able to do is to pray, but you can do your share, once you're free of this burden. Can't you, my dear?'

'I'll do what I can,' I said cautiously, because her face had become so intense and dangerous-looking.

'I can put you in touch with people who are working for the cause,' she said. 'It is good to find meaning in your life when you're trying to get over the sad business of giving up a child.'

I was tempted to ask if she had sent Maureen on a quest to save Ireland and Maureen had heeded the call, but I decided to keep quiet until I knew more. But one thing I had to ask.

'Sister, I believe I saw you when I was in New York,' I said. 'You were walking alone through the Lower East Side.' The image came into my head quite clearly. Me stepping out of the shadows on the crowded sidewalk and almost bumping into the nun with the beak-like nose. But she had been wearing a different kind of habit.

She shook her head. 'Not me. We are an enclosed order. Part of our vow is never to leave the convent again. Our nuns never go outside these walls. We are even buried here.'

'I must have been mistaken then,' I said. 'But I saw a nun who looked very like you. Although I'm sure many nuns look alike when all one can see is the face.'

'I tell you what,' she said. 'It was probably my sister that you saw. Folks say that we look alike, although I've not seen her for several years so I can't tell you how she looks now.'

'Is she also a nun?'

'She is.'

'In your order?'

'No. Not in the same order. Our parents thought that I was suited to the contemplative life and my sister could face exposure to the wickedness of the world. I don't know if that was a correct assessment of our personalities. We were too young to know what was good for us and nobody gave us a choice. Shipped off to the convent, we were, when we were sixteen. I think I would have been well suited to life outside these walls. But I have made full use of my talents here. The other sisters have no notion of the outside world, no head at all for business or organization. I make sure this place runs as it should.'

It was on the tip of my tongue to suggest that pride was a sin. But she seemed to have taken to me and I had to make the most of that. I nodded in agreement when she looked at me.

'I'm sure it's not an easy job that you do,' I said, buttering her up even more.

'Oh, I enjoy making this place run like clockwork,' she said. 'But I'm currently having to train another sister to take over this section, which means that I sometimes have to act as midwife, until she gets the hang of it – and I'm not sure she will ever have the gift. That's not a job that comes easily to me. I am not used to – the messiness of it all. I am extremely fastidious by nature. I was brought up to believe that cleanliness is next to godliness. It is a real penance to have to assist with the delivery of a child. And a devastating blow if I lose either the mother or the child. We lost a child recently. It still haunts me that maybe I should have done something differently.'

'Could you not have called in a doctor?' I asked. 'Could you not have taken the girl to a hospital?'

'The doctor was summoned, but he was out on another case, some miles from town. Things go wrong so quickly sometimes and I don't have the gift like Sister Francine did.'

'Sister Francine, who was she?' I asked.

'She ran the maternity ward and delivered the babies until she died three months ago. A true saint – beloved by everybody and with a gift of knowing exactly what to do when it came to babies. I find her shoes very hard to fill and pray daily that one of our novices may hear the call to take over this task.'

We continued walking down the hall. 'These are my quarters,' she said, indicating a closed door, which she did not attempt to open. 'I no longer live and sleep with the rest of my sisters. Since my job calls for me to be available at any hour of the day or night it would be unfair to disturb their few hours of repose. My office is here and my cell beyond. You will find me here if I am not among you and you need me in an emergency.'

'Thank you, Sister,' I said again.

She looked at me with her head on one side, reinforcing the bird-like impression. 'I don't know why I'm talking so much to you. I don't usually chat with our young charges. It must be that you're a fellow Irishwoman and I feel a bond between us.'

'Have you not had any other Irish girls here then?' I asked innocently.

'Not at the moment,' she said. She went to move on, then added, 'We had one girl here recently direct from Ireland like yourself. It's a pity you two didn't get a chance to meet.'

'What a pity,' I reiterated. 'I'd love to have had someone from home here. It's all rather frightening to me to know I'm all alone in a strange new world. So she's had her baby and gone then, has she?'

'She has,' Sister Jerome said in clipped tones.

'Is she living somewhere nearby?' I asked. 'I'd love to meet her after I get out of here. We'd have a lot in common to talk about, wouldn't we?'

'I've not the slightest idea where she went,' Sister said curtly. 'And you probably wouldn't have gotten on at all, now I think about it. She was not at all like you. A difficult girl, if you want to know. Stubborn. Wouldn't be led or advised. Then ran off without a word of thank you. Disappeared during the night.'

'How awful,' I said. 'That must have been worrying for you.'

'Disappointing,' she said. 'After all we did for her.'

'Perhaps it was hard for her to give up her child,' I suggested. 'I know I wouldn't find it easy.'

'None of the girls finds it easy,' she said, 'but most of them want what's best for their baby and they see that a good, stable home, with loving parents, is the only practical solution. Maureen was always too headstrong.'

I remembered the fight Emily had reported to me with Maureen shouting, 'You can't make me. It's cruel.' Was that about giving up her baby? Had she changed her mind at the last minute? I couldn't think of any way to ask any more questions at this moment without making Sister Jerome suspicious of me.

'I know I'll want what's best for my child,' I said, continuing to play the good obedient girl. 'How could I possibly hope to support the little dear?'

She gave me another approving nod. 'Now let's get you settled with a uniform and a place to sleep. Your dormitory is up these stairs.'

There was a flight of stairs at the end of the hall past Sister's office. She went ahead of me, up the steps at a great rate. She must have been at least fifty, I reasoned, if she was born at the time of the famine, but she seemed remarkably agile for her age, especially wearing that heavy and cumbersome habit.

Our footsteps echoed with the sound bouncing from the stone steps to the stone walls as we came out to a hallway above. It was the only sound I had heard here apart from the swish of her robes. I looked down the deserted hallway. The windows on this hall were frosted so that light came in, but there was no view – obviously to prevent the girls from seeing beyond that wall into the world outside.

'It's really quiet in here, isn't it?' I said. 'Not a single sound.'

'We usually maintain a rule of silence at all times,' she said, 'and that applies to you girls as well as our sisters. No talking or whispering at any time in the hallways or in the dormitory after lights out. Only minimal talking on the job when a question needs to be asked. Silence also at meals when the girls take it in turns to read from a holy book. You know how to read, do you?'

'Of course,' I said, a little too readily. Would a girl in my situation really know how to read?

'Some of the girls are barely literate,' she said with a sniff of disapproval. 'And some of their personal cleanliness habits – well, they leave a lot to be desired.' She pointed down the hallway. 'The last door on your left is the bathroom. And there is a WC beside it. We expect girls to wash themselves well daily and take a bath at least once a week. Towels can be found in the laundry closet next to the bathroom.'

'So where are the other girls?' I asked, realizing I had seen no one apart from Blanche.

'They are all at their daily tasks,' she said. 'Either

Rhys Bowen

working in the laundry or out in the garden or in the kitchen. There is a lot to do at this time of year – preserving and bottling our fruits and vegetables to keep us going through the winter. We like to be almost self-sufficient here.'

It seemed I was doomed to do my share of bottling and preserving wherever I went!

'Of course we do not have the grounds to keep any animals except our hens, but we eat little meat anyway.'

She pushed open the first door we came to. I noticed it must be directly above her quarters. So she'd hear if anyone got up during the night, I thought. The room was dark, with only a couple of high windows sending shafts of sunlight to the top of the opposite wall. It contained a row of narrow iron bedsteads, eight in all, a small cupboard beside each, and a row of hooks on the far wall. Here there was a large crucifix, and a statue of St Anthony, holding the child Jesus, stood on a shelf in one corner. These were the only decorations, except that one of the beds had a small vase of flowers beside it and one other held a photograph.

'Now we have to decide where we can put you,' Sister said. 'Not much room, as you can see. I doubt that we could squeeze a cot in here if we tried.'

At the sound of her voice a figure rose up from one of the beds. My heart skipped a beat and I stepped backward involuntarily.

'Blanche, what are you doing here?' Sister demanded angrily. 'You should be at your assignment. Aren't you supposed to be our porter this week?'

'I am, Sister, but I started feeling dizzy again so Sister Perpetua said I could go and lie down for a while.'

'Blanche, you have to stop this malingering,' Sister said angrily. 'It won't help you in the long run. You are fully recovered from the birth and you have to put it behind you. No amount of grieving will bring that baby back, and there is no point in wallowing in guilt and self-pity. In fact I think it would be far better for you if you went back to the outside world and got on with life.'

A terrified look came over Blanche's face. 'Don't make me go yet, Sister. I'm not ready. I can't face it.'

'Pull yourself together, girl,' Sister snapped. 'You'll be just fine.'

'But I've nowhere to go,' she wailed. 'They won't take me back at home. I've nobody.'

'I will give you a letter to take to my sister in New York,' Sister Jerome said. 'Her convent has been most helpful in placing girls like you in domestic service. But if you can't buck up and pull yourself together, who would want you?'

Tears were now running down Blanche's pale face. 'I try to buck up,' she said. 'But I just feel so awful all the time. So sad. As if nothing good will ever happen to me again.'

'Of course it will, you silly girl. You'll get a job and soon this will all seem like a bad dream. Now then, pack up your things and change the sheets on your bed. Molly will be sleeping here from now on.'

'Oh, Sister,' I intervened. 'I'm sure I wouldn't want to take Blanche's bed. If she's not feeling strong enough to go yet, then I really think she should stay. I'm sure we could find a place to put a cot for me until she's ready. Or I could sleep on the sofa in the common room for now. I really don't mind.'

'Blanche can sleep in the sisters' guest room tonight,

while we get together her letters of reference and a new outfit of clothes for her. Pack up your things, Blanche, and make your bed for Molly, then take her to the clothes closet and find her a uniform. I have letters to write, but I'll be back for you in half an hour.'

As she turned to walk out of the room I heard the swish of those robes again and I realized what had struck me as strange about her from the first. Her habit was made of silk.

Chapter 24

'I'm so sorry,' I said to Blanche as soon as I heard the sister's feet going down the stairs. 'I would never have turned you out. I'd rather sleep on the floor.'

She gave me a sad smile. 'It's not you,' she said. 'She hates me. She can't wait to get rid of me. It has really angered her that I've been allowed to stay for so long.'

'What has she got against you?' I asked as I helped her pull the sheet from the bed. She seemed a frail and delicate little thing, like an expensive French china doll.

She looked up at me. 'My baby died,' she said.

'She blames herself for her own failure as a midwife?' I asked.

She shook her head. 'In her mind she never fails,' she muttered. 'No, she blames me because I let her down. She had a good home waiting for that particular baby, you see, and she didn't want to lose out on that money.'

'What money?'

She moved closer to me so that our shoulders were touching. 'The convent gets requests from couples who want a baby that they can pass as their own,' she said.

'This couple wanted a fair-haired child with blue eyes and of course she was sure my baby would be light-haired – which it was, poor little thing.'

'And couples pay for this?'

'Oh, yes. From what we've heard they are asked to make a donation to the convent and sometimes it's a generous donation. That's why sister was so angry with me. I suppose the convent really needs the money.'

'As if you could have done anything to stop your baby from being born dead!' I said indignantly. 'It must have been really upsetting for you.'

She nodded and her light blue eyes filled with tears. 'I can't seem to get over it. I hate this place, but I have nowhere to go. I don't think I'm strong enough to get a job yet.'

I was so tempted to say that I'd take her on and look after her and nurse her back to health and wholeness, but how could I, when I was supposed to be in the same position as her?

'Look,' I said. 'I think I might know some people in New York who could help you. But they won't be home for a few days. If you go and stay with the nuns as Sister suggests, then by the end of the week you can safely go to this address and tell them that Molly sent you.'

'So what are you doing here if you have friends in New York, people who can help you?' she asked. It was a good question and I had to think before I answered.

'They are women who help destitute young girls to find employment,' I said. 'They suggested I come up here to the convent and then go to them when I've had my baby.'

'I see.' She looked almost hopeful.

'Do you have a pencil and paper?' I asked. The only

thing I had in my bag was my calling card and that would never do.

She looked around and shook her head. 'Then repeat after me,' I said. 'Nine Patchin Place. Can you remember that?'

She repeated it. I nodded. 'Good. Keep repeating it to yourself. Any constable in New York will tell you the way. It's in Greenwich Village and it's where these women live.'

'Thank you,' she said.

We finished stripping the bed and Blanche led me down the hall to a linen closet for clean sheets. 'And there should be a clean uniform in here for you.' It was more like a small room than a closet, with shelves of neatly folded linens on all sides. She looked around the shelves then reached up, hauled down some folded gray-and-blue cloth and handed it to me. It was a gray dress with its gray-ish-blue overgarment like the one she was wearing made of coarse cloth. It was hard for me to take it, knowing that I wouldn't be needing it and that some girl would have to launder it again, but I couldn't find a way to refuse.

As I took it she said, 'I think that one will fit. That must have been Katy's and you're about the same size.'

'Was Katy one of your friends?' I asked. 'Has she had her baby and left?'

Blanche shook her head. 'She died.' Her voice dropped to a whisper. 'She fell down the cellar steps and broke her neck.'

'How terrible,' I said. 'Poor girl.'

She nodded. 'It was an awful shock, especially when I was feeling so low anyway. Katy was a lovely girl. So friendly and nice.'

'What was she doing going down to a cellar?' I asked.

'I've seen how dark and old some parts of this building are. Why would you ever send a pregnant woman down there?'

'As to that, I don't know what she was doing. Perhaps Sister Angelique had something against her as well. Perhaps she found out that Katy was scared of mice or rats or spiders so she sent her down to clean some part of the cellar where there are bound to be plenty of them. She does things like that.' She shrugged.

'Sister Angelique?' I asked.

'She's being trained to take Sister Francine's place. Sister Jerome only likes running things and bossing people around – not the actual day-to-day work. But between ourselves,' and she lowered her voice, leaning close to me, 'I don't think that Sister Angelique is the right person for the job. She volunteered, I understand, but she's difficult. Moody. Strange. She didn't take to Katy, although I can't think why. Katy was a lovely person.'

'You don't think . . .' I began hesitantly, 'that she maybe took her own life out of despair?'

She looked shocked. 'Take her own life? Katy would never do that. She was a cheerful sort of girl, although . . .' She broke off.

'Although what?'

'She definitely did have something on her mind the day before she died. She was worried about something. I remember now. I asked her what was wrong and she said, "It's nothing. Just something that's bothering me and I'm not sure what to do about it. She never takes them off, you see."'

'Who never takes what off?' I asked.

Blanche shrugged. 'She wouldn't say. She just said,

"Forget about it," and walked off. And then we heard that she'd fallen down the steps that evening. But she would never have taken her own life. Never.'

'I'm sorry,' I said, because I could see she was distressed. 'I should never have brought it up. It was simply a sad and terrible accident.'

'That's right,' she said. 'Poor Katy. Such a waste of a life.'

She was about to lead me out of the closet when I moved closer to her and whispered, 'Sister Jerome told me about another Irish girl called Maureen. I gather she didn't like her much.'

The ghost of a smile crossed Blanche's face. 'She didn't. Maureen stood up to her and she didn't want to give up her baby, so I heard.'

'And Sister already had a good home for it?' I asked.
She nodded.

'But Maureen didn't have any option, did she? I mean she couldn't just go out into the world with no money and a baby to look after?'

'Of course not. That's what Sister told her, but for some reason she wouldn't see sense.'

'So what happened to her?' I asked.

'She ran away and nobody found out until she didn't show up at breakfast.'

'Did you know her?'

She shook her head. 'Not really. She'd already had her baby when I arrived and the new mothers stay in the maternity wing with their babies. But a couple of the girls heard her yelling and shouting at someone. She said awful things, I gather – that she'd rather kill her baby than let it go to those people.'

'But she didn't kill it, did she?' I asked in a horrified whisper.

'Of course not. Sister wouldn't let her see it again. Took it and locked it up in her own room until the new mother could come for it. That's probably why she ran away. She had nothing to stay for.'

'What are you two gossiping about?' came a shrill voice behind us, the accent still with a trace of French to it. We turned guiltily to see another nun standing behind us. She was small, thin, with dark eyes and arched eyebrows that gave her a surprised look. She looked at me with interest.

'This is Molly, a new girl, Sister,' Blanche said.

'Ah, yes.' The nun continued to examine me. 'Sister Jerome informs me of your arrival.' It was hard to tell how old she was. Not that young anyway, with a sallow complexion and a thin line of mouth. 'And were you not showing a bad example to the new girl by gossiping with her during silence hours, Blanche?'

She was glaring at us, those dark eyes boring through us. Blanche gave a little whimper.

'I'm sorry, Sister,' I said. 'My fault. I was asking Blanche about where the laundry was done. And she said it was all right to ask questions about our tasks.'

'Yes, that is correct.' She was still staring at me. I wondered how much she had overheard. We had been talking in low voices, hardly more than whispers, but maybe she had been standing just outside the laundry closet door listening for some time. I felt ridiculously afraid.

'I am Sister Angelique, in charge of you from now on. Go into the bathroom and get yourself changed, Molly,' she said. 'And then I'll have you taken out to the garden. They could use some extra help picking beans. And you,

Blanche – Sister tells me you are to move to the guest room. Are your things already packed to leave?'

'No, Sister. I haven't had time,' she said.

'Time for idle chatter, I notice. Then hurry and do it now and then meet me down at the nun's guest room.'

'Yes, Sister,' she said. She gave me a regretful glance and then scurried back to the dormitory. I prayed that she would remember Patchin Place and turn up on my doorstep in a few days. I didn't think she'd be an ideal servant, but I was going to give her a chance anyway. I went into the bathroom, took off my crumpled muslin, and tucked it into my bag. Then I splashed water over my face and put on the gray dress and blue overgarment. They were made of coarse cloth, heavy and itchy. I wondered if the rest of the nuns wore silk and whether they all enjoyed a good life thanks to the donations Sister Jerome was taking in for them. So much for poverty, chastity, and obedience.

I noticed there was no mirror on the bathroom wall. Clearly vanity was a sin. I ran a brush through my hair, then, on a sudden impulse, I reached into my purse, took out my calling cards and tucked them into the pocket of my dress. I wondered if anything else might give me away. I remembered my wedding ring, and decided to remove that from my purse and hide it likewise in the pocket of my muslin with the calling cards. Luckily I had not brought too much money with me, nor any form of cosmetic that might brand me a hussy. Sister was waiting for me outside the door. I wondered if she might have been spying on me through the keyhole and seen me hide my calling cards. However, she gave no hint of suspicion, but nodded in approval at the uniform. 'Now you look suitable and ready for work,' she said. 'Go and put that bag in the cubby beside your bed and we'll be off.'

I did as she said, feeling awful again that this cubby had been Blanche's until a few minutes ago. I wondered if she'd managed to find all her things, and it occurred to me that perhaps the same thing had happened to Maureen. Had she been told to vacate her bed and had to pack up her possessions so rapidly that some of them got left behind? I realized that I'd probably never know now. I had heard the same story of her quarrel and departure from three people. It had obviously been discussed among the girls so it would have come out if anyone had seen her go. I supposed it all made sense. She had no chance of saving her child and so she had simply slipped out of the place that night. Story solved. I had come all this way and gotten myself into this ridiculous situation for nothing. But then I remembered that Katy had been worried, had had something on her mind, and had ended up falling down the cellar steps.

Chapter 25

Having deposited my bag in the cubby, I followed Sister Angelique down the staircase and through a door at the end of the downstairs hallway. It had been surprisingly cold in that building and the sun on my face felt welcome. We crossed an area of gravel on which lines of laundry hung limply in the hot afternoon sun. On my left a wing jutted out from the square main building and from an open upstairs window came the sound of a baby crying. I looked up at it. Sister Angelique frowned. 'I don't know what they think they are doing, leaving the window open like that. I'll speak to them.'

Beyond the gravel we could hear the sound of voices coming from between the rows of plants in the kitchen garden. They fell silent as we came past a trellis of pole beans and I saw three young women, all heavily pregnant like myself, busy at work picking the beans.

'It seems as if there was more talking than picking going on here,' Sister said, peering down at a half-full basket. 'I hope you will set a good example to our new girl. Her name is Molly and she comes from Ireland.'

They were staring at me with blank, unfriendly faces.

'I thought we had no room for another girl,' one of them said. 'All the beds are full.'

'Blanche will be leaving us in the morning,' Sister said, 'and tonight she has been transferred to the sisters' guest room to prepare herself for going out into the world.'

'Blanche?' A tall, angular girl asked. 'Is she really ready to go then?'

'Blanche needs to pull herself together and get on with life,' Sister said. 'Anyway, this is not for you to query, Peggy. I have made my decision and that is final.'

'Don't we get a chance to say good-bye to her?' a frail-looking, little scrap of a girl asked.

'Better for her if you don't. She would only get emotional again and that is not good for her. Now, back to your work. They are waiting for more produce in the kitchen, and you need to show Molly how things are done.'

'We've almost finished, Sister,' one of the girls said hastily. 'Three buckets full this afternoon. That's good, isn't it?'

'How about the raspberries?' Sister asked. 'Are they all picked?'

'No, Sister. We were going to get to them next,' the same girl said.

'You'll find the birds have eaten them all if you don't get a move on. You, Elaine. Take Molly and make sure those raspberry bushes are stripped by the end of the afternoon. You other two come and help them as soon as the beans are finished. And pick carefully. Don't crush them, you hear?'

'Yes, Sister,' they muttered.

She turned on her heel and stalked off.

'Old cow,' one of the girls muttered.

'Careful, Elaine. She might hear you. You know she's got unnatural powers of hearing.'

A tall, rather striking-looking brunette tossed back her head. 'What do I care? What can she do to us after all? We're only here for a few more weeks. And I'm actually paying for the privilege.'

'You are paying to be here?' I blurted out.

She turned those amused dark eyes on me. 'I was a bad girl,' she said. 'Got rather tipsy at a party and let a boy take a few too many liberties. Unfortunately I'm betrothed to someone else and he wouldn't have taken kindly to walking down the aisle with a girl with a large belly.' She laughed and the others smiled nervously.

'You're still going to marry him?'

'Of course. His family is rich. I'd be a fool if I didn't. However, he's in the Navy and luckily for me his ship is deployed to the Philippines for a year. So he'll return. I'll greet him on the pier and he'll be none the wiser.' She looked at me with a smirk. 'I can tell why a bed suddenly became available, can't you, Aggie?'

'Why?' the frail-looking one asked.

'Because Sister has her redhead at last.'

'Oh, of course.' They were all smirking now.

'What do you mean?' I asked, my face turning red under their scrutiny.

'She's been waiting and waiting for a red-headed baby,' the striking girl called Elaine said. 'You don't see too many of them.'

'What does she want a red-headed baby for?' I asked. Although I knew that I wouldn't be here and that my child would be born within the safety of my own home, I felt a jolt of fear go through me.

The scrap of a girl, Aggie, leaned closer to me. 'She's got a couple waiting for a red-haired baby. And you can bet your life the donation will be most generous.'

'So you'll probably be all right,' Elaine said. 'A fellow Irishwoman and a redhead. She'll probably make sure she takes good care of you.'

'Doesn't she take good care of all the girls?' I asked innocently.

Elaine moved closer. 'She leaves it mostly up to Sister Angelique, and let's just say that one has her favorites and her non-favorites. Me, I'm fine because I am paying to be here and because I could leave whenever I wanted to. But if you cross Sister, or she thinks you will probably have an ugly baby, she can make your life hell.'

'She didn't seem too nice to Blanche,' I said. 'I felt terrible. I certainly didn't want to turn anyone out of her bed for me and I told Sister I could sleep on the sofa in the common room until someone left, but she wouldn't hear of it.'

'It's not your fault,' the tall one said. 'She's been dying to get rid of Blanche since her baby was born dead. Furious with her, she was. We reckon the nuns must have been going to lose out on money that was promised them.'

'I don't know why she stayed so mad,' Aggie said. 'I hear she found herself a pretty, fair baby to take the place of Blanche's.'

'You know Sister,' Elaine said. 'Once she carries a grudge, she's not going to let up on it.'

I was trying to find a way to bring Maureen or Katy into the conversation.

'Come on, back to work, I suppose,' Elaine said, 'Or we'll never hear the last of it.' She picked up a basin and walked ahead of me past the beans and tomatoes to a line of raspberry bushes.

'Elaine,' I whispered, falling into step beside her. 'Are you saying that the nuns make money from our babies?'

'Of course,' she said. 'I'd say Sister has a nice little business going here.'

'But why would people pay for a baby?' I asked. 'Surely they can go to the foundling institutions and find babies aplenty, free for the taking.'

'There are several reasons, I suppose. The prospective parents that these girls have been vetted and don't have any awful diseases, and they can request a particular type of child. Sometimes a couple wants a baby that looks like them – a redhead like yours, for example. Other times they are paying for a baby with no questions asked.'

'What do you mean?'

She looked at my puzzled face and laughed. 'You're rather green behind the ears, aren't you? You know – a society family and the wife is worried that her baby might look like the Spanish gardener and not the fair-skinned husband, for example. Or if a touch of the tarbrush resurfaces after a generation or two.'

'"A touch of the tarbrush"?' I looked confused.

She laughed again. 'My dear, where have you been all your life? There are plenty of families, especially in the South, with Negro ancestry they'd rather forget. And it does resurface at the most inconvenient times.'

'You mean these people trade their own child for one from here?'

'Exactly. And they feel justified in donating to the good sisters, knowing that the truth will never get out.'

We had reached the raspberries. She surveyed them

and shook her head. 'Not much here,' she said. 'I love that talk about their vegetables and fruit having to last the sisters all winter. The ground is so poor here that they never get a decent crop of anything. We're on a rock, you see. The soil is just not deep enough.' She started plucking raspberries and dropping them into the basin. I followed suit.

'Why do they need enough vegetables for the winter if the convent has money coming in from these donations?' I asked.

'Good question. I've had to help prepare the sisters' meals and frankly they don't eat too well – lots of soups and beans and coarse bread. Of course they may like it that way, as a continual penance.' She grinned. 'But the ground is so rocky they can't even dig graves for the nuns to be buried here, because they can't get down far enough in the solid rock.'

'So where are the nuns buried then? I thought I was told they never left this place after they made their profession.' I looked around at the rows of plants and then the small orchard beyond. Someone had been digging up a patch of bare earth over by the orchard. On one side of us was the severe façade of the building with its turrets in the corners and sloping slate roof, and on the other three the high brick wall. I saw no cemetery.

'They aren't,' she said, then laughed when she saw my surprised face. 'There's a crypt under the chapel and the dead nuns are put in big stone coffins down there. Poor old Sister Francine was taken down there only a few weeks ago.'

'I gather she was very kind.'

'And a good midwife too,' Elaine said. 'To be honest

with you, Molly, I'm not looking forward to having this baby with those sisters helping with the delivery. I don't think either of them has much idea what to do. And they are both horribly impatient. If there's an emergency then God help us all.'

'Couldn't you ask to send for a doctor if there was an emergency?' I asked.

'Jerome sent for a doctor with Blanche's baby in the end,' Elaine said, 'but we have no telephone or means of communication with the outside world so sending for a doctor requires somebody to run to the nearest house. By the time he got here it was too late.'

I couldn't take my eyes off that high wall. Now that I was close to it I saw that it was topped with broken glass. I wondered whether this was to keep intruders out or the occupants in.

'So are we ever allowed out to go down to the town or for a walk?' I asked. 'Or do the girls sometimes slip out when Sister isn't looking?'

Elaine laughed. 'Allowed out? Slip out? Honey, we are prisoners here. Haven't you noticed Sister and her keys? We can't even get to the nuns' part of the building.'

'What about the chapel?' I pictured it in my mind's eye, with each half open to the altar. 'All one has to do is go up to the altar and walk around into the nuns' half and leave through their door.'

'I tried that,' Elaine said. 'When they are at one of the services in chapel they lock our door. When they are not they lock their door.'

The tension that had been steadily growing inside me was ready to explode. This charade had gone on long enough. I would go to Sister now and tell her that I had changed my mind and no longer wanted to stay. Blanche could have her bed back and I'd be leaving.

'I need to go and find Sister Jerome,' I said.

'I wouldn't if I were you,' Elaine warned. 'She'd think you were trying to get out of work, and you don't want to annoy her on your first day.'

'But I've changed my mind. I don't want to stay,' I said.

This made Elaine laugh. 'Oh, that's a good one,' she said.

'What do you mean? She can't keep me here against my will.'

'My dear sweet innocent, she wants that red-haired baby. She wants it badly. There is no way she is going to let you go,' Elaine said. She threw another raspberry into the basin, then paused to brush back a wayward curl from her face.

'Surely, if I went to the other nuns and explained to them – Sister Perpetua seemed nice enough. They'd understand, wouldn't they?' As I said this it occurred to me that perhaps they enjoyed their share of the money that Sister Jerome earned for them and they too were looking forward to the money this red-haired baby would bring in.

'You'd never have a chance to speak to them. We're cut off from them; in fact the only time we see them at all is through the screen at morning mass.'

'What about all the other times they go to pray? Don't nuns have services in chapel all the hours of the day and night?'

'They do, but I told you – they lock our door when they are in chapel.'

My indignation was now rising. 'This is ridiculous,' I

said. 'I'm not going to stay against my will. What about those girls who act as porters? They can open the front door. Doesn't she worry about them getting out?'

'You'll soon notice that the only girls selected to be porters are those who really want to be here and have nowhere else to go. Also those who aren't likely to have a beautiful baby.'

I listened to this in stunned silence. It was almost too much to believe. Then I shook my head. 'Very well, if she thinks she can keep me locked away in here, I'll escape. There must be a way to climb out somewhere.' As I said this I looked at the wall with its broken glass on top.

Elaine shook her head. 'In case you haven't tried yet, none of the downstairs windows open and the upstairs windows only open onto this garden. And there is only one door that connects our part of the building to the front part where the nuns live, and that door is always kept locked.' She moved conspiratorially closer, lowering her voice even though we were far enough away from the bean pickers. 'To tell you the truth I've been itching to get out of here myself. Not to run away or anything. I know I've got to see this through if I want to have a chance at a normal life. But just to be part of the outside world for a while – for the hell of it. So now that you're here, we can maybe work on something together. There may be a way to climb over the wall from the roof of the hen house. We'll have to experiment.' She grinned. 'Yes, that sounds like fun. You've cheered me up a lot.'

She hadn't cheered me up at all. I looked across at the chicken run, tucked in the corner against the far wall. It was completely exposed to the convent building with not a single tree or bush in front of it, and what's more,

I couldn't see any way that we could climb up to the roof of the hen house unless we could get our hands on a ladder to use – but if the nuns locked us in so securely, I doubted that they'd be careless enough to leave a ladder lying around. And then there would be the small matter of hauling ourselves over that wall with its broken glass – and lowering ourselves down the other side. I didn't fancy my chances of climbing or dropping down the other side in my current condition.

But one thing was sure. I was leaving this place one way or another. Keep calm and think logically, I told myself. There was no need to panic. I would first ask Sister Jerome if I could leave. She seemed to have taken to me, as a fellow Irishwoman. If she denied my request, I'd have to think again. Then I realized that I did have a way to contact the outside world and let Sid and Gus know about my predicament. Blanche was due to leave in the morning. All I had to do was to find a pen and paper and write a message to them which Blanche could deliver to The Lighthouse Inn or even mail to them. It was at the most only a matter of waiting. Thus relieved, I went back to work.

Chapter 26

I went back to picking raspberries, my hands trembling a little. Now I knew that I had to tread very carefully. From everything I had seen, Sister Jerome was a ruthless and determined woman. I had to make sure that she did not suspect I wasn't who I claimed to be. I had to play the sweet, obedient Irish girl and look for my chances. She had to sleep sometime. Where did she put those keys when she slept? Did she lock her own door at night?

Now that I realized I was probably committed to spending the night here, my thoughts went to Sid and Gus again. They would be so worried about me. I just prayed that they didn't try to send a message to Daniel about me. I'd never hear the last of it if he knew what a stupid thing I'd done. *Hear the last of it.* I toyed with the words. They had such a ring of finality to them. Then I told myself that I was perfectly safe for now. Sister wanted that red-haired child. She would do anything to keep me alive and healthy, at least until my baby was born.

I went back to my raspberry picking until a bell started tolling from the chapel tower.

'What's that for?' I asked.

'It's four o'clock. Time for the nuns to head back to chapel,' Elaine said. 'They have an office every four hours, day and night. You wouldn't catch me wanting to be a nun.' She laughed. 'Not that I have the temperament for it. I enjoy the pleasures of the flesh too much. In fact if Sister only knew how wicked I really am, I'd probably be kicked out tomorrow.'

'So we don't have to stop and pray or anything?' I asked.

'We just keep on working until suppertime at six,' she said. 'Then it's bedtime at eight-thirty, up at six in the morning, breakfast then mass then work. It's like school, isn't it?'

I nodded, distractedly, because something had just struck me. I had my escape route – my way out of here. It was the chapel. All I had to do was to go up to the altar and then cross into the nuns' side of the screen. A priest would be there. He would surely come to my aid if I appealed to him for help. Now I felt a little better. And hungry. I realized I hadn't eaten a proper meal all day. When the bowl of raspberries was full I volunteered to carry it through to the kitchen. The kitchen was a cavernous room with only a high window that showed a square of blue sky. It was like a Turkish bath in there with big pots bubbling away on a woodstove and three girls stirring away at them, looking like the three witches in *Macbeth*.

They looked at me inquiringly as I came in.

'Where did you spring from?' one of them asked.

'I just arrived,' I said. 'I'm Molly. Here are the raspberries Elaine and I picked.'

'And where's Elaine?' the same girl asked with a belligerent tone to her voice.

'Where do you think?' another girl said, chuckling. 'Off lollygagging somewhere to get out of her share of the work. That's what we'd expect from Elaine. Never done a real day's work in her life.'

'Welcome to the female answer to Sing Sing, Molly,' one of the girls said. 'I'm Gerda, this is Alice and Ethel. When is your baby due?'

'Another month,' I said, trying to remember exactly what I had said to Sister Perpetua.

'Same for me,' the skinny, undernourished creature called Alice said. 'Maybe we'll be lying side by side, calling out to the saints to save us.'

'What a charming prospect you paint,' I said and all three girls laughed.

I looked around the kitchen. 'I don't suppose there is any food I could have, is there? I arrived at lunchtime and I haven't eaten a bite all day. I don't think I can hold out until supper.'

Gerda, who seemed to be in charge, pointed at the shelves along one wall. 'There's bread and butter there, and cheese and tomatoes. Help yourself. The one thing they don't stint on here is food. They recognize we're eating for two and they want healthy babies. So we can eat all we want.'

I was already on my way to the bread box and started carving myself a hunk of bread. It was freshly baked and I was positively salivating as I spread thick butter onto it and then a good slice of cheese.

'And Sister likes us to drink plenty of milk,' Gerda said. 'To make sure we've got enough of our own to feed the baby. The milk is kept down in the cellar while the weather is as hot as this. It's nice and cool down there.'

'The cellar?' Images of rats, spiders, and cockroaches jumped into my head, and those broken steps down which Katy had plunged to her death. 'Oh, no thanks,' I said. 'I don't fancy going down to the cellar by myself. Water will do.'

'Oh, it's not bad,' Gerda said. 'Come on. I'll show you where things are kept. You'll have to go down there all the time when you're on kitchen duty.'

She went across the room and into a scullery where clean plates were drying on a rack beside the sink. In one corner a stair led down by the outside wall of the building. I followed her cautiously, then saw that the stair was broad and smooth from continuous wear. What's more, it consisted of six steps, then a little landing, then a ninety-degree turn, and six more down to a narrow room. It also had a good handrail. Surely nobody could have fallen to their death down these stairs?

And when I reached the cellar I saw that it had a high window near the ceiling that let in a shaft of natural light. Gerda went ahead of me, took a dipper from the wall, and ladled milk from a churn into a tin mug. 'Here you go. Get that down you,' she said. 'We also keep the meat, fish, and fruit down here. As you can see it's always cool. Apart from that window it's all underground, sort of cut into the hillside.'

I was staring up at that window. If I piled boxes on the kitchen table it was just possible that I could reach it. However, was it wide enough for me to climb through in my present state? And there didn't appear to be any way to open it – unless I smashed it. I tucked it away as a last chance solution. I drank the milk gratefully, then came up the steps again to the kitchen. After I had eaten heartily of bread and cheese I supposed I should go out to the garden again to do more fruit picking, but it was the first time I'd found myself alone.

As I came out of the kitchen I could hear the sound of chanting coming faintly from the chapel. I went over to try the door for myself. It was indeed locked. I wondered if Sister Jerome was in there with the other nuns. I was sure the door locking must be her idea. I wondered if the other nuns had any idea that she went to such great effort to make sure that none of her charges escaped. But then of course they would all be glad of the money that our babies brought into the convent. They might know everything that was going on with us. If only I could find a chance to talk to one of them. . . .

I walked the length of the downstairs hallway but found no door apart from the one that led through to the chapel and the nuns' part of the building. I went through to the extra wing that contained the laundry room downstairs and the maternity ward upstairs. Again I could hear the pathetic cry of a newborn. I felt a wave of contraction through my own body in reaction and tears came into my eyes. I could feel all too strongly what it would be like to go through the pains of labor, to hold a precious child in my arms, and know that it was about to be taken from me. No wonder Maureen changed her mind.

I have to get out of here now, I thought. The only windows in the laundry room opened onto the garden with its high wall. It seemed my only option was the chapel. If I could find somewhere to hide when the nuns weren't occupying it, then I could slip out while they were concentrating on their office. I hadn't really taken in the details but surely chapels always had side altars and statues and banks of candles – and enough shadow to hide me. If they were currently chanting in there then the next opportunity would be when they returned for the next service at eight o'clock tonight. Elaine had said there was one office every four hours, day and night. Night-time would be a better idea, as I could melt into shadow more easily in a poorly lit building.

As I stood looking out of the laundry room window I noticed a patch of bare earth. It looked as if someone had started to build something – maybe a raised bed for vegetables. *Not deep enough to bury anybody*, Elaine had said. And then suddenly a thought came to me, so awful and violent that I had to grab onto the window ledge to support myself. Another patch of bare earth and the maid Anna saying that Mrs Mainwaring had suddenly taken it into her head to build a summer house. Mrs Mainwaring, usually so cold and withdrawn, who had been quite emotional that Maureen had not returned. I had been blind and naïve about the Mainwarings' baby. Had I been equally blind about what happened to Maureen? What if she had returned to the Mainwarings unexpectedly and tried to take back her baby? And what if the Mainwarings weren't about to give it up and had killed her . . . and buried her on their own property, building a summer house to cover the evidence forever? Now that this thought had entered my head it seemed entirely possible. Perhaps Mrs Mainwaring did meet Maureen when she came to the convent and the almighty row Maureen had was with her former employer. What if Mrs Mainwaring took the baby and Maureen followed, tried to take her child back and . . .

I now had an even stronger reason to get out of here

immediately. I had to tell Daniel right away and let him take it from here.

'You, girl, what are you doing?' asked a voice right behind me. And there was Sister Angelique right behind me. 'I thought I assigned you to garden work.'

'I just brought in a full bowl of raspberries to the kitchen,' I said, 'and I wanted to see if there was a way out to the garden through here. But there wasn't.'

'No, there is only one way out to the garden. You must realize that we are an enclosed order. This convent was created to keep the outside world at bay and to protect ourselves. We are a band of defenseless women, *ma petite*. That's why we take such precautions. And we have to protect our young women from threats. We have had abusive and drunken louts hammering at our doors before now, demanding the return of their womenfolk.'

It was an uncanny feeling, almost as if she could read my mind. Had she spoken with Elaine, I wondered. Did she know that I had been querying being locked in here? I decided I had to act now.

'I'm so glad I've found you, Sister,' I said. 'I'd like to be taken to Sister Jerome, because I've changed my mind. I've decided that I don't want to stay here and give up my child. I'm going to go home to Ireland and ask for my family's forgiveness.'

She put a hand on my shoulder. 'My dear, you are saying the same thing as every girl who comes to this place. It's that moment of panic after they realize what they have committed themselves to do. They know it makes sense to give up their child so that it can have a better life, but they don't think they can go through with it. And this

convent is not the most inviting of settings for those who
have come from a warm and friendly home, is it?'

I nodded. 'I miss my family so terribly,' I said. 'I really
can't stay here. I know you've been so kind to me in allow-
ing me to just come in off the street, but I have to go.
Please let me go.'

'Of course, my dear,' she said. 'We never would dream
of keeping anyone against her will. But don't make a hasty
decision you'll regret one day. There is no future in this
world for an illegitimate child and no hope of his mother
making a good marriage. No man will want you or your
child. You will be outcasts – shunned, scorned. Is that
what you really want for your baby?'

'No, but . . . my young man may still be alive in Panama.
If he hears about his child I know he'll return home and
do the right thing,' I said. 'And if he returns home and
hears that I've given up our child, then he'd never forgive
me.'

I wished I was the kind of woman who could cry at will.
But I couldn't. 'I was too hasty in coming here. It was a
moment of panic and I'm thinking clearly now. This is
not what I want. So if you don't mind, I'll take off this
uniform, pack up my things, and go before it gets dark.'

The bony hand was still on my shoulder. I felt pressure
now, those fingers digging into me. 'All in good time. I
think you should at least stay the night. I will speak with
Sister Jerome about your dilemma and suggest to her that
we discuss it in the common room tonight with the rest
of my sisters. We will pray together and let their wisdom
advise you on what is truly the best path for you and for
your child. We will let the Holy Spirit guide us, don't you
agree?'

I sensed the hand on my shoulder trembling and I found myself wondering if this scene had happened before. Had Maureen come to her in the same way and announced that she was going to leave? And Sister had been reasonable and gentle and holy in trying to persuade her to give up her child as promised. And the moment Maureen came into my mind I realized something – something that should have been so obvious that I wondered why I hadn't seen it before. Sister had said that Maureen ran away during the night, before breakfast. But Elaine, daring, resourceful Elaine who didn't mind breaking rules, had confirmed that there was no way out of here, unless one stole Sister Jerome's keys from her belt. I remembered something else too – something that Blanche had told me. She'd said Katy had been worried about something before she died. Katy had said, 'She never takes them off.' Did she mean those keys that hung from Sister's belt? Had she realized, as I had also now done, that Maureen hadn't gone anywhere, that it was impossible? And had it cost Katy her life? I wanted to escape as urgently as ever, but I made myself a vow. Before I left this place I had to do my best to find out what had become of Maureen.

'Very well, Sister,' I said. 'I'll stay just this one night. But then if I want to go in the morning, you and your sisters will agree that I can leave.'

'Of course,' she said. 'We only want what is best for you, you know. You and the little one inside you.' The hand now slid down from my shoulder and took my arm. 'Come along, let's go and see how those lazy bean pickers have been doing.'

And I was led back outside.

Chapter 27

Now that I realized it was possible that Maureen had never left the convent, I wondered what had become of her. Was she shut away somewhere – a prisoner in the nuns' part of the building? Had she decided to join the order and now lived among the novices, or was it possible that she was no longer alive? If the latter, then who had killed her and where had they hidden her body? In an old building of locked doors like this it wouldn't be hard to find a place to dispose of an unwanted body. I stopped my work as I watched Sister Jerome coming out of the building, her black veil and silk robes flying out in the evening breeze like an avenging angel.

I tried to tell myself that I was again being overdramatic and reading too much into this. Perhaps there was a perfectly logical explanation. After all, if I had come up with possible ways to escape, couldn't Maureen have done the same – she who had been here long enough to know the workings of the convent and the secret places of the building? Also she was no longer pregnant and encumbered, making it easier for her to slither through a window, climb along a ledge, or hoist herself over a wall. Perhaps she had climbed through that open window in the maternity room and managed to work her way around the outside of the building somehow. The stone was certainly rough enough for footholds and there were drainpipes and window ledges to hang onto. I'd have to check that out for myself if I could somehow get into that maternity room.

But there was one small thought that kept creeping back into my mind. If Maureen had managed to escape then what was Katy so worried about? And how could she have fallen to her death down those shallow, safe cellar steps?

I went back to harvesting crops with Elaine. It crossed my mind that Elaine might be the kind of person who was Sister Angelique's informant. She wasn't well liked by the others and Sister had certainly said some things to me that made me think she knew what had worried me. We filled the final basket of beans and carried it into the kitchen. New smells were now coming from the stove – onions frying and potatoes bubbling away. Dinner was being prepared. My next task was to write a letter to Sid and Gus and get it to Blanche without letting it fall into Sister's hands. I could hardly ask her for paper and envelope since I had declared my intention of leaving in the morning.

'Is there anywhere we can find paper and envelopes to write a letter?' I asked Elaine.

'Sister Jerome has some in her office,' Elaine said.

'I don't really want to ask her,' I said.

'I suppose I could let you have a sheet of mine. It's in my cubby beside my bed – the one by the door,' she said.

'Thank you.' I beamed at her. 'And do you happen to have a pencil or something to write with?'

'I've my fountain pen,' she said. 'Only be careful with it.'

'A fountain pen! My word.' Fountain pens were a luxury I could never dream of affording.

'Given to me for my twenty-first birthday last year by my father,' she said.

'What a kind father you have.'

'Not really,' she said. 'He always does the right thing – like giving generous presents for birthdays, but otherwise showed no interest in me whatsoever. I wasn't a son, you see. He made it clear he was disappointed in me. That's why a good marriage is so important.'

'Does he know about the baby?'

She gave a bitter laugh. 'Of course not. None of them do. They think I'm off visiting friends out West. What's more they will never know. I'm making my donation to the sisters out of a small legacy on my twenty-first.'

As I went up to find the writing paper it struck me how many secrets Sister Jerome knew and what a perfect opportunity she had for blackmail. I found Elaine's cubby, stuffed with sundry little luxuries from eau de cologne to lace-trimmed handkerchiefs, and located the paper and the wonderful fountain pen. I sat on my own bed and wrote the note – short and to the point.

Trapped in convent. Come and get me out. Demand to see Sister Perpetua, not Sister Jerome. Tell her the truth – I'm not Molly, the deserted Irish girl.

I sealed the envelope, addressed it, and tucked it away into the pocket of my dress. Now I had to find a way to get it to Blanche. That way came just before dinner. I came downstairs in time to hear Sister Angelique saying, 'Aggie, I suppose you'd better take some food through to Blanche. She's spending the night in the nuns' guest room. You've been the porter. You know where that is, don't you?'

'Yes, Sister,' Aggie said.

'Could I go with Aggie?' I asked. 'I'd really like to apologize to Blanche one more time about taking her bed and to wish her well.'

'Not necessary,' Sister said. 'You were in no way to blame for turning her out of her bed. It was high time she left. She knew that as well as anybody.'

'Oh, but I'd like to bid her farewell.'

'Molly, Blanche is a highly emotional young woman. We don't want to set her off crying again, do we? Go and fix her a tray, Aggie.'

I was not going to be allowed to join her, whatever I said. I waited until Sister moved away and then I wandered through into the kitchen. Aggie was ladling potatoes onto a plate. I crept up beside her. 'Aggie,' I whispered. 'I have to get a note out to friends. It's really important. Can you give it to Blanche to post for me?'

'Put it on the tray, under the plate,' she said. I put down the letter and the plate came down on it in an instant. She picked up the tray and set off with it. I heaved a sigh of relief. In the hallway a bell rang and we were summoned to supper. The sisters came in to join us, standing at the head of the table. We said grace and then we sat down. Plates of food were carried in – liver and onions, beans and potatoes. Not bad at all. I glanced at the head of the table and saw that Sister Jerome had a large pork chop instead of our liver. What's more, she was tucking into it with relish, smacking her lips as she ate.

I had barely taken two bites when I heard the sound of running feet and a horrible wail echoing down the hallway. Aggie burst into the dining room.

'Sister, come quickly,' she shouted. 'It's Blanche. She's hanged herself.'

Sister Jerome jumped up. 'Sister, come with me,' she said. 'You girls stay where you are. Get on with your meal.'

Aggie was as white as a sheet, her hand over her mouth, and breathing heavily. Other girls helped her to sit down and poured her a mug of milk.

'It was awful,' she gasped at last. 'I'll never get that picture out of my mind. Never. I went in and there she was – hanging from a stone buttress on the wall. All blue her face was and her tongue all swollen and sticking out. Horrible.'

And she started to sob. Arms came around her. She sat there with her head in her hands, her whole body heaving.

'I can't say I'm surprised, can you?' Elaine said.

'Sister was wrong to make her leave before she was ready,' one of the other girls muttered. 'Anyone could tell she wasn't strong enough to face the outside world alone.'

I felt sick. I could sense the other girls staring at me and I knew what they were thinking. I told myself I had not forced Blanche to leave, but it was my coming that had precipitated things. So I couldn't help feeling responsible. I also realized something else. Aggie had come back without Blanche's tray.

'What happened to the tray you took?' I asked.

'I think I just dropped it. I was so shocked. There's probably food everywhere and I'll get into trouble.'

'No you won't,' Elaine said. 'Of course you were shocked. Anyone would be.'

So my letter to Sid and Gus was somewhere on the floor of that room with the spilled food. It would be only a matter of time before it was found and then Sister would know the truth about me. I didn't have time to wait for rescue by Sid and Gus, or to find out about Maureen. I had to save myself somehow tonight.

'Do you think someone ought to go and clean up that tray?' I asked.

'I'm not going back in there,' Aggie said.

'I think we all ought to stay well away,' Gerda said. 'They won't want us getting under their feet and spilled food is the least of their worries.'

I just prayed that a letter hidden under liver and gravy would be the least of their worries enough to be overlooked until morning.

Nobody felt much like eating. I managed a couple of spoonfuls of rice pudding because that slipped down easily, but most of the food went back to the kitchen. The kitchen crew did the washing up and the rest of us went through to the common room. But nobody felt like talking either. It was growing dark in the room. A lamp had been lit and a couple of girls sat beside it, working at their sewing, one darning stockings, one mending sheets. One other was knitting a baby jacket. I had no work to do and perched on a hard chair, feeling awkward, wondering if there was any way I could get to the room where Blanche killed herself and retrieve that letter. They would have to summon a doctor to certify her death. And maybe a policeman too. The other sisters would have been called in. Would this be my chance to get out? It didn't seem right that I should use poor Blanche's death for my own advantage, but I worried what would happen if Sister read that letter and found out that I wasn't who I claimed to be.

I left the other girls to their sewing and walked quietly down the hall toward the one door that led through to the other half of the convent. That door wouldn't open. Even in her haste, Sister had remembered to lock it. It was almost dark now in that windowless stairwell. A little light came down the stairs from above, enough for me to make out the shapes of the various doors. I went across the hallway and pushed open the chapel door. It swung open easily and I stepped into dark silence, breathing in the sweet incense smell. The chapel had been gloomy even in full daylight. Now that the sun had set, it had faded into darkness. My heart was beating fast as I felt my way past the rows of pews, up to the altar steps then crossed to the nun's portion of the chapel. I realized I hadn't retrieved my things from the bedroom. But there was nothing of great value among them apart from my wedding ring and I wasn't going to turn down a chance at freedom.

My eyes had now accustomed themselves to the fading light. I walked past the prie-dieux with their kneelers until I reached the door in the back wall. It was locked. It wouldn't be opened again until the next office at eight o'clock, which must be quite soon now. If I could find somewhere to hide until then, I could wait until all the nuns were at prayer and slip out behind them. I looked for a place to hide. Day was fast dying now and in the gloom the chapel became a frightening place. Statues loomed out at me from their niches and I realized something unnerving – there was no form of proper lighting in this chapel – no electric light or even a gas bracket. There were occasional sconces for candles along the walls, and of course there were candlesticks on the high altar but I had nothing to light candles with.

I could not bring myself to stay here alone in darkness. Call me a coward, but I've always been afraid of the dark. I suppose it was the Irish upbringing with all our tales of ghosts and ghoulies and things that go bump in the night. During my life in New York I hadn't really had to face this fear, with well-lit streets and electric lights. But in a place like this – a place of such tension and secrets, where girls had died – it resurfaced with a vengeance. I could feel panic gripping at my throat, making it impossible to breathe. As I stood there I felt a cold draft creeping around my legs and feet and it seemed as if I could hear someone breathing. The wind had picked up and was rattling at the tall windows, scratching at them like bony fingers, and through the sigh of the wind I thought I could hear voices – one voice maybe, whispering, 'Come and find me, Molly. Come and find me.'

I didn't wait a second longer. I stumbled my way back to the altar steps then all the way to the back of my side of the chapel. For a horrible moment my fingers touched rough stone wall where I thought the door should be. I felt my way around until finally I made out the doorframe and pushed open that door. I came bursting out to relative safety, still breathing hard. Then I hurried back to the other girls. Safety in numbers, I muttered to myself.

Of course, once I was back in a place of light and company I felt ashamed of my moment of panic. If I had only held my ground, I might have found a hiding place and been out of that door within the next hour. I reasoned with myself that it would be more sensible to plan my escape for the eight o'clock mass in the morning, when girls and nuns were in the chapel at the same time. When a priest was here – an outsider who would surely help me. I would rise early and find my hiding place, and if I couldn't find one, then I'd be ready to go up to the priest the moment mass had finished and beg for his help.

I realized too that I probably only had one chance. If that failed, Sister Jerome would take stronger measures to keep me here.

Chapter 28

No sooner had I returned to the other girls than the bell began to toll. Those girls who had been sewing and knitting put down their work, the lamp was extinguished, two candles were lit, and we followed the candlelight upstairs to the dormitory.

'I know I'll never be able to sleep,' Aggie said, sinking down onto the bed next to mine.

I nodded sympathetically. 'It must have been awful for you. I feel so badly. I didn't want Sister to make Blanche leave, but she wouldn't listen to me.'

'Of course not. She wanted Blanche out and nothing was going to change that.' She pulled off her uniform dress and knelt beside her bed to say her prayers. I was touched by her innocence and found myself wishing that my religion still meant something to me and that I could pray like that. I had plenty I wanted to pray for tonight, the most pressing item being that I'd be able to go back to my real life, my friends, and my husband, in the morning. That my baby and I would be safe. I too undressed and lay in bed, feeling the coarse roughness of the nightgown against my skin and breathing in the unfamiliar smell of damp and mold, mingled with a tinge of carbolic soap from the laundry and just a hint of antiseptic.

One of the girls went over and blew out the candles, plunging us into complete darkness. Used to a place of streetlamps and city noise that never died down completely, the silence and darkness were overwhelming.

Daniel, I wish you were here, I thought. *I wish you'd come and take me home. I wouldn't care how much you shouted at me for my stupidity. Because I have been stupid, and proud and overconfident in my abilities. As usual, I haven't thought things through to see what might go wrong. And I promise I'll never do it again if only I get out of here safely.*

One by one the other girls fell asleep and I lay there listening to their heavy rhythmic breathing. From outside came the hoot of an owl. Images danced in front of my eyes in the darkness. And that whispered voice in the chapel, *Come and find me.* Was that my heightened imagination or had I really heard something? How could I hope to find Maureen if I was locked away here, I thought. And my first task is to save myself and my baby. I can't risk lingering any longer to see what might have happened to her. If she is among the novices, I'll spot her during mass in the morning. If not, then I'll have to admit that I've failed and she will never be found.

I suppose I must have been drifting off to sleep when I was awoken by a bloodcurdling scream. I sat bolt upright. Moonlight was coming in through that high window and I could see Aggie standing beside her bed, doubled over, clutching her stomach and screaming. On the floor at her feet I could make out a dark puddle.

'I'm dying!' she screamed.

Other girls were sitting up now. 'She's gone into labor. Get Sister,' one of them said. 'You're not dying, Aggie. Stop making a fuss. It's only labor pains.'

'I'll get Sister,' I said. My fingers trembled as I tried to light the candle. I felt my way along the hall, down the stairs. I knew which door belonged to Sister Jerome and I hammered on it now. It opened with great force and Sister herself stood there, dressed in a voluminous nightdress and a white cap on her head. 'What is it?' she demanded.

'It's Aggie. She's gone into labor, I think. She says she's dying.'

'Stupid girl. Always inconsiderate, going into labor in the middle of the night,' she snapped. 'Hold that candle up so I can see.'

She took her habit from a hook on her wall, pulled it over her head, then tied her belt with the keys on it. Lastly she draped the veil over her head. 'The wimple will have to wait,' she said, as she stepped into carpet slippers.

'Do you want me to wake Sister Angelique?' I asked.

'She sleeps in her cell with the other sisters,' she said. 'I'll go and wake her after I see what's happening with Aggie.' She slammed her door behind her and took the stairs at a great pace. I tried to keep up without letting the candle be blown out.

'Stop this nonsense at once, Aggie,' I heard her say as she came into the dormitory.

'But I'm dying,' the girl gasped. 'Look, there's blood all over the floor.'

'That's not blood. Your water broke, silly girl. Quite natural. Come on, let's get you across to maternity.'

'I'll help if you like,' I said.

'You can stay and clean up that mess on the floor,' Sister said. 'Gerda. You help me bring her across.'

I went downstairs to get a bucket and mop from the scullery, but I'd only gone halfway along the downstairs hall when something struck me. Sister hadn't locked her door behind her. And she'd be safely over in the maternity ward for a while yet. It was a chance I couldn't resist. I tiptoed back along the hall to Sister's room and turned the door handle. The door swung open and I stepped inside, closing it quickly behind me. In the candlelight there was nothing outstanding about the room. Exactly what I would have expected from a nun's quarters, in fact. Simple in the extreme. Narrow bed, chest, and wardrobe. No sign of decoration on the walls, only the obligatory crucifix. There was a desk in the corner. I went to that and opened the drawers. Nothing incriminating that I could see.

I opened the top drawer of her chest, feeling most uncomfortable at this prying, and saw only neatly folded black lisle stockings and undergarments. The other drawers contained nothing of interest. However, in the drawer of her bedside table I found a surprise. Among the rosaries, prayer book, and holy cards was a pretty little enamel brooch-watch and some good pieces of jewelry. Surely nuns weren't allowed to wear jewelry? Where did she acquire it, and did she ever wear it under her habit?

Then I saw something that made me pause. A pretty little statue of Our Lady, hand carved in wood. I knew with absolute certainty that it was Maureen's statue. Katy had said she found it in a wastebasket, so Sister must have taken it from Katy's things, unless Katy had handed it over. Why was Sister keeping it? Just because she liked the look of it? Or because she didn't want anyone else to see it? I closed the drawer quietly and went over to the wardrobe. An ordinary, coarsely woven habit hung there, plus a dressing gown. Again nothing unusual. Then on the top shelf I noticed an attaché case. I brought it down carefully, put it on the bed, and opened it. It was full of papers. They seemed to be letters. I held the first one up to the candlelight and read.

Again my wife and I wish to express our deepest thanks for our lovely baby girl. She is all we ever dreamed of and more. As agreed, I am enclosing a check for a thousand dollars . . .

I put the letter down. Elaine had mentioned generous donations, but I had thought in terms of one hundred dollars at the most. A thousand dollars was a fortune. The convent could run happily on it for years. They could afford to install electricity, proper heating, to repair the crumbling outside of the building. I went through other letters, all promising large sums and expressing satisfaction with the baby they had received. This was a veritable business, and a very prosperous one. At the bottom of the case I came to an oilskin pouch. I opened the clasp and gasped. It was full of money – a lot of money, possibly thousands of dollars. And I knew right away that the money donated to the convent was never seen by the other nuns. Sister Jerome was keeping it for herself, for reasons I couldn't fathom.

I stood with the envelope in my hands, wondering what to do next. Should I report what I had seen to the police? Then I reasoned that she hadn't committed a crime. Those babies had been legally obtained and the couples had paid up willingly. Her only crime was a moral one – exploiting desperate girls for her own ends. And cheating her sisters out of money they could certainly use. And it struck me that Maureen might have posed a threat greater than just wanting to reclaim her own child. Perhaps Maureen had figured out Sister's neat little business and had threatened to go to Mother if she didn't get her child back. And had possibly made a fatal mistake in doing so.

I had sensed that Sister was a ruthless woman, but it was only now that I appreciated the real extent of the danger I was in. I was safe as long as I behaved like an obedient Irish peasant girl who was about to deliver a red-haired baby. But if Sister had stumbled upon that letter to Sid and Gus by now, and had worked out that I was here undercover, spying on her, then my life wasn't worth a fig. I was suddenly alert and afraid, imagining Sister standing on the other side of that door at this moment, observing everything I had done, and then quietly entering the room to silence me . . .

I stuffed the envelope back into the attaché case, put the letters back on top of it, and returned it to the top shelf before I half tumbled out of the room, almost knocking over the candle in my haste. The downstairs hall was dark and silent. I remembered the bucket and mop, found them and cleaned up the floor as instructed. The other girls had either gone to sleep or were feigning it. As I mopped I could hear screams coming from the other wing. A new fear added itself to the others: I had always known that childbirth was an uncomfortable business. My own three brothers had been born at home and I remember my mother moaning and invoking the saints, but it hadn't seemed too terrifying. But in this place Blanche had experienced complications that led to a dead baby and now Aggie was still screaming. Was this what I had to look forward to in two months' time? My hand went to my belly and I felt the reassuring little flutter of a kick against my fingers.

I emptied the bucket down the WC, cleaned the mop, and left them to be taken down in the morning. I'd had my fill of dark, empty hallways and I needed the safety of my sleeping companions. But I could not sleep. I lay still, hands on my belly, hearing an occasional scream in the distance. At least she was still alive, I thought. The night went on, interminably. I heard the convent bell tolling out midnight and then four o'clock. Soon it would be light. Soon I would be able to check out the chapel for a place to hide.

I must have drifted into exhausted sleep because I woke to find sunlight streaming in and birds chirping on the roof. I scrambled to my feet. It must be still early as my companions were still asleep. I could hear no more screams coming from the maternity wing and wondered if Aggie had had her baby and whether they both survived the ordeal. I got out of bed, making no sound, and crept down to the chapel. The door opened and I stepped inside, feeling the cold stone of the floor on my bare feet. I went around to the nuns' sanctuary and started to look for a hiding place. There were a couple of statues but both were in niches with no place big enough to hide a person. It seemed impossible. I'd just have to come forward to intercept the priest when he finished mass.

Then I came up with a brilliant idea. I'd ask him to hear my confession. No priest could ever refuse that, and no sister could condemn it or even try to stop it. I felt a huge wave of relief flood over me. I could go back to breakfast, act as if nothing was amiss, and bide my time until mass.

As I was about to leave the chapel I noticed something I hadn't seen in the darkness. A black hole in the floor in the furthest corner. I went over to it and saw a flight of steep narrow steps going down into darkness. Then I remembered what Elaine had said: the nuns were not buried because the ground was all rock. They were laid to rest in big stone coffins in the chapel crypt. I started down the stairs, holding onto the wall on one side to steady myself. And it came to me that Katy hadn't fallen down the cellar steps at all. These were the steps down which she had tumbled to her death, because she had come to suspect what really happened to Maureen and had gone to find out for herself.

A glimmer of light shone in through a small high window like the one in the cellar. It was not enough light to show clearly what lay below. Instead it hinted at large rectangular shapes lying on the floor, looking almost like giant sleeping animals. I stood, halfway down the stair, as I realized these were the stone coffins in which the nuns were buried, one still standing in the center of the floor with wilted flowers on it. And I knew what Katy had come to check for herself. She had suspected that Maureen had been hidden down here and I thought I knew where. Sister Francine had died at about the time Maureen had vanished. It was all too possible that Maureen was lying in Sister Francine's coffin, placed in there, covered in a sheet, before the stone lid was put on.

A draft of cold air swirled around me. I didn't wait a second longer. I needed to get back to the safety of the dormitory. As I came back up the stairs I found the light ahead of me blocked by a great black shape. A nun stood at the top of the steps, staring down at me impassively.

Chapter 29

'And what were you doing where you'd no business to be?'
Sister Jerome asked me. 'I came into chapel to pray.' I tried
to keep my voice natural and calm. 'I thought I heard a
noise. An animal whimpering. So I came to investigate.'

'And did you find an animal whimpering?' she asked.

'I was too scared to go any further,' I said.

'Very wise of you. You never know what you'll find in
old buildings like this,' she said, 'and the stairs in poor
repair too. You wouldn't want to slip, in your condition.'

'Certainly not,' I said. I started up the steps toward her.
She hadn't found me out. She was going to let me go. Or
she wanted my baby so badly that she was prepared to
keep me alive for now.

I reached the top step. She still loomed over me – tall,
black, threatening.

'Now would you mind telling me exactly what you are
doing here?' she asked. Her voice still sounded calm and
pleasant enough. But she was still blocking my path.

'What do you mean? You know why I'm here.'

'It really is true about the Irish and their blarney, isn't

it,' she said. 'I never forget a voice. I didn't get a good look at you through the grille when you came asking about Maureen, but I remembered your voice. You've been putting on the Irish accent good and strong with me, but when you were chatting with the other girls you let it slip and there was something about the way you expressed yourself that brought back where I'd seen you before. And Sister Angelique said you were asking the girls questions about Maureen and about Katy. At first I wondered why, and then I realized it wasn't the first time you'd been here snooping around. So out with it – who sent you here?'

I hesitated, unsure what to say. If I still professed my innocence, that nobody sent me, then she would know that nobody knew where I was. But if I told her that I'd been sent by the police, that they were told to come to my aid this morning if I didn't appear, would that guarantee my safety?

'Nobody sent me,' I said in such a manner that it could have implied the opposite.

'And what are you trying to find down in our crypt? There are nothing but bodies down there, you know. Bones and bodies.'

'I know what you've hidden down there,' I said, staring at her defiantly even though I was still two steps below her.

'How can you know?' she asked scathingly. 'You're not strong enough to shift that coffin lid by yourself.'

'What coffin lid would that be?' I asked.

She glared that I'd caught her out. 'Think you're so clever, do you?'

Emboldened now, I went on, 'You must have had an

accomplice yourself, Sister. If I'm not strong enough to move the lid, then neither are you.'

I saw a scornful smirk twitch at her lips. 'It was no problem at all, my dear. The coffin was open from Sister Francine's viewing. I came down to make everything ready to close the coffin and found that stupid girl, trying to hide down here. She shoved me aside and tried to run up the steps. I caught her pinafore and jerked her back. She fell and hit her head. I finished her off and laid her in the coffin. Francine was only a small person. Plenty of room for two.'

I shuddered at the matter-of-fact way she was telling me this, almost as if it was a good joke she was sharing.

'But someone must have seen when they came to close the lid.'

Again the smirk. 'I covered the body, and my sisters and I shut the lid together. They rely on me for everything.'

As she talked I had come slowly up the rest of the stairs until I was at her level.

'You made a big mistake in coming here,' she said. 'In putting your nose where it's not wanted. I'm not letting anyone stand in my way.' Without warning she lunged at me, trying to give me an almighty push. I had been expecting something of the kind. As she came at me I threw myself to one side, bracing myself against the rough stone of the wall. She grabbed at my nightgown. For a second I felt myself pulled downward with her. With all my strength I leaned back and sat down heavily on the stone step. Her fingers slipped from the fabric and she plunged down the steps, hitting the stone floor with a sickening thud that echoed around the vaulted ceiling of that crypt.

* * *

For a long moment I stood at the top of the stairs, not moving, not daring to breathe. I could just make out the black shape of her body, sprawled on the floor below. My first instinct was for self-preservation. I told myself I should go back to my bed as quickly as possible and pretend to be asleep. Then when her body was discovered, I could profess surprise and shock like everyone else. But somehow I couldn't just leave her there.

I could go down to her and get her keys, a voice now whispered in my head. I could let myself out of the building and nobody would be the wiser, except that I would now be incriminating myself if the police were called in and the other girls described the red-haired Irishwoman who vanished in the night. Also I had left my dress, with my calling cards hidden inside the pocket, in the cubby beside my bed. I peered down at the body again. She hadn't moved, but there was a chance she could still be alive.

My Catholic heritage came surging to the fore. I knew then that I couldn't leave her to die without the last rites. Not that I thought she'd be all that ready to confess her sins, but I had to give her a chance to do so. The priest would be here soon. I turned and ran back the way I had come, out of the chapel, along the hallway, and up the stairs. 'Come quickly,' I shouted. 'Sister Jerome has fallen down the chapel steps.'

Several of the girls were on their feet in an instant, running ahead of me to the chapel. Gerda, always the leader, went down the steps first.

'She must have tried to go down the steps while it was still dark,' she said. I noticed that nobody had asked me what I was doing in the chapel alone at this hour or what I was doing down in the crypt myself. She reached Sister's body first and knelt down beside it while I loitered at the top of the steps, unwilling to come any closer.

'Is she dead?' I asked. My tongue didn't want to obey me.

Gerda put her face close to Sister's. Then she scrambled to her feet again.

'We've got to get help. She's still breathing,' she said. She made her way back up the steps to the rest of us then led us to the nuns' entrance.

'It's locked, of course,' she complained. 'Somebody get Sister's keys.'

'Not me,' the skinny Ethel said. 'I'm not going down there for all the tea in China.'

'Oh, very well.' Gerda marched over and went down the steps again, coming up with Sister's bunch of keys in her hand. She tried one key after another in frustration until a voice behind us demanded.

'You girls – where do you think you are going? And in your night attire too.'

We spun around guiltily to see Sister Angelique standing behind us. She was staring in horror and disbelief at us and it came to me that maybe they were in the money-making scheme together and we were somehow in danger.

'Return to your dormitory immediately,' she said. 'I shall report this to Sister Jerome.'

'Sister Jerome fell down the steps of the crypt,' Gerda said. 'We were trying to get help.'

'Sister Jerome? *Mon dieu.*' She ran over to the steps, disappeared into darkness then reappeared again. 'We

must summon a doctor immediately. She is badly hurt,'
she said. She took keys from her own belt and opened
the door. Then she scurried across to the far wall of the
tower and began to tug on a rope that hung there. Far
above us in the tower the bell began to toll. The result
was immediate. I heard doors opening and closing on the
floor above, the sound of feet tapping along the corridor
and then down the stairs. Nuns came toward us, looking
with amazement to see us standing huddled together in
their hallway.

'Sister Jerome has fallen,' Sister Angelique gestured
toward the chapel. 'In the crypt.'

'Is she badly hurt?' Sister Perpetua pushed through the
crowd.

'She may be dead by now,' Gerda said. 'She wasn't
moving.'

Sister Pepetua took immediate control. 'You, Angelique,
go and fetch Mother. Help her to come down. Gerda, go
and get dressed, then wait for Father Bernard. When he
comes, take his pony and trap and go for the doctor. You
know where he lives, don't you?'

'Yes, Sister.' Gerda ran off, back through the chapel.

The rest of us made our way down the steps behind the
nuns. 'Help me to turn her over. Gently now. We don't
want to do more damage,' Sister Perpetua said, kneeling
beside Sister Jerome's lifeless body.

I watched in horrified fascination as they turned Sister
Jerome over onto her back. Her face was a bloody mess,
hardly recognizable as a face at all. The nuns and several
of the girls crossed themselves. I heard a whimper from
the back of the crowd.

Sister Perpetua put her own face close to Jerome's

battered one. 'Sister, can you hear me? The priest will be here in a few minutes. Don't go before you've had the last rites.'

Sister Jerome's eyes opened, the left one half-swollen shut and bloody. Her eyes searched the group and fastened on me. 'That girl,' she said in a croaking voice as she raised a hand to point at me. 'She tried to kill me. She pushed me down the stairs. She's mad. She needs putting away, locking up.'

They turned to look at me. 'Not true!' I shouted and my voice echoed from the vaulted ceiling. 'It was Sister Jerome who tried to kill me, the way she killed Katy. She came at me and tried to push me down the steps. But I managed to keep my balance and she went flying down the stairs instead of me.'

'Katy fell. I was nowhere near,' Sister Jerome said, gasping out the words in a rasping whisper. 'You see, she's mad. Quite mad. I don't know what I was thinking when I let her in here.'

'Yes you do,' I said. 'You wanted to make money from a red-haired baby, just like you've been making money from all those other babies you've sold.' I turned to the girl next to me. 'Take the keys and go to Sister's room. In the wardrobe on the top shelf you'll find an attaché case. Bring it here. Quickly.'

I looked back at the others. 'I'll show you proof of what Sister Jerome has been getting up to behind your backs.'

One of the young nuns had returned with water and was sponging Sister's face. Her breath was now ragged.

'Mad and dangerous. Lock her away before she hurts someone else,' she gasped.

I could sense hands waiting to grab me. The girl came

running back with the attaché case. 'Open it,' I said. I took out the oilskin pouch. 'Look at this. It's full of money.'

'Of course it is, foolish child,' Sister said with surprising force. 'I'm the convent banker. We've been saving up for a new roof. We almost have enough, thanks to my business acumen.'

'Do your sisters know how you've been amassing this money?' I asked. 'That you've essentially been selling babies?' I looked up at faces staring at me with puzzled fascination. 'Maureen O'Byrne threatened to let out your secret, didn't she? Unless you let her keep her child.'

'Maureen O'Byrne?' Sister Perpetua asked. 'What has she to do with this?'

'Do you want to tell her, Sister?' I asked, staring down at Sister Jerome.

'I don't know what she's talking about. Mad.' The voice was little more than a whisper now.

'Take the lid off Sister Francine's coffin,' I said, 'and I'll show you what Sister Jerome is capable of.'

'Open Sister's coffin?' one of the nuns said. 'The girl really is mad.'

'Do as she says,' Sister Perpetua said quietly.

'But she's not been dead long. Think of the stench.'

'See if we're strong enough to move the lid,' one of the younger sisters said, going across to the nearest stone coffin. 'Come on, help me.'

Several girls and sisters pushed and strained together at the big sarcophagus, grunting with the effort. There was a grinding sound as stone moved against stone, then one of them exclaimed, 'Holy Mother of God!' They backed away hastily as we all recoiled at the smell. Hands were pressed against noses. There was the sound of retching.

Some girls went hastily back up the steps. I took a deep breath and went over to the coffin.

They had only succeeded in moving the lid several inches. With much trepidation and not at all sure what I would find, I reached my hand in, touched something soft, and pulled out a long strand of red-blond hair.

'I don't think Sister Francine had hair like this, did she?' I asked.

Nuns crossed themselves.

'Who is it?' one of them asked.

'It's Maureen O'Byrne,' I said. 'She didn't run away after all. She must have figured out what Sister Jerome had been doing and threatened to expose her if Sister didn't let her keep her child.'

There was a collective gasp. Sisters and girls alike turned back to stare at Sister Jerome.

'You stupid girl.' She spat the words. 'I was doing it for you.'

I stared down at her, feeling a mixture of pity and revulsion. 'For me? How were you doing this for me? You'd never met me until yesterday.'

'For the cause, the Irish cause,' she said, speaking the words slowly now as if it hurt her to breathe. 'The money was going to the Republican Brotherhood. To Irish freedom. And now you've ruined everything.'

'Stand aside, please. Here's Mother now,' said a strong voice. The crowd parted and at the top of the stairs stood an old, hunched, and wizened woman in a nun's habit, supported by a younger nun. Beside her was a young priest.

'Help me down the steps,' she said, and she came down, with the priest supporting one arm, the sister the other.

She stood over Sister Jerome. 'Jerome, what is this? What have you done?' she asked. She smelled the stench and her gaze went to the half-open coffin. 'And who has desecrated Sister Francine's resting place?'

'It's Maureen O'Byrne, Mother,' Sister Perpetua said. 'Maureen O'Byrne's body has been hidden in Francine's tomb.'

'Who did this terrible thing?' Mother asked.

'Sister Jerome.' I could hardly get the words out. 'And she killed Katy too. Pushed her down these very stairs.'

The old woman looked at me with surprise and interest, not knowing who I was. 'She tried to kill me,' I added. 'But she misjudged and fell down the steps herself.'

The old woman shook her head sadly. 'Oh, my dear Jerome. I warned you, didn't I? I saw the signs – the secrecy, the way you tried to distance yourself from us. I feared that you would betray all that the order stands for. The sin of pride, my daughter. You had too much pride. Make amends for that now. Repent before you go to your maker. Father Bernard will hear your confession.'

'I don't wish to confess,' Sister Jerome said. 'I have suffered my own hell for twenty years. I never wanted to be here. I never truly believed. I have been locked away, deprived of a normal life. It is you who should be begging my forgiveness.'

Father Bernard knelt down beside her. 'I beg you to reconsider, Sister,' he said. 'You cannot go to your maker with these terrible sins on your conscience.'

'I have no conscience,' she said. 'And I am not sorry for anything. Go away. I wish to die alone.'

'You should all leave now,' Mother said. 'Father Bernard

and I will stay at her side until it is time for mass. Bring the doctor down to us as soon as he gets here.'

'Mass, Mother?' one of the girls said. 'Surely we won't be having mass now?'

'Nothing will ever stand in the way of the order of this house,' Mother said firmly. 'Our primary purpose is worship and prayer. We will prepare ourselves to pray for Sister Jerome's soul, even if she will not.'

'There is no point in bringing a doctor,' Sister Jerome said. 'My body is broken.'

As we started to walk away she said to no one in particular, 'Such a waste. I could have done so much more. Somebody tell my sister, but not my parents. They don't deserve to know.'

'Should we perhaps call the police, Mother?' one of the nuns asked.

'Not yet, Sister,' the old nun replied in a low whisper and she glanced over at Sister Jerome who was now lying there with her eyes closed.

I understood her wisdom. She wanted to make sure that Sister Jerome died in peace. She wanted to protect the convent from outsiders. I joined the others going back up the stairs and I didn't look back at the woman who had tried to kill me.

We walked back to our dormitory in silence, took our day clothes from the pegs on the wall and began to dress, all too stunned to talk. A head reared up from the end bed. 'Is it time for breakfast yet? I'm starving.' Elaine asked drowsily.

'Yes, who is on breakfast duty?' someone else joined in. 'Come on, hurry up. We want something to eat before mass.'

'What was all the fuss about?' Elaine asked. 'Where did everyone go running off to?'

'Sister Jerome. She fell down the steps to the crypt. And it turned out she killed Maureen and Katy.'

'That's what you thought all along, wasn't it, Molly?' Elaine asked. 'That's why you came here.'

I looked at her with surprise. 'All those questions,' she said. 'Frankly I'd wondered myself, but I thought it wiser to stay silent. Has someone called the police in?'

'Sister Jerome is dying,' someone said quietly. 'I think Mother's going to let her die in peace.'

It seemed that everyone today was putting on her day dress without bothering to wash first. I did the same. As some of them went down to the kitchen I looked at the rumpled empty bed beside mine and suddenly remembered about Aggie and her awful screams. There had been no sounds coming from the maternity wing when I went past earlier. And Sister had left her to follow me to the chapel. Did that mean that she was alive or dead? I prayed that just one of last night's dramas had a happy ending. I decided to go and find out for myself.

I walked down the hall, and as the others descended the stairs to breakfast, I went in the opposite direction, through that forbidden door. As I pushed open the door I heard the sound of a baby crying. The first room I came to had eight beds in it, but only three were occupied. At the foot of each bed was a crib. Three faces looked up at me expectantly as I came in.

'You're new,' one of the girls said. 'Have you brought breakfast? It's late and we're hungry.' She was nursing a baby and didn't bother to cover herself as I came in. 'And where's Sister this morning?'

'Sister has had an accident,' I said. 'I'll see about breakfast. I wanted to know what happened to Aggie.'

'Aggie? The one who kept us awake all night with that awful row?'

'Yes.'

'I expect she's still in delivery, sleeping.'

'Where's that?'

'Two doors down the hall. But get a move on with breakfast, won't you?'

I went on down the hall and pushed open the door cautiously, not sure if I wanted to see what was awaiting me. A still, white form lay in the bed. She looked so pathetically young and frail that a lump came to my throat. She had claimed she was dying and it was true. I looked across at the cot where a tiny baby lay, apparently asleep. As I tiptoed over to it a voice said sharply, 'Hey, what do you think you're doing? Get your hands off my baby.'

And Aggie sat up, glaring at me.

'I came to see how you were,' I said. 'I was worried.'

'Oh,' she said. 'It wasn't too bad in the end. Went quite quickly really. And I've got a baby boy. Fancy that. A baby boy – me!' And a big smile spread over her thin, pinched face. At the sound of her voice the baby stirred. Dark eyes fluttered open and I could have sworn he stared straight at me. And I knew that I had to go home, back to loved ones and normality.

Chapter 30

Later that morning I rode beside the doctor, back down the hill to the town. Sister Jerome still lingered on and as far as I knew had not died by the time I left. I did not go to see for myself. They had taken her on a stretcher to the nuns' guest room where Blanche had killed herself the night before, so that she didn't have to endure the bumping of going upstairs. The doctor had said that little more could be done for her and it was only a matter of time. Her fellow nuns were praying beside her whether she wanted it or not. I thought it ironic that she would die in the same room where Blanche had taken her life, thanks to Sister Jerome's callous behavior. Or had she? I wondered if Sister might have had a part in that death too. Now we'd never know.

After mass I had been summoned for a long interview with Mother. She listened to the whole story, her boot-button eyes surprisingly alive and alert in that old face. When I had finished she said, 'Our order came here almost a hundred years ago. Our mission was to pray for the sinfulness of the world from which we had shut ourselves away. Then a few years ago a young girl came to our doorstep, with child and desperate. Her family had cast her out and she had nowhere to go. We took her in and decided that we would never turn away a girl in similar circumstances. Clearly God had sent her to us. Word got out and more girls came. Suddenly we found ourselves not only praying the offices, but caring for mothers and babies. We were no longer cut off from the world, however hard we tried. It was a mistake. We should never have strayed from our original purpose.'

'But you are performing a wonderful service here, Mother,' I said. 'Those girls here would have nowhere to go if you hadn't taken them in. They would have wound up dead or eventually in prostitution.'

She nodded. 'Maybe you are right, but by opening our door to the outside world we also let in evil. It is easy to be seduced by money, however noble the cause.' She sighed. 'Poor Sister Jerome. She had no vocation, I'm afraid. But once she had renounced the world she could no longer return to it. And because I have been in frail health recently I see now that she usurped my authority. Sister Perpetua warned me . . .'

'Sister Perpetua pleaded with her not to turn out Blanche, but she didn't listen.'

'The sin of pride. She thought she knew best.'

'But you won't report this to the police, will you?' I said.

'Given the circumstances I think it's best not to. Nothing can be gained by it and the sanctity of our convent will be violated. My daughters and the order must come first.'

'Even though Sister Jerome murdered at least two people?'

'She has given her own life in return. It is her soul I

grieve for. Her poor twisted soul.' She looked sharply at me. 'You took a big risk to your own safety and that of your child for someone you didn't even know. That was either extremely noble or foolhardy.'

'I didn't realize the extent of the risk I was taking,' I said. 'Otherwise I would never have come here.'

A slight smile twitched at her lips. 'Yes, you would, I suspect,' she said. 'But may I now suggest that you go home and take no more risks. Your first obligation now is to your husband and child, and frankly you'll need all your strength for a new baby.'

And so I had left the convent. The other girls hung back, rather in awe of me now that they knew I was not one of them. I overheard one of them whisper that perhaps I was an angel sent to avenge Maureen and Katy. At least that made me smile. Only Elaine had the courage to come to say good-bye. 'Think of me in this place when you have your own baby, won't you?' she said. 'I'm glad to know that you won't have to give yours up. You obviously care much more about it than I do about mine. I don't think I'm the motherly sort.'

'Why don't you leave and go to a refuge in the country?' I said. 'You don't have to stay here and endure this.'

'I think things will get better now that Sister Jerome is no longer in charge,' she replied. 'Mother says that the doctor will be called in for future deliveries until a new midwife can be properly trained.' She gave me a brave smile. 'And I really can't leave, you know. I couldn't risk being found out, however slight the chance would be.'

'I wish you all the best, then,' I said. 'And I hope you have a happy life with your fiancé when he returns from his sea voyage.'

'I intend to. Maybe I'll come and visit you in New York, but I don't think we'll discuss old times.' She grinned, then turned away as I walked toward the front door where the doctor awaited me.

'That place has always intrigued me,' the doctor said as the horse *clip-clopped* down the hill at a slow and steady pace. 'No good can come from shutting a lot of women away together. All their worst qualities come out.'

'Not all of them,' I said. 'Those who truly chose to be there are probably quite happy. It's those who didn't have a vocation like Sister Jerome who were eaten away inside.'

I was deposited outside The Lighthouse Inn and went in cautiously, not sure what kind of reception I'd find. As I came up onto the porch I heard a scream. After what I had been through that night my heart nearly jumped out of my chest. But it was Bridie, running toward me, arms open.

'She's here. She's come back!' she shouted in her high little voice.

Immediately the lady innkeeper appeared from the kitchen as Sid and Gus came running down the stairs.

'Thank God, oh, thank God,' Gus said and joined Bridie in hugging me.

'Where have you been?' Sid demanded. 'We have been worried out of our minds. We were about to go to the police and to send a wire to Daniel. Gus wanted to do so last night, but I didn't want to contact Daniel until we really had to – for your sake.'

'I'm so sorry,' I said. 'I got myself locked away in that confounded convent. I tried to send you a message, but the girl who was supposed to deliver it killed herself.'

'But you were going down to Irvington.' Sid was still

glaring at me. 'You were going to visit the Mainwaring household, so you told us. We telephoned Mrs Mainwaring and she said she had been out all day and had not seen you.'

'I did go there,' I said, 'and I learned the whole story of Maureen and her baby and the baby's father.' I glanced down at Bridie who was clinging onto my skirt like a rock. 'Bridie, love, why don't you run upstairs and find me a handkerchief in my bag?' I said.

As she went Gus asked, 'And? Who was he? Did she run off to be with him?'

'Quite the opposite,' I said. 'Her employer, Mr Mainwaring, had his way with her, as they say. He had a lecherous eye and apparently couldn't keep his hands off the servants. They wanted that poor girl to give them her child as they had no child of their own. They'd adopt it and she would be hired back as its nurse. Imagine her dilemma – wanting to be close to her baby, but not wanting that monster to get his hands on her again.'

'There is no justice in this world for women,' Sid said angrily. 'Why should a woman be shunned by society and condemned for her act if she gives birth to an illegitimate child, even if she was forced, against her will? And the man walks away, whistling merrily.'

'When we have the vote you must run for Congress, Sid,' Gus said. 'You'll be able to change things.'

'Maybe,' Sid said, 'but go on with your story, Molly. You went back to the convent and they dragged you inside and imprisoned you?'

'No, I confess that I behaved as usual without thinking clearly. Too impetuous by half, my mother always said. Too hot-headed.' I grinned. 'I pretended to be a wayward girl and got myself admitted. I sensed that Maureen had never left the place and I was right. One of the nuns had killed her and hidden her body in another nun's coffin.'

'God Almighty,' Sid said.

'Killed her, what on earth for?' Gus asked.

'I don't know exactly what happened but she changed her mind at the last minute and wanted to keep her child. Sister Jerome was privately making good money from placing babies with suitable families – essentially selling babies to childless couples. I think Maureen threatened to spill the beans if she wasn't allowed to leave and Sister Jerome couldn't have that happen.' I stopped, staring out at the peaceful scene in front of us – the broad river, flowing lazily past, and in the distance a sailing ship. Already the convent seemed like a bad dream.

'So let me get this straight,' Sid said. 'You admitted yourself to that convent, knowing that at least one girl had already been killed? Are you out of your mind, woman? What in heaven's name possessed you?'

I shrugged. 'I didn't think I'd be in any danger. I thought I could snoop around and then say that I'd changed my mind and wanted to leave again. What I didn't count on was that Sister Jerome had had a particular request for a red-haired baby. There was no way she was going to let me leave.'

'At least she wouldn't have killed you, then,' Gus said.

I was about to answer when that whole scene on the chapel steps replayed itself in my head. In all the excitement that had followed I had struck that memory from my mind. Now it came back to me with full force and I realized: I had literally been one inch away from falling to my death. I kept silent.

'So how did you manage to escape?' Gus went on.

'The truth came out. We found Maureen's body.'

'So you solved the whole thing by yourself?'

'I suppose so,' I agreed.

'Molly being brilliant as usual,' Gus said proudly. 'And what happened to your evil nun? Has she been dragged away in chains?'

'She had an accident. When I left she was dying,' I said.

Sid was looking at me critically. 'I can see there is more to this than Molly is willing to tell,' she said. 'But the only thing I can say to you, Molly Murphy Sullivan, is this: don't you ever do something as stupid as this again, do you hear me? Because if you try then Gus and I will personally lock you up in our attic until you see sense.'

I started to laugh. She laughed too and gave me a big bear-hug embrace.

'Here's your handkerchief.' Bridie came in just as I was wiping away tears. 'What's wrong?' she asked. 'Are you sad?'

'Never happier,' I said. 'I'm safely back among friends. What could be better.'

'And tomorrow we're taking you back to your mother-in-law where nothing can happen to you other than a surfeit of jam making,' Gus said.

'Oh, no.' I shook my head firmly. 'I have to get back to the city and tell Daniel . . .'

'You're going to confess all this nonsense to Daniel? Are you quite mad, woman?' Sid demanded.

'I'm not going to tell him the actual details, but I think I've found out something that will help him with his investigation. Before Sister Jerome died she said that she had been sending money to aid the Republican cause in

Ireland. Now it seems to me that the only person with whom she would have contact outside the convent would be her sister, who is also a nun but works in the Lower East Side. In fact I think I passed her sister in a carriage on the road when I was staying with Mrs Sullivan.'

'So you think her sister would be handing the money to the Republican Brotherhood?'

'That's what I wondered. At least she'd be a middleman along the chain and through her we might be able to find out where they meet and what exactly they are planning.'

Sid looked at Gus and shook her head. 'She never gives up, does she? Now you want to go from one dangerous situation to the next. What are we going to do with you?'

'Oh, I'm not intending to do this myself,' I said. 'But as Sister Jerome lay dying she did ask that somebody send a message of her death to her sister. So I thought that I could legitimately do that, find out where her convent is, and then pass along the information to my husband. There is no harm in that, is there?'

'With you there is always the potential for harm,' Sid said. 'But to be on the safe side we're coming with you. From now on we're not letting you loose in the Lower East Side alone.'

'We are not letting her go anywhere alone,' Gus added firmly.

Chapter 31

We spent the rest of the afternoon beside the river, sitting in the shade, watching Bridie splash about at the edge of the water – in short, exactly what I should have been doing all the time I was here. I couldn't help thinking how pleasant it was and wondering why I felt so driven to put myself in difficult situations and get involved in other people's problems. And for what? I asked myself. What exactly had I achieved? I had found out what happened to Maureen O'Byrne and I could now write to her family, but I would be bringing them only heartache. I had stopped Sister Jerome's money-making scheme, but I would now be depriving the Republican Brotherhood of funds when I was really all for their cause. At least I had stopped girls who came to the convent in the future from being abused by Sister. I hoped I had prevented any future tragedies like Blanche's suicide. So a little good was done then. Something achieved.

I turned my attention back to Bridie who was now standing on a rock, waving her arms. 'Look at me, Molly,' she called.

'Mrs Sullivan would have a fit if she saw you showing your arms and legs like that,' I called back. 'And getting freckles to boot.'

'Then we won't tell her, will we?' Bridie said with a cheeky smile on her face, and I read into her expression that she was hinting, 'I won't tell about you if you don't tell about me.' The child was growing up fast!

We had a lovely dinner of locally caught fish out on the porch, under the stars, and stayed up late watching lights dance on the water as a pleasure craft made its way upriver. Then the next morning Sid and Gus came with me to take Bridie back to my mother-in-law and pick up the rest of my things. Bridie was bursting with enthusiasm and couldn't stop talking about the splendid time she had had with the ladies. I noticed she carefully avoided mentioning those things that might have distressed my mother-in-law.

'My goodness, child, you're going off like a steam train.' Mrs Sullivan put a hand on Bridie's shoulder. 'It's not polite to hog the conversation when there are adults present. I think we need to get you back to some good honest hard work as soon as possible. I've the silver waiting to be polished in the dining room. On with your pinny and get to it.'

'Yes, Mrs Sullivan,' Bridie said meekly and went off.

My mother-in-law turned back to us. 'I can't let her get too uppity, can I?' she said. 'But I'm so glad she was able to let her hair down and be a child for a while. She's been worrying so much about her father and brother.' She moved closer. 'And between you and me, I've just heard a report from Panama that the conditions on that canal they are building are deplorable. Men are dropping like flies.'

'Let's pray for the best, shall we,' I said.

She looked at me critically. 'I can't say the stay by the river has done you good, my dear. You look positively tired and pale. Never mind, a few days of rest and feeding you up will do the trick, I daresay.'

I couldn't look her in the eye. 'Actually I'm going straight back to New York with Miss Walcott and Miss Goldfarb,' I said. 'I'm feeling guilty about leaving Daniel alone when he's been working so hard. A man should have a good meal waiting for him when he comes home from work, don't you think?'

She had to agree to that one. 'I always made sure there was a meal in the oven waiting for my man,' she agreed. 'But don't you think he'd rather that you stayed up here and I took care of you?'

'I'm not an invalid, Mother Sullivan,' I said. 'He worried about me in the heatwave but it's cooled down remarkably, wouldn't you say? Besides,' I added before she could answer, 'I'll maybe only stay down there for a few days, make sure he's well stocked up with food and come back here again – if you'll still put up with me, that is.'

She looked flattered, as I hoped she would. 'You know you're always welcome here, my dear.' She patted my hand. 'And I find it heart-warming that you're so concerned about dear Daniel. He's married a good woman, that's for sure.'

Of course I felt guilty after that, because Daniel wasn't my prime reason for wanting to return to New York. But at least I had managed to escape without any hurt feelings, and that was the main thing, wasn't it? Bridie helped me pack my bags, no longer bright and chatty but silent and morose.

'Why do you have to go?' she asked at last. 'Why can't I come with you?'

I stroked her hair. 'I'll be back soon, I promise, and it's better for you to be out of the city in the good fresh air.' She shrugged. 'And Mrs Sullivan is very kind to you. If you mind her well, you'll grow up to be a fine young lady.'

A tear trickled down her cheek. 'I don't want to grow up to be a young lady,' she said, wiping it away with the back of her hand. 'Then my da and my brother won't know me when they come back.'

I wrapped her in my arms. 'Oh, sweetheart, they'll be proud to know you. They just want what is best for you.' (This wasn't exactly true, as her father had asked me to find her a servant's position at the age of ten, but it was good that she thought it true.)

'I wish I were your daughter,' she said, her voice barely bigger than a whisper. There – she had voiced the thought that had gone through my own mind more than once.

'I love you like a daughter,' I said, 'but I have a new husband and soon I'll have a new baby of my own. Maybe when the baby comes and things are more settled then you might be able to come and live with us for a while, but for now you really are better off with Mrs Sullivan. Remember how hot and crowded it is in the city?'

Bridie didn't say another word, but insisted on carrying down my bag for me and giving it to Jonah to load into the trap. Then she stood solemnly waving as we set off for the station.

New York felt hot, sticky, and smelly after the country idyll and I almost regretted my decision to return home. However, when I turned the key in my front door and entered my little house I changed my mind. The house had an unused feel to it and smelled of decaying fruit and stale coffee. So then I felt sorry that Daniel had had to fend for himself and looked forward to surprising him with a good meal. But first I had a task to perform. Sid and Gus insisted on accompanying me and even insisted on taking a hansom cab to the Lower East Side.

'At least it shouldn't be too hard to track down a nun in this part of the city,' I said to them as we climbed down from the cab on the corner of Broome and Elizabeth Streets. 'Last time I was here the place was crawling with nuns and priests.'

'You'll probably find it some kind of feast day and they are all on their knees in their convents,' Sid said dryly as she scanned a street remarkably devoid of nuns. I looked around and my gaze fastened on the butcher shop on Elizabeth where I had come down the stairs just too late to witness a kidnapping.

'I wonder if that woman ever had the right baby returned to her?' I said.

Gus shook her head. 'If she did, there has been nothing about it in the *Times*.'

'How terrible for her.' I couldn't take my eyes off the door of that butcher's shop. 'I wonder what she'll do. Would she keep a baby that she knows isn't hers and spend her life wondering who is raising her baby?'

'It may not be as nice as that, Molly,' Gus said quietly. 'Did it not occur to you that perhaps they killed her child by mistake and found a baby to take its place?'

'Yes, Daniel suggested that might have happened.' I turned away. 'It just doesn't bear thinking about it, does it? I don't know what I'd do if . . .'

'Then don't think about it,' Sid said firmly. 'Frankly I don't know that it was a good idea letting you come to this part of the city, even if it is just to deliver a message. It's too distressing for you. Maybe we should take you straight home.'

'No. I have to do this.' I shook my head firmly. 'There may be a lot at stake here. Let's find the convent and get it over with. I'm sure almost any of the women around here can tell us where the Foundling Hospital is located.'

We stopped several women as they did their shopping. We asked in several stores. Yes, they knew there were nuns in the neighborhood. There was a convent attached to the church on Prince Street – the convent of the Immaculate Conception, but those nuns ran a school, not an orphanage. Their own daughters attended. You couldn't miss it – big, imposing brick building. We thanked them and made our way there, sure that one set of nuns would know about others. These turned out to be the nuns with the big white coifs we had seen on the street and we encountered a pair of them coming out of the school yard just as we approached.

'Why is it nuns are always in pairs?' Sid muttered. 'Are they only allowed out in twos, in case they get up to sinful behavior alone?'

'I don't know,' I whispered back, 'but it's true. You do usually see them in twos.'

We stopped them and asked about the Foundling Hospital.

They smiled with sweet unlined faces. 'It's up in the East Sixties, my dear.'

I stared at them, confused. 'The East Sixties? Not around here at all then?'

'That's right. Sixty-eighth and Lexington, I believe. And a fine job those sisters do too, taking in poor abandoned babes and even finding good homes for some of them.'

'Then I must have misunderstood,' I said. 'I thought there was an order of sisters living in this part of the city who took in abandoned babies.'

One nun looked at the other, turning the coifs carefully so that they didn't bump into each other. 'She must be thinking of that little convent on Broome Street. Aren't they the same order as the Foundling Hospital? They probably do find babies left on their doorstep, in this part of the city.' I could tell she was examining us – my friends in their bohemian garb and me in my present condition, and trying to work out why we'd be looking for the Foundling Hospital. But she was too polite to ask.

'Thank you,' I said. 'I have been asked to deliver a message to a particular sister. I was told she works in this area and I somehow associated her with foundlings. Do these nuns on Broome Street wear a habit with a black bonnet?'

'I believe they do,' one said. 'Aren't they Sisters of Charity? Yes, I'm sure they are. Mother Seton's girls.'

'And where on Broome Street is their convent?' I asked.

Again they turned to each other in a cautious, stately fashion. 'Close to Chrystie Street, do you think Sister?'

'I believe you're right, Sister.'

'Thank you again,' I said. 'We just came from Broome Street. We'd better go back and see if it's the right place.'

'God bless you, my dear. And the little one you're carrying,' she said and they resumed their walk, hands tucked in their habits and heads down. We made our way back to Broome Street. At first glance it wasn't obvious which building was a convent. It was a street of a mixture of old brownstones and ugly new brick tenements. Laundry was draped out of upstair windows. At street level there was the usual mixture of shops, all doing a lively afternoon trade. There was no church to which a convent would be attached. No clear display of a cross or religious statue. But then I noticed a door at the top of a flight of steps with a cross on it and beside the door was a plaque that read: SISTERS OF CHARITY. VINCENT HOUSE.

I turned to my friends. 'Look, I appreciate the way you are keeping an eye on me, but I don't think you should come in with me. I want to find out if this nun has connections to the Irish Republican Brotherhood and she certainly wouldn't tell me in front of you. Would you mind waiting for me somewhere nearby?'

'If you're really sure . . .' Gus began.

'I'm sure I'll be just fine,' I said. 'It will only take a few minutes.'

'We'll wait out here for you then,' Sid said. 'On the other side of the street where we can keep an eye on the building. Just in case we're needed to rush in and rescue you.'

Gus laughed. 'It's a convent, Sid. She's not going into Eastman's den.'

I pretended to laugh too, but I hadn't told them about a nun who had tried to kill me and successfully killed two other young women. Convents were not always safe places. But this nun would not see me as a threat. I'd be the bringer of bad news to her of course, but I'd be seen as a fellow champion of the Irish cause – an ally, not an adversary.

'I don't think I should be more than a few minutes,' I said, 'but I don't like you having to stand on the busy sidewalk in the heat. Why don't you wait for me at one of the cafés on the Bowery?'

'We'll wait here,' Sid said. 'We are not delicate violets who will faint in the heat. We can stand under the awning of that tailor's shop. I'm sure the tailor won't mind.'

'If you're sure . . .' I repeated.

'Oh, go on with you. Get it over with and we can all go for a nice, cool drink,' Sid said.

I nodded, then went up the steps, and rang the bell. The door was answered by a fresh-faced young nun in the severe black habit I had remembered. I told her I was looking for a nun who had a sister in a convent in Tarrytown and her face broke into a smile immediately. 'That would be Sister Mary Vincent,' she said. 'Very fond of her sister she is too. She'll be happy to receive a message from her. Won't you come in?'

I stepped in a dark, narrow hallway and she closed the door behind me. Inside it was so cool it was almost cold. 'I believe Sister is still in her office upstairs. If you'd like to go up, it's the door on the right at the end of the hall.'

I made my way gingerly up an extremely narrow flight of stairs. The irreverent thought crossed my mind that it was a good thing these sisters didn't wear coifs or they'd get stuck in the stairwells. At the top of the stairs a hallway disappeared into darkness in both directions. I peered around the corner cautiously and started as I saw a figure coming toward me, only a few feet away. The nun's black habit melted into the darkness of the narrow corridor so that it looked as if a disembodied face was coming toward me. After my initial shock I recognized her. It was Sister Mary Vincent. There was a distinct resemblance to Sister Jerome, but this face was softer and kinder. She started too at the sight of my face appearing around the corner in front of her. And she shot me a look of horror and surprise.

'What are you doing up here in the daylight?' She hissed the words at me in a whisper.

'I'm sorry,' I said, coming up the last of the steps to meet her, 'but they told me to come up to you. Was that not the right thing to do?'

She stood there like a statue, staring at me, then shook her head. 'I must apologize. You gave me quite a turn. I mistook you for someone else. Now, what can I do to help you?'

'My name is Mrs Molly Sullivan,' I said, 'and I've come from the convent in Tarrytown with news of your sister.'

'How very kind of you. How is the dear woman?'

'I'm sorry to be the bringer of such distressing news, but I'm afraid your sister died yesterday.'

'Joan is dead?' she asked and crossed herself. 'I mean Sister Jerome, of course. Joan was her name at home and I still think of her that way.' She paused to compose herself. 'How did she die?'

I looked at her kind, concerned face. 'An accident,' I said gently. 'A tragic accident. She fell down a flight of steps.'

'She always was in too much of a hurry,' Sister Mary Vincent said. 'Always taking too much upon herself. She wore herself to a frazzle, I'm sure. Ah, well. She's gone to her heavenly reward and it's not right to grieve, is it?'

'I think it's perfectly all right to grieve,' I said.

'You're very kind,' she said and I saw her fighting not to cry. 'But where are my manners? It's so good of you to take the time to bring me the news in person, rather than the shock and coldness of a letter. Won't you come down to the parlor and have something cold to drink?'

'Thank you,' I said. 'That would be very nice.'

'Watch your step,' she said. 'These stairs are horribly steep.' She led the way back down the stairs and into a room that overlooked the street. I couldn't actually see Sid and Gus, but I presumed they were standing in the shade of that awning. I reminded myself that I shouldn't leave them there too long as I took a seat at the battered table that was at the center of the room.

'So did you actually know my sister?' she asked. 'Are you connected to that convent?'

'I can't say that I really knew her. They are an enclosed order, after all. But I spoke with her several times,' I said. 'She mentioned you. And I can see that you were obviously fond of her.'

'We hadn't seen much of each other since we were girls,' Sister Mary Vincent said. 'But we were close in age. She was the bossy one, of course.' And she smiled. 'But I relied on her and it was a blow when we were sent to different convents.'

'Why was that?' I asked.

'It was what our father decided was best for us. And in those days we didn't argue with our father. There were ten of us, you see, and we were sitting around the table one night and father told us that we two were the homely ones. He said we'd never be likely to find ourselves a husband with faces like ours and it would be best if we went into the convent right away and gave them two less mouths to feed. Then he said that I had a pleasant way about me and should do well working with children while Joan was more suited to the intellectual and contemplative life.

And so our destinies were chosen for us. Nobody ever asked us if it was all right with us, but off we went, without a word of complaint. That's just the way it was in those days. I have to say I've been happy enough. I expect Joan has too. I know she had been running their ministry of mothers and babies, and running it very well too. Joan always did like to be in charge of things.'

I decided to take the plunge. 'I understand that Sister Jerome was a keen supporter of the Irish cause for home rule,' I said.

'She was indeed. She was able to send me small donations from time to time from the contributions they received at her convent, and asked me to pass them along to the cause, which, of course, I was happy to do.'

The amounts of money I had seen would have amounted to more than small donations and I wondered if Sister Mary Vincent was lying to me, or if Sister Jerome had indeed hogged most of the money for herself. I would have to be extra diplomatic in my questions.

'So you yourself are also involved with the Republican struggles are you?' I asked, the Irishness in my voice becoming more pronounced. 'God love you.'

She nodded as she carried two glasses of some kind of pink cordial to the table and placed one in front of me. 'Our parents raised us to be passionate about the cause,' she said. 'After what they went through in Ireland – seeing their home destroyed and cast out into the street with nothing but the clothes on their backs. The English land-owner ordered that, you know. He wanted the land and didn't care a fig that people were living on it. Living from it. It's about time we threw out the invaders and claimed what's ours by birthright.'

'You're right,' I said. 'I was involved in a small way myself once when I returned to Ireland.'

'You were?'

I declined to elaborate but went on, 'So you presumably are in touch with members of the Brotherhood here in New York, if you're raising money for them. How might I get in touch if I wanted to send my own contributions?'

'If you'd like to give me the money, I'll make sure it goes to the right people,' she said.

'And if I might want to get involved personally? Is there an address where I can meet them and volunteer my services?'

'I wouldn't be able to tell you that,' she said. 'They're secretive with good reason. The government here is in cahoots with the English. I just have to send on the money to a certain post office box and somebody picks it up. That's all I know. If you'd care to write a note with your name and address, I could send it along next time there is a contribution.' She paused, reconsidering. 'Not that there will be more contributions with my dear sister gone. I work among the poor here. Nobody has money to spare.'

Obviously I couldn't give her my name and address. It occurred to me to give her a fake one, but I couldn't see what that might achieve. 'I probably shouldn't do that,' I said. 'My husband is a New Yorker and doesn't understand the Irish cause as I do. He'd be angry with me.'

'I understand. But any time you can spare a little money, you can bring it to me and I'll make sure it goes to the right place. Every little bit helps, doesn't it?' She drained her glass and got to her feet. 'I should be getting back to work. I have to go and pick up a baby from St Peter's church. That's become a prime spot for dropping off unwanted infants, I'm afraid. I'll bring it back here to clean it up and then take it to our Foundling Hospital. So many unwanted children in the city. There's almost not a day goes by that someone doesn't hand me a child, found in a doorway. Make sure you treasure yours, my dear. Is it your first?'

'It is.' I smiled and got to my feet too. I was trying desperately to think of other things to ask her, but it could well be that she really did know no more than she was telling me. She opened the door for me.

'Thank you again for bringing me my sad news, my dear,' she said. 'I appreciate your coming here. Let me just get my basket for the baby and I'll be off too.'

We stepped out into the blinding sunlight of the day and came down the steps together. Then she nodded to me. 'God bless you then.' And she set off down the street with a basket over her arm.

I stood on the steps and it was almost as if I was having a vision. I was recalling the first time I had seen her, nearly colliding with her as I went up to the employment agency. She had had a similar closed basket over her arm then. And I remembered what Sid had said about nuns always going around in twos. She had been alone – the exception to the norm. And she was not there when the woman had started screaming that someone had stolen her baby.

And I knew with utter certainty that Sister Mary Vincent had taken that baby from its baby carriage.

Chapter 32

Why? I thought. *When there were so many unwanted infants in the city, would she want to steal another?* And I knew the answer to that too. Because Blanche's baby had died. Sister Jerome had promised a couple a fair, blue-eyed baby and she didn't have one to deliver. So her sister in the city had obliged, presumably thinking that the money was going to the Irish cause. And I had actually seen her going past in a small black carriage, bringing the baby with her. I wondered whether she had been responsible for any of the other kidnappings.

Before I could take this thought any further Sid and Gus had come across to join me. 'Well, that didn't take long at all,' Sid said. Then she frowned. 'Are you all right, Molly. Is something wrong?'

'I've just realized something shocking,' I said. 'I know who stole that baby and why a different one was returned. I have to go home and wait to tell Daniel.'

'Thank God for that,' Gus said. 'You look as if you've seen a ghost. You're as white as a sheet.'

A ghost. Images flashed through my mind – the

disembodied face of Sister Mary Vincent floating toward me down the hallway and her expression when she saw me. Almost as if she was seeing a ghost. Why was she so shocked to see me? Who did she think . . . ?

'Oh, no,' I said, looking back up those steps. 'I have to go back into the convent. I've just realized something.'

'What?'

'I think that my brother might be hiding in there.'

'In that convent?' Gus sounded shocked. 'Don't you think the nuns might have found him by now?'

'Oh, I think at least one of the nuns knows quite well that he's there,' I said. 'Sister Mary Vincent mistook me for someone else when she came upon me in the darkness. She thought she was looking at my brother. We look very alike. And she said, "What are you doing up here in the daylight?" *Up here*, she said. That must mean that he's supposed to stay down in a basement during the day. I've got to go down and find out.'

'Molly, is that wise?' Gus said.

'He's my brother, Gus. I don't want him captured and arrested and killed. I've got to try to persuade him to leave the country, or at least leave New York, before the police find him. And I should also make him see that he's placing a group of nuns in danger.'

'But what if he's with a group of ruffians down there,' Gus said. 'Didn't you say that he was working with anarchists? Those men wouldn't think twice about killing you.'

'I can't believe that nuns would let a group of anarchists hide out in their convent. This particular sister is passionate about the Irish cause and that's why she must be hiding Liam. I'll go cautiously.'

'We're coming with you,' Sid said.

I shook my head. 'Liam would surely hear more than one person coming. He'd hide or escape.'

'If you think we're letting you go down into the bowels of a building alone, you can think again,' Sid said.

'I must speak with him alone. Don't you see that?' I pleaded. 'I tell you what. You can stand at the top of the stairs and watch out for me. You can delay any nun who might want to go down to the basement. And you can hear me if I call for help.'

'I suppose so,' Sid admitted grudgingly. She looked across for affirmation to Gus.

'I think Molly has to go the last bit alone,' she agreed. 'And we don't even know that he really is down there. It's just Molly's hunch.'

We went back up the steps. I had seen Sister closing the front door behind us and was pretty sure it wasn't locked. We turned the handle and stepped back inside to the cool gloom.

'What do we say if one of the nuns catches us?' Gus whispered.

'We'll tell them we've come to inspect the place as our ladies' club is considering a charitable donation,' Sid said breezily. 'People are always pleasant if they think you're going to give them money.'

There was a flight of stairs going down where I had previously gone up. I glanced back at my friends then began to descend. At the bottom were several doors, and I heard women's voices coming from what had to be a laundry judging by the sounds and smells. This was only the floor halfway below street level, I concluded. It probably housed the kitchen and scullery as well as the laundry. I moved along as silently as I could, looking for the way down to a floor below this. I didn't think it was likely that anybody would choose to hide here, when this level was so obviously in use. I prowled most of the hallway, but discovered no stairs. I opened one door quietly and found myself staring at a broom closet. Another room had chairs stacked up in it. I had almost given up when I peered into a scullery and saw what looked like more steps in a far corner. I crept across, realizing that it would be increasingly difficult to explain my presence if I was spotted now. The stone steps did indeed go down into darkness, turning a corner so that I couldn't see what lay beyond. The wall felt cold and damp to the touch as I inched my way down. The small square hallway at the bottom was in almost complete darkness, the only light coming from a tiny grating up at the top of the wall. I stood still, wondering what to do next. I felt my way along the right-hand wall until I made out the shape of a doorway. I tried the handle. It was locked. I tried a second doorway. Also locked.

Of course, I thought. If I were hiding out from the authorities, I'd keep the door locked too. I was just about to give up in frustration when I heard soft footsteps approaching. I stepped back hastily up into the stairwell and pressed myself against the wall as I heard one of the doors open with a click.

'Don't stay outside too long this time,' a voice whispered. 'Sister said you were almost spotted.'

'A man's got to take a pee, doesn't he?' the closer voice answered. 'Besides, I'm going mad, cooped up in here like a caged beast. How much longer, do you think? Why won't they tell us anything?'

'We'd have been out of here by now if those explosives had made it through safely, wouldn't we?' The voice sounded remarkably like Liam's. 'Go on. Hurry up, for God's sake.'

I was conscious of a figure moving past me. Then one of the locked doors clicked open and daylight came in. He had gone into a narrow area between buildings, where I supposed the WC was to be found. I didn't wait a second. I darted through the half-open door into the room where I had heard the voices. It smelled of stale food and stale sweat and my senses recoiled. It was lit by one small oil lamp on a packing case on which the remains of two meals also reposed. Apart from that there were only two cots in the room and on one of these my brother was sitting. He leaped to his feet as I came in, fists up, ready to defend himself, and a look of utter horror crossed his face as he saw me.

'For the love of God, Molly, what are you doing here?'

'I worked out who was hiding you. I have to speak to you, Liam, before the police find you. You're a wanted man. They know you're here, Liam. You have to get away while you can.'

'Do you think I don't know all that?' He gave a bitter laugh. 'And I would have been long gone if our original plans hadn't been stymied. But I'm not leaving, Molly. I'm seeing it through.'

'What exactly is it you're seeing through?'

'Something big, Molly. Something that is going to make the world sit up and notice that we Irish can't be trodden on any longer.'

'Something that needed a lot of explosives,' I said.

'How the devil do you know that?'

'I heard your friend talking,' I said. 'You're going to blow something up, Liam.'

'No sense in denying it. We are.'

'You're planning to destroy innocent lives to make your statement? How will that make the Irish look to the rest of the world?'

'Sometimes innocent lives have to be lost in a war. You know that. And this is war, Molly. War against the English until they give us home rule.'

'You put me in a difficult position, Liam. I'm married to a policeman. I can't let you do this. But you're my brother. I have to try and save you if I can. I don't suppose I can make you come forward and tell the police what is being planned.'

'Damned right you can't. Do you think I'd betray the cause? It would be more than my life is worth.'

'Then I'll give you twenty-four hours to escape before I tell my husband. That's my best offer, Liam.'

He looked at me and I saw he was crying. 'You give me no alternative,' he said. 'You know I can't let you go, don't you? I should kill you now, but you're my sister and you've the little one coming too and I can't bring myself to do it. But I can't let you get in the way of our plans either.' He glanced at the doorway then back at me in an agony of indecision. 'My pal will be back any second. Go while you still have a chance to leave. You have to do what you think is right, just as I do.'

'You're a brave man, Liam. Our mother would have been proud.' I stared at him for a long moment, taking in the features of his face. I longed to hug him, but I knew he wouldn't want me to. Then I turned to go. But the doorway was blocked by a big man standing there.

'What's this then?' he asked, coming inside and shutting the door behind him. 'Having visitors now, are we?'

'She's my sister, Barney. She came to warn me the police are onto me.'

'Did she now?' The big man was looking at me with cold, animal eyes. 'And how did she find you? Did you contact her? Have you let your mouth run away with you again?' He lunged at me and his hand came over my mouth. 'So will you do it or shall I?'

'Do what?'

'Kill her, of course. We can't let her go. She'll bring the police straight here.'

'I'm not killing my sister, Barney. And neither are you,' Liam said. 'She's on our side. She's fought for the cause before now.'

'And you don't think she'll give us away? We can't risk that, Liam. Nobody is supposed to know we are here. Nobody.'

'She said she'd give us twenty-four hours. They can find us another safe house in that time.'

I was finding it hard to breathe with that big hand crushing me. I wriggled and tried to break free.

'Let go of her,' Liam said. 'I don't want to hurt you, Barney, but I will if I have to.'

'A little squirt like you? And what could you do about it, that's what I'd like to know. You're worth nothing to us, Liam Murphy. That's why they picked you to push the plunger on the explosives. You're expendable.'

With a roar of rage Liam flung himself at the bigger man. There was a sickening thud as fist connected with jaw. Barney staggered and released his grip on me. I fought myself free as he swung at Liam. Liam ducked nimbly and another punch found its mark on the side of Barney's head.

'Go on. Run,' Liam shouted to me. 'Get out of here now!'

I didn't want to leave him, but I could see the sense in getting away when I could. I darted out of the room. As I came up the steps I heard Sid shouting. 'Molly, watch out! The police are here . . .'

And before she could finish the sentence, men in blue uniforms swarmed down the stairs around me.

'Where are they then?' one of the police shouted to me.

'Liam, run!' I screamed.

Liam came bursting out of the room and made for the back door. As he ran out into the yard a single pistol shot sounded. Liam pitched forward and went sprawling onto the cobbles.

Chapter 33

'No!' I heard myself yell as I forced my way back down to him. Several policemen were standing around him as he lay there. There was a bright red stain spreading across the back of his white shirt. I ignored the police as I dropped to my knees beside him.

'Liam,' I said gently and stroked his hair. 'I'm so sorry.'

His eyes opened and he looked at me, puzzled. Then the ghost of a smile crossed his face. 'Molly,' he said and he fell back, dead.

'Molly, dearest, come away.' Sid's voice brought me back to the present. She lifted me to my feet. 'There's nothing more you can do. Let us take you home.'

From inside the building came sounds of curses and a scuffle. Then Barney was dragged out past us.

'Yer traitorous devil woman,' he shouted as they went past. 'Curses on you. Curses on you and your family. May you rot in hell.' And he spat at me.

'Come on, Molly. Let's go home,' Gus said, coming to take my other arm. Together they led me out of an alley-way and back into the busy street. As we emerged I saw

John Wilkie standing outside the house. He came over to me.

'Mrs Sullivan, please allow my men to take you home,' he said.

I glared at him. 'How did you know I'd be here?'

'We were awaiting your return to New York and naturally we took the liberty of having you followed.'

'You made me betray my own brother,' I said angrily.

'Believe me, it's better this way. I wouldn't recommend either the noose or the electric chair as a pleasant way to die.'

'He didn't have to die at all,' I said. 'He'd done nothing wrong.'

'Nothing wrong? Is that what you think?'

'He might have been plotting and planning a crime, but it might have been all talk. He hadn't actually committed any crime in America that I know of. You'd no right to shoot him in the back like that.'

'As to that, we always try to cooperate with our English allies and they were the ones who alerted us to his presence. He is a wanted man in his own country, you know.'

'In the eyes of his own people he's a hero.'

He looked at me quizzically. 'Do you happen to know exactly what he was planning, Mrs Sullivan?'

'Some kind of bomb explosion.'

'Precisely. He was part of a cell of anarchists planning to plant a bomb in the English Houses of Parliament. Hundreds of innocent people blown to pieces. A fine historic building reduced to rubble. Do you call that heroic?'

'I didn't say I agreed with him. But the Americans also behaved in similar fashion during their own war of independence, I expect.'

'They fought army to army like gentlemen,' he said. 'We won our independence fair and square, Mrs Sullivan.'

'Molly, we have a cab waiting.' Sid tugged at my skirt. 'You're only upsetting yourself by lingering here. Let's go home.'

'I just want to reiterate that I'm sorry you had to witness this, Mrs Sullivan,' Mr Wilkie said. 'I'm sure you were fond of your brother.'

I gave him a curt nod as I was led over to the waiting cab.

Sid and Gus came with me into my house. I looked around hopelessly. 'I meant to make Daniel a nice dinner,' I said. 'And now . . .' and to my shame I burst into tears. My friends were kindness itself. They sat me down and made me a cup of tea with plenty of sugar.

'Don't worry about cooking anything,' Gus said. 'We will provide the dinner tonight.'

'You're too kind and I'm a horrible friend to you,' I said. 'I make trouble for you. I inconvenience you.'

'Nonsense,' Sid said. 'Our little lives would be quite dull without you. Where would we find drama and excitement? How else could we live vicariously as sleuths? And you know that we adore you.'

I looked up and gave them a watery smile. They went off, presumably to prepare a meal. I went upstairs to change my clothes. When I took off my dress I saw that there was blood on the skirt. I crumpled it up and threw it into a corner. I knew I could never wear it again without remembering. I had just changed into a clean skirt and shirtwaist when I heard the sound of approaching feet. The front door was thrown open and Daniel came striding in.

He looked up and saw me coming down the stairs. 'Then it's true,' he said, and a look almost of despair flooded his face.

'What's true?'

'So you have returned and it appears I'm the last to know.' His voice was icily cold. 'For the second time now I had to hear from John Wilkie that my wife had slunk back into the city and gone to see her brother behind my back. What sort of marriage is this, Molly? Are you constantly going to be sneaking around doing things you know I wouldn't approve of?'

He was yelling now, his face red with anger. In truth he was rather frightening, but I wasn't about to let him know I was scared.

'Do you want to hear my side of this story or have you already made up your mind to condemn me without a trial?' I shouted back.

'Your side of it? You came back home without telling me and the first thing you did was to go to your brother. I'd say that pretty much condemns you in any court of law.'

I pushed past him, making for the front door.

'Where are you going?' he demanded.

'Over to my friends. I'll stay with them until you can behave like a civilized human being.'

He grabbed my arm. 'You're not going anywhere.'

'You can't stop me!' I yelled at him. 'I'm a free human being. Just because I'm your wife you do not own me. Now let go of me. If you don't let go I'll . . .'

'You'll do what? Call the police?' He was glaring down at me until suddenly his face twitched in a smile. That was a final straw for me. I swung at him and my hand connected with his cheek in a resounding slap. I stepped back in utter horror at what I had done. He had released my hand and stood stock still.

'Daniel. I'm sorry. I didn't mean . . . you were laughing at me. Laughing at my helplessness. And I've just been through a most harrowing time. I have just watched my brother die.'

'I heard about your brother. I wish it hadn't had to happen that way.'

'John Wilkie was tailing me,' I said. 'I'd never have gone near the place if I'd known Liam was there. I'm responsible for my brother's death, don't you see?'

'No, Molly. He brought about his own death by becoming an enemy of the state. It was either now or later. The moment he embarked upon this venture he was a doomed man.'

'I tried to warn him,' I said. 'But he wouldn't listen.'

'So you are trying to say that you didn't go to that place to see your brother?'

'Of course that's what I've been trying to tell you! But apparently you don't trust me enough to listen to my side of the story.'

'All right. I'm sorry. I'm ready to listen.'

I turned away from him, staring out of the window at the deserted street. 'I did not go to see my brother today. I had no idea he was hiding at that convent. I went there to tell one of the nuns that her sister had died at a convent in Tarrytown. And in the darkness she mistook me for my brother, thus betraying that he was hiding there.'

Daniel came up behind me. 'You were delivering a message from one convent to another and just happened to bump into your brother who has been eluding the police?'

'That's right.'

'And exactly why did this convent in Tarrytown happen to ask a complete stranger to deliver such a poignant message?'

'Because I was visiting there,' I said. 'Remember I told you that I'd been given a commission to track down a missing Irish girl? You yourself gave me permission to pursue this and ask among our friends, didn't you? Well, by chance I ran into her employers in Westchester County and learned that she had been taken in by this particular convent to have an illegitimate child.'

'I see. And it was just an amazing coincidence that out of the whole of the New York City area a nun who died in this convent just happened to have a sister who was hiding your brother?'

I turned back to face him. 'You still don't believe me, do you?' I took a deep breath. 'I was a little shocked myself, but looking back on it, I can give you the connections. Both sisters were passionate about the Irish freedom movement. They were supplying the Republican Brotherhood with money. So, yes, I knew that the sister in New York might have some ties to the Brotherhood and thus might be a future useful contact for you in your investigation. So when I was asked to take the message to her sister in the city as this nun lay dying, I agreed, thinking that I might learn some information for you and your investigation.'

He was looking at me long and hard, still trying to assess if this could possibly be true and if there was more I wasn't telling him, I suspect.

'You say these sisters were supplying the Irish freedom fighters with money? Where exactly do nuns come up with surplus money? What about poverty, chastity, and obedience?'

'This particular nun in Tarrytown was rather good at making money. She sold the babies that were born to unwed girls. And when she couldn't deliver a particular type of baby, she had her sister kidnap one from the Lower East Side. I think you'll find the baby from that last kidnapping is with a couple who thought they were getting it from an unmarried girl.'

'You're telling me that this nun was responsible for the kidnappings on the Lower East Side as well?' Daniel was staring at me.

'I don't know if she was responsible for any of the other kidnappings. Maybe they just gave her the idea of an easy way to find the baby her sister particularly wanted. Her sister was a forceful woman, Daniel. Perhaps this Sister Mary Vincent was under her sister's thumb and afraid not to carry out her orders. She seemed like a nice, gentle woman. Not the sort to go around kidnapping for money.'

'We'll soon find out,' he said. 'I'll be around there in the morning.'

I nodded. 'I suppose so.' I wondered what would happen to her – whether she'd go to prison. Whether the whole convent would be shut down. And the thought passed through my head that if only I'd minded my own business they'd have been free to carry on their good work, and Liam would still be alive. But then I reminded myself that a baby would now be safely returned to its rightful parents and that hundreds of people would not die in an explosion. So at least some good would come of it.

Daniel stood there, awfully quiet, staring past me at the

window where the last rays of the setting sun streamed in, bathing our narrow hallway with a rosy glow. At last he said, 'I've been fourteen years on the police force. I've learned from seasoned veterans. I've handled all types of criminal cases. But my wife, newly arrived from the backwoods of Ireland, manages to tie up all my unsolved cases for me with apparently no effort at all. I should just quit my job and stay home looking after the babies while you go out to work for us.'

I tried not to smile at his exasperated face. 'You might like to consult me when you get a particularly tricky case in the future,' I said.

'I'd just love to know how you managed it.'

I took a deep breath, thinking of the strange coincidences and underlying links that had brought me to that convent on Broome Street. Maureen O'Byrne. She had been the link. But I agreed that the whole story was a little hard to believe.

'You can just call it the luck of the Irish, Daniel. It certainly wasn't through my brilliance in deduction. I heard a name mentioned at a tea party. I followed up on it. One thing led to another. And unfortunately they led to my brother. I led the police to my brother. I'll never forget that or get over it.'

'Molly, did John Wilkie tell you what your brother was planning to do?'

I nodded. 'He was part of a plot to blow up the Houses of Parliament. Don't think that I condone such acts for a second. But I wanted to save him. I wanted him to get away and he refused.'

He put his hands on my shoulders. 'Don't blame yourself. Tell yourself that your act actually will save lives.

Rhys Bowen

Then try to put it behind you. Oh, and Molly, if another letter arrives for P. Riley Associates . . .'

'Don't worry. I'll hand it straight to you and you can find another detective agency.' I looked at his cheek, still red, and put my hand up to it tenderly. 'I'm sorry I hit you.'

'So am I. You pack quite a punch, woman.'

'I don't know what got into me.'

'I do. I pushed you too far. But you're lucky I didn't put you over my knee and give you a damned good hiding – with a good-sized stick. I'm allowed to by law, you know. Rule of thumb.'

'Why didn't you?'

He shook his head. 'I've seen enough of violence to know that it achieves nothing. There will be no hitting in this house, neither parents nor children. Is that clear, Molly?'

'Yes, my lord,' I said meekly.

He laughed and wrapped me into his arms. 'I knew marriage to you wouldn't be boring.'

'I'll try to make it a little less exciting in the future,' I said. 'I really am sorry I've been neglecting my wifely duties too. One of the main reasons I came home was to make you a slap-up meal. I didn't quite manage that.'

'Then I suppose we'll have to make do with what's in the house. There isn't much. I've been too busy.' Then his face lit up as an idea came to him. 'We could always go out. How long has it been since we had a meal at a restaurant together?'

'Not since our honeymoon,' I said.

'Well, then, come on. Get your hat.'

'But Sid and Gus promised to take care of dinner.'

'Oh, Molly, I don't feel like being polite to your friends tonight. I'd like a dinner for just the two of us. Can't we sneak out and leave them a note?'

'It does sound tempting.'

'Well then, what are we waiting for?' He took down my hat from the peg in the front hall and opened the door. Then he said, 'What in heaven's name?'

I came to see what he was staring at. A procession was approaching us down Patchin Place – waiters with black suits and white dickeys, each bearing a covered dish. At the back of the procession came Sid and Gus, one carrying flowers, one wine.

'We decided that we were not feeling inspired enough to cook you a good meal tonight. Besides, Giovanni's Italian Restaurant prepares a better meal than we do,' Gus said. 'Go and lay the table before it gets cold. I hope you like gnocchi.'

Even Daniel had to laugh. 'Molly said she'd try to make things a little less exciting around here,' he said as the waiters passed us, one by one, into the house. 'I don't think somehow that's ever going to happen.'

The next day I sat down to the sad task of writing to the family in Ireland, bringing them the news about Maureen. I spared them the most heart-wrenching details, telling them that she died after giving birth to a baby at the convent. That would be distressing enough for them, I realized. Still, I suppose it's always better to know the truth than to spend one's life worrying, isn't it? And I waived my fee. Then I suggested that if they wanted to repay me, they might like to light a candle and say some prayers for my brother's soul. Then I decided that I'd go to church and do the same. I had abandoned my religion for so long, but suddenly I felt a strong need for it.

When Daniel came home that night he reported that Sister Mary Vincent had denied having anything to do with the other kidnappings and bitterly regretted the one she had carried out. Daniel didn't know what would happen to her. She had knowingly harbored fugitives, after all. And only a few days later Daniel's men were lucky enough to catch a low-level gangster in the act of stealing a baby. So that case was closed, Lower East Side parents could breathe easily again, and Daniel got the credit. Oh, and Martha Wagner's baby was returned to her, so all ended well. Just not for my brother.

Postscript

William Joseph Sullivan was born on September 14, 1904. He came into the world bawling, his little fists clenched and ready for a fight. He had his father's shock of dark hair and dark blue eyes. So Sister Jerome would have been disappointed in her anticipation of my red-haired child.

Liam is a good baby, eating and sleeping well, and the household runs smoothly, thanks to Aggie, whom I acquired from the convent maternity home. I could have had the efficient Gerda, I suppose, but I thought she might turn out to be a trifle too bossy for my liking. And a little too efficient as well. It would be like having my mother-in-law in the house. I took Aggie initially out of pity – she seemed such a scrawny, undernourished little scrap with nowhere in the world to go, but she has turned out remarkably well. It seems she grew up looking after any number of young siblings and knows exactly what to do to quiet a fussy baby. A lucky find indeed. Which gives me time on my hands, of course. Not always a good thing for me as I start looking for things to occupy me outside of the home.

At Liam's baptism my old friend Miss Van Woekem came up to congratulate us. 'This seems to be the year for babies,' she said. 'I've just had a visit from a young cousin who lives out in Westchester County. Harriet Mainwaring. She also has a beautiful baby. Looks a little like you, my dear, come to think of it. Such an Irish face.'